GUERRILLA BEACH

GUERRILLA BEACH

BY

OAKLAND ROSS

CORMORANT
BOOKS

Published with the assistance of the Canada Council
and the Ontario Arts Council.

Edited by Gena K. Gorrell.

Cover shows a detail of a wall mural painted by local
children at Garden Centre, a Street Kids
International project in Lusaka, Zambia. Used by
permission of Street Kids International.

Cover design by Artcetera Graphics, Dunvegan,
Ontario.

Published by Cormorant Books Inc., RR 1, Dunvegan,
Ontario K0C 1J0

Printed and bound in Canada.

Canadian Cataloguing in Publication Data
      Ross, Oakland, 1952-
        Guerrilla Beach
      ISBN 0-920953-75-1
        1. Latin America--Fiction. I. Title.
      PS8585.08404G84 1994 C813'.54 C94-900413-8
      PR9199.3.R68G84 1994

For my mother and my father

Contents

Bang-bang

The last thing that Josefina Velásquez Ochoa needed to do on the morning of March twenty-fourth—a hot brittle morning when the earth sprawled like cracked old leather beneath the dry-season sun—was to tread upon a landmine. Let someone else tread upon a landmine. Josefina wasn't interested.

So, when she first caught sight of a band of guerrillas digging up the dirt road at the bottom of a rock-cluttered hill about half a kilometre ahead, Josefina very nearly decided right then and there to turn around and march straight back home, even though she was now more than halfway to Gotera. It was evident what the guerrillas were doing. They were planting a landmine in the road.

Josefina had troubles enough as it was. She had half a dozen mouths to feed and very few hands to help her. She had two younger sisters who did their best but

9

they were small. She had a younger brother, and a son of her own who cried all the time—she didn't know why. The son had a father, but Josefina remembered him only by his rank (lieutenant), his first name (Rodrigo), and his sweet talk (lies). He hadn't come around, despite all promises, since that one rash and fateful night in San Miguel exactly a year ago, so what was the use in thinking of it?

Josefina never thought of it any more. She had too many mouths to feed and too little time. He had bought her flowers from a stall, flowers and a lovely floral parasol, bowing as he bestowed them upon her. But that was past now, not worth thinking about. There was far too much work to be done. Her little baby cried all day, all night. Her mother had arthritis and could hardly move. His hands had been strong and sure. Gentle, his touch. He had whispered to her of love, foolish boy, her big foolish boy. But that was forgotten now. She didn't think of it. Her father was dead, three years ago now, the less said about that the better, and Josefina had mouths to feed. The way his upper lip turned down when he smiled.

Now the corn in the milpa had got to be planted, and someone had got to help her do it. Josefina had been counting on Miguel, her younger brother—a good hard worker as boys went. But last night the soldiers had come and taken him away. They were going to make Miguel into a soldier, they said. "Right, Miguelito?" Then they jabbed him in the sides with their rifle barrels and laughed with a sound like shovels striking rocks.

They would make Miguel into a soldier, all right, thought Josefina, so that he could carry a gun and point

10

it at people who annoyed him, and fire it if he wished. Then off he would go to fight the subversives and defend the honour of the fatherland and get himself killed, while weeds sprang up amid the rocks in the milpa, and the rains fell and washed the soil away, and the Velásquez family was reduced to rags and to gnawing roots and bark until they all starved to death, as was apparently God's will and divine plan, so good riddance. Men.

That was what Josefina had thought, a little before dusk, when they took her brother away. She had stood in front of the family's sagging adobe house, not moving, just plain helpless, clutching little Rodrigo to her side. The soldiers lumbered off on foot, hustling Miguel before them, his thumbs bound behind his back with twine. Narrowly avoiding a kick, the good-for-nothing rooster darted across the path, its neck stuck out, its wings upraised. The hens cowered sensibly off to the side, and the soldiers clambered down past the torn green fronds of the banana plants, kicking up currents of red dust, laughing among themselves.

"Why don't we go back and fetch your pretty older sister, Miguelito?" one voice cried. "We have room for her in the garrison."

Another said, "Ah, yes, Miguelito, but does she have room for us!"

They all laughed again. Their voices faded, and the sun smouldered red through the evening mist. It quickly sank beneath the dark webbing of forest on the western hills. Within minutes the sky was black. Dogs barked in the distance.

The following morning, Josefina took one long tired look at the mouths she had to feed, all crammed at that moment with a mush of tortilla and fried egg. She imagined them empty—and decided what she was going to do. She immediately felt an unfamiliar but not unpleasant stirring between her legs.

She put on her pale yellow church dress, the one with the chiffon fringe at the collar. She unfolded her pretty blue shawl and draped it over her shoulders. Now she hesitated, thinking of the crucifix she always wore around her neck, suspended on its slender chain. At first she considered removing it, afraid of sacrilege, but soon she changed her mind. The little figure on the cross remained in its usual place, tucked between her breasts.

From a drawer she removed her green plastic handbag, the one she had purchased that terrible day a year earlier in San Miguel, with part of the money from the sale of the pig. The handbag was empty except for her rosary and a ten-*colon* note, but she decided to carry it anyway—a young woman should carry a handbag. Had there been a mirror in the tiny adobe house, she would have been able to gaze at her reflection before she set out, searching for the woman she sometimes imagined she would yet become—finely dressed, still slender, still soft of skin, fragrant, shapely, like an advertisement in one of the Mexican women's magazines she had pored over so many times at the general store in town.

There was one picture that she especially loved, an advertisement for a perfume with a French-sounding name—a vision of cool dappled waters on whose banks she too would lie, swooning and blurry, bare-breasted and pure, in a fountain of willows, lilies, and marigolds.

But the sun beat down hard on the morning of

12

March twenty-fourth, so Josefina took her lovely floral parasol from its hook by the wooden door—it was her sole memento of Rodrigo, apart from the howls of his son—and announced to all that she would be back late that afternoon, or perhaps early the following morning. The younger ones would have to care for little Rodrigo.

Josefina set off on foot, bound for San Francisco Gotera, a two-hour walk away. All around her, near the dry season's end, the land crackled in the sun. The sun had sucked the moisture from everything, turned every living thing to ashes or tinder. The earth was strewn with the shards of leaves. In a faint breeze, the broken corn stalks clacked.

Josefina opened her parasol and set it against the sun. She strolled away along the Osicala road, enclosed in a filmy oval of shade. She felt fresh and cool as water. As she walked, she thought of men. If there was one thing that Josefina believed she understood, it was men—men and their ways. Think of boys. Multiply. When there was important work to be done—such as keeping a family fed and clothed—there was nothing to be gained by relying on men. Men were good for just four things, and one was drinking, and another was killing, and another was giving speeches. But there was a rough kindness to the weight of a man's hands upon a woman's skin, or there could be if the woman was careful, and a woman had better be careful, for there was no point in treading on a landmine.

Josefina stopped where she was, at the crest of a lightly forested hill, and observed the rebels in the hollow beneath her. She had no interest in landmines. She had one firm rule—stay out of the war. It was by getting mixed up in the war that her father had come to his sad sorry end. Three years earlier he had taken part in the seizure of the Chávez coffee estate south of Gotera, on behalf of the peasantry and the masses. Like the others, he had been drummed into it by the leftists. Like the others, he had been killed when the army came. It was terrible—but, as with most things involving men, it was predictable.

Now Josefina had half a mind to turn around and march straight back home.

"Hello, *compañera.*" A young rebel lookout emerged from a copse of trees and strode over to her. His wooden-stocked carbine dangled from his shoulder by a length of twine. "Where are you going?"

"To Gotera. I have some business there. Is the road safe?"

"It is now. But pretty soon it won't be." The rebel smiled. His cheekbones pushed out against his raw brown skin. He leaned closer, lowered his voice. "We're planning an ambush, a special little surprise for our friend Colonel Guerrero." The young man stood back, nodded impressively. "We'll just direct the ordinary traffic around and wait for some soldiers to come. With luck, we'll get Colonel Guerrero himself. Then—bang!"

What nonsense, thought Josefina: if they kill one more colonel the army will simply send another and another—and another after that. It never ends. It just goes on and on, like a children's game with no purpose. She said, "I wish you every success. May I pass?"

"Of course. But remember: not a word of what you have seen."

"Of course." And Josefina strolled down the hill

and past the group of young rebels working in the road. Without paying close attention, she saw that they were digging a shallow trench. More guerrillas were piling rocks atop a nearby hummock, evidently an ambush post. The rebels were always up to some mischief or other, but this was the first time that Josefina could remember them planting a mine this far south, this close to town. Normally they kept to their liberated zones farther north.

The young men stopped work to gaze at the pretty woman with the floral parasol. They rested against their shovels, brushed the sweat from their brows, shielded their eyes from the sun. They nodded to each other and whispered. One released a low whistle that struck the air and was gone. Soon they shrugged and went back to their digging, smacking the blades of their shovels against the hard surfaces of rocks. Josefina set her parasol upon her shoulder, gave it a little twirl, and continued her march to Gotera. Now she knew about the landmine in the road, something she had not known before.

Men.

The film being shown at the crumbling cinema on the main square in San Francisco Gotera on March twenty-fourth was *Rambo II.* Typical, thought Lawrence Pozniak. War in the countryside, war on the screen. A fine little republic, El Salvador. He shifted his weight against the side of the dusty white Volkswagen minibus. He crossed his feet at the ankles, shoved his hands into his pockets. Already he and the others had been waiting more than an hour.

"Hey, Larry," said Bob Carling, the producer, whose tangled brown moustache was an obvious compensatory mechanism for his fast-encroaching baldness, now largely obscured by a pale blue terrycloth hat. Apparently, he also had noticed the cinema's makeshift hand-lettered marquee. "If nothing else pans out, at least we can catch a flick."

"I've seen it already," said Larry, who was the reporter in the crew. Larry also wore a moustache—a crisp and tidy flourish of urbanity and manhood. It had no visible compensatory purpose, a point that Larry liked to stress by reaching up and pushing both hands back through his hair, ruffling the ample waves with his fingers. He did so now.

"Any good?" said Bob. He evidently meant the film.

"How should I know?"

"I thought you said—"

"Oh, give me a break. *Por favor. Rambo . . .*? Are you kidding?"

"I was only asking."

"Well, don't."

"Jesus. Shoot me for asking a simple question."

"Don't tempt me."

"Gee, thanks. Thanks a lot."

Larry reached up, removed his tinted glasses, and began to knead the bridge of his nose. He closed his eyes. He was having a bad day—a bad day near the end of a bad assignment in a bad country. He had been recruited for the Salvador job when Gloria Reynolds came down with hepatitis—courtesy of her last Central American

16

swing. Gloria was based in Washington, Larry in Ottawa. Larry would like to be based in Washington.

But right now Larry would settle for Canada. He put his glasses back on and peered over at Bob, who was sipping purified water from a plastic bottle. Larry felt a sudden poignant longing for Ottawa—he had a vivid image of skaters twirling or tottering along the Rideau Canal surrounded by drifts of ice-cream snow. "Say, I wonder if the Rideau is still frozen," he said to Bob. "How would you like to be skating on the canal right now?"

Bob snapped the plastic cap back onto the mouth of the water bottle. "If it meant getting out of this dump, I'd go *swimming* in the canal right now."

The others nodded. The pervasive badness of their situation was probably the one thing they could all agree on—all of them, soundman Pete McArthur, cameraman Daniel Rivard, their Salvadoran driver, Guillermo Palacios, whom everyone called William ("*Mal*," he agreed. "*Todo está muy mal*"), and their translator and guide, a toffee-voiced Englishwoman named Sally Gillespie who lived in San Salvador and was the only one in the group who spoke Spanish, apart from William—and Larry, of course, who had taken Spanish in grade twelve.

This gig was bad.

About almost everything else, the Canadians differed, which was perhaps inevitable, Larry thought. It was the result of having spent seven days together bouncing around in a minibus in a hot dry country where most of the bridges were blown up and the phone lines knocked down; where the cicada sang with a sinister wail, like strands of zinging wire being drawn back and forth through your brain, right between your ears; where a miserable dose of gastroenteritis lurked just beyond every meal; and where at any moment they were all apt to be ambushed or pinned down in cross-fire—either of which might be a welcome prospect at the moment, on the whole, considering how desperately they needed bang-bang and how little time they had left to get it.

Larry had mixed feelings about bang-bang.

It now appeared, for example, that the Canadians would wind up having to buy some bang-bang off the shelf from one of the U.S. networks, which was negative in the sense of being unspeakably demeaning but positive in that it involved no personal risk.

Bang-bang meant pictures of horrified peasants streaming from their sagging little mud-brick communities on foot, balancing their boxes and baskets on their heads. It meant trails of smoke writhing above palm trees and crumbling walls. It meant helicopter gunships racing overhead, barking like dogs. It meant rebels and soldiers and corpses and guns.

No bang-bang, on the other hand, meant zip. It meant no footage of the combat, no mournful shots of the bloody wounded, the dazed survivors, the weeping relatives, the silent corpses. It meant no tape of crack-crack, pow-pow, thud-thud, whomp-whomp, bang-bang.

Ending up bang-bangless in Salvador, as Larry knew, was much like going to Canada in mid-February and failing to turn up snow. Explain that to Toronto.

So here they were, members of a television crew

from the Canadian Broadcasting Corporation, slouching by their minibus in the main plaza in sleepy San Francisco Gotera on a Sunday, waiting for an interview with Lieutenant-Colonel Antonio Guerrero Campins, commander of the Salvadoran army garrison in the remote eastern province of Morazán. Most of the province north of Gotera was controlled by rebel forces of the Farabundo Martí National Liberation Front. In theory, it was a good part of the country for bang-bang.

The Canadians had already presented their business cards at the garrison gate, along with Sally Gillespie's scribbled request for an interview. Now there was little to do but wait. They had driven up that morning from San Miguel and were determined to stick it out because Lieutenant-Colonel Sigifredo Castañeda had mentioned to them only yesterday, as a sort of consolation, that he understood Colonel Guerrero was planning a major offensive into the north in the next few days.

Sigi, as the Americans called him, had imparted this information in a low voice while stubbing out a thick cigar, just before striding across a sloping lawn to climb aboard one of two olive-green UH-1H helicopters that were waiting to whisk him and a pair of U.S. network crews—ABC and CNN—off on an aerial tour of trouble spots north of the capital. Bang-bang guaranteed. Unfortunately there had been no room for the Canadians. Very sorry. Maybe next time.

The Canadians had piled back into their minibus for a long, risky, but uneventful drive east to San Miguel, where they had spent the previous night. Now, Larry thought, it looked as if Sigi had been wrong. Except for a few pigs grovelling in the gutters and the occasional

19

pariah dog limping past with tilted head and baleful eye, there was nothing going on in the main plaza of San Francisco Gotera. There was certainly no sign of a major military mobilization. There was little sign of human activity at all, apart from a slender young woman in a yellow dress, carrying a parasol. They'd watched her venture through the garrison gates shortly after they arrived.

The only other people in the square now were a pair of sombre-looking army sentries with automatic rifles at the entrance to the garrison. Something in that direction caught Larry's eye, and he turned in time to see a cocky-looking little kid of about twelve years of age shuffle out between the two sentries and into the square. The kid was wearing camouflage khaki and a floppy olive-green hat. He carried a compact automatic rifle and immediately pointed it at the Canadians. "Bang-bang!" he shrieked. "Bang-bang!" Then he scowled and motioned with his rifle barrel over to the left.

"Just ignore him," said Sally. "He's Guerrero's personal mascot. His name's Carlitos. He's incorrigible."

"Bang-bang!" the little boy howled again. He unleashed a fierce-sounding tirade in Spanish. He glared at the Canadians.

"What's he saying?" asked Pete, the soundman. "What's he want? Does he want something? What?"

"Just ignore him," said Sally. "He's just—it's nonsense. He's telling us to line up against the wall over there so he can search us. Otherwise he's going to kill us."

"Bang-bang-bang!" the youngster roared. "Bang-bang-bang!" He waited, with his rifle lowered. He tilted his head to one side. Then he suddenly swung on his heels and trained his rifle at a pig snouting through the gutter across the square. "Bang-bang-bang-bang!" he shouted. "Bang-bang-bang-bang!" He stamped his feet and called out something in Spanish.

The pig looked up for a moment, its snout twitching in the air. Then it went back to snuffling through a clutter of rubbish and dirt, ignoring the boy entirely.

"Bang!" the boy screamed. He reared back on his heels. "Bang-bang-bang-bang-bang!"

Eventually the boy seemed to lose interest in the pig. He turned and sauntered back towards the garrison, through the tall iron gates. He shot both the guards—"Bang-bang! Bang-bang!"—and vanished into the darkness. The guards neither moved nor said a word.

"Ignore him? How do you ignore a spoilt little brat when he's carrying a gun?" asked Pete, who kept his pack of Marlboro cigarettes tucked above his right elbow in the roll of his shirt-sleeve and had three days' growth of beard. Like Larry, however, Pete had never been to a war zone before. "Do you think it was loaded?"

"Probably," said Sally. "This is El Salvador."

Larry had heard that line before, but now he found himself pondering it as a kind of revelation. This was El Salvador. This was—

Something moved near the garrison entrance. A woman appeared, the same woman as before—a tallish young woman with a high bronze complexion. She seemed shaken, wobbled as she walked. She wore a light blue shawl and a yellow dress with a chiffon fringe at the collar. She carried a little green purse. Now, at the edge of the square, she stopped. For several moments she didn't move. She just stood by the raised terrace at the garrison entrance, put out her hand to clutch the steel gates, for balance. She had thick arched eyebrows, an erect carriage, trim round breasts, and a dazed expression. She started to move, seemed to hesitate again, then stepped forward into the sunlight.

The woman carried a floral parasol. She tried to open it, with some effort, finally succeeded. She raised the parasol above her head and hurried away across the square. For no particular reason, Larry waved at her, as one civilian to another, but she did not wave back.

Larry watched her go. What was wrong with these people?

Colonel Antonio Guerrero Campins was in a state of high agitation. On his large wooden desk, he had the business cards of two Canadian journalists—Lawrence Pozniak, reporter, and Robert Carling, producer. The cards raised more questions than they answered.

After receiving the cards along with a request for an interview, jotted in Spanish on a leaf of lined notepaper, Colonel Guerrero had immediately dispatched his orderly to determine whether CBC signals could be received on the satellite dish mounted on the garrison rooftop, guarded by two machine-gun nests.

Ten minutes later the orderly returned, clicked his heels at the door. He saluted and gave a complete report. "*Negativo*," he said.

Colonel Guerrero waved the man away without

a word. He proceeded to brood, with his chin cupped in his hands. It had once been said by someone—and news of this had gotten back to Colonel Guerrero—that if they were making a movie about El Salvador and Colonel Guerrero was in it, he would ideally be played by Peter Lorre. Ha. Ha. Ha. Very funny. Whose idea was that, anyway? Was it that bastard Sigi Castañeda? Probably.

Peter Lorre. Each time the colonel thought of it, the comparison seemed even more deeply unjust. Peter Lorre—a small sullen man with a raspy voice and bugged-out eyes, a wormy little character. The colonel knew Peter Lorre from the old movies that he sometimes watched on his personal VCR, a top-of-the-line Sony. Peter Lorre—wasn't he dead?

But enough of that. Right now Colonel Guerrero had more important things on his mind. He was trying to think of a way to exploit his latest opportunity, as he had been taught to do many years before, at counter-subversion school. But it wasn't easy.

Fact. Here was a foreign television crew. They had shown up in the plaza like an apparition of the Virgin, who, in the colonel's mind, always presented herself as a slender young boy swathed in translucent veils of cotton. A foreign television crew. It was something the colonel had long dreamed of—except that, in his dreams, the foreign TV crews had always been American, either ABC or CNN, whose signals came in clearly via the satellite dish on the garrison rooftop. He often watched the American broadcasts, especially when they concerned El Salvador.

What times of reverie those were. What moments of pain and rapture. How Colonel Guerrero longed to

23

appear on the screen himself—fielding questions from foreign journalists in idiomatic English, surveying the columns of smoke upon the horizon, leading his own troops into battle on American TV....

That bastard Sigi Castañeda was forever doing all those things—on ABC, on CNN. That bastard Sigi Castañeda had been trained in the Panama Canal Zone. He spoke fluent English, and commanded an elite battalion—formed by the gringos and based near San Salvador, so it was convenient to reach—whereas he, Colonel Guerrero, had received most of his counter-subversion training in Taiwan, in Spanish translation, and was stuck way out here in Morazán, where the American TV crews never came.

But, now, at last, here was a foreign television crew—albeit Canadian, a word that triggered imprecise associations in Colonel Guerrero's mind—and its members were seeking to interview him. What was he to do?

He glanced down at the handwritten note once more. He knew what that bastard Sigi Castañeda would do. He would take the visiting journalists out in one of his helicopters and show them the war. But Colonel Guerrero had no helicopters, and right now he had no war. In their note, the Canadians mentioned something about an operation to dislodge the subversives to the north, but Colonel Guerrero knew that nothing was going on, nothing at all, aside from occasional and unpredictable skirmishes between his patrols and small bands of Communists. It had been months since his last major campaign and it would be weeks at least until the next.

They were always the same anyway, those

campaigns. His men moved in, the subversives moved out. There was lots of shooting, and people died. His men moved out, the subversives moved back in. It was what the gringos wanted. They called it gung-ho.

Still, Colonel Guerrero believed passionately in the cause. He hated Communists and delighted in their deaths. He would love to fight Communists on TV, even Canadian TV if there was no choice. But right now—with a Canadian TV crew parked on his doorstep—he didn't see how it could be managed. He didn't see how he could exploit this opportunity. And so he brooded.

As the colonel brooded, Carlitos wandered into the office and flopped down onto one of the fuzzy brown chairs across the room from the officer's desk. The little boy glowered at the floor and fidgeted with the safety catch on his rifle, flicking it off and on, off and on. "There's nothing to do," he moaned.

The colonel glanced up again. For a few moments he gazed with what was almost affection at the small boy, whose parents he vaguely remembered having tortured to death two years earlier. He considered taking Carlitos back into the small apartment that adjoined the office, where, without shame or ceremony, the boy would strip and kneel, little round buttocks raised in welcome, and for a few short dizzy moments all care would cease. Then the colonel remembered the Canadians waiting outside.

"I said," repeated Carlitos, "there's nothing to do." He released the magazine from his rifle and pried a single cartridge out onto his hand. He held it up to one eye, closed the other, and examined the long narrow bullet for signs of imperfection. He pouted. "There's never anything to do around here."

"What about your new friend, the one we brought in last night?" asked Colonel Guerrero, thinking: two boys, two little boys. It made him tremble. "Why don't you play with him?"

"He cries all the time. They had to lock him up again. That's no fun."

"Well, maybe you could cheer him up."

Carlitos grunted, pushed the cartridge back into the magazine, punched the magazine back into the butt, and aimed the rifle at a point behind Colonel Guerrero's head. "Bang," he said. "Bang."

"Don't do that," said Colonel Guerrero. "How many times do I have to tell you?"

The thought of the new little boy—Miguel was his name—made Colonel Guerrero remember the boy's older sister, who had visited him in his office a little earlier that day, with her heavy accusing breasts. At first, the woman had demanded her brother's release—straight out, just like that.

Colonel Guerrero had been equal to this approach. "No," he had said. He shook his head. "The fatherland demands. . . . "

But the woman suddenly removed her shawl, narrowed her eyes, and offered to . . . negotiate. That's what she'd said. "Can't we," she said, "negotiate . . . ?"

Colonel Guerrero stood upright, felt the wall at his back. What was she suggesting? She was approaching him now, with that sly accusing look. That look. That look. The colonel thought at once of his mother—his mother embracing him, the heat of her body, her loose rounded flesh, and his own head pressed between those two great. . . .

He couldn't even say the word. He couldn't breathe.

The colonel shuddered at the memory of what happened next, at the memory of those . . . breasts. Exposed and wanton, bulging right there in his office. She was taking off her dress! "Stop! Young lady! Stop that this instant . . . ! Orderly! Orderly!"

But he was too late. It all happened so fast, before he could prepare himself, take preventive action. A jug of water flew from his desk, his chair fell over. A flurry of yellow material, parting, opening. And . . . those breasts.

He struggled free, groped his way towards the window. He needed air. He needed to breathe. He threw open the window. That was all he remembered. That, and the clatter of heels—dwindling, dwindling—and the rasp-rasp-rasp of his lungs.

Now, almost an hour later, Colonel Guerrero struggled to erase the memory of those breasts. Could he ever forget them? They made him think of the heat of his mother's body, the press of her flesh, her voice cackling in his ears. "Baby, my own darling ba—"

"Mother!" he'd cry. "Let me go! Let me—!"

And suddenly he had an idea. He had an idea for a way to exploit his opportunity. Of course! It was perfect! "Orderly!" he called. "Orderly!"

The orderly soon appeared in the doorway, clicked his heels, and saluted. "*Sí, mi coronel.*"

"Go," said Colonel Guerrero, "and find that woman again, the one with the . . . you know. The parasol. Tell her I want to see her. Tell her I have reconsidered. Oh, and the foreign television crew, the Canadians—tell them I will see them. I will see them now."

A few minutes later, the orderly returned to report that the young woman with the parasol could not be found. But Colonel Guerrero decided that it didn't matter. Even better, really. The woman had probably started home on foot. They would meet her along the way. "Just get me the television crew," he said.

Josefina put out her hand to support herself against the terrace railing in front of the garrison. She waited for her heart to slow, but her blood kept racing. It had all been so unexpected, so contrary to what she'd foreseen. The officer had recoiled, pushed her away, knocked over a jug of water, bellowed for his orderly.

Josefina remembered her frantic efforts to pull her brassiere back into place. She'd tugged at the white chiffon fringe on her dress. She must have caught her fingers in the chain around her neck. The clasp broke, and the tiny golden crucifix flew away, collided against the scrubbed concrete floor. She left it there, turned, and ran.

A dark labyrinth of corridors. Shadows. Murky courtyards. She twisted through them in a daze. At last she emerged past the pair of sentries, out into the swirling afternoon light of the main plaza. Her heart beat like a motor, exactly like a motor. She nearly fell, reached out blindly to keep her balance. She closed her eyes, waited for her heart to slow, but it didn't slow. It just kept pounding.

Josefina struck out across the plaza, out into the sun. She fought with her parasol. It flew open with a thump, nearly splitting the fine floral fabric. She barely glanced at the party of strange gringos who were lounging at the edge of the square, by their white bus. She saw them only from the corner of her eye. One of them waved. She did not wave back. She kept on walking, holding her parasol above her, just like a lady.

Josefina decided she would go to the presbytery behind the Roman Catholic church. There, she would seek out one of the Catholic fathers from Ireland and she would plead with him to hear her confession. She suddenly wanted desperately to say her confession.

Her mind spun, but Josefina knew that she had sinned. In all the hours that had passed since the abduction of Miguel, she had thought only of herself, of the mouths she had to feed, and of the sacrifice she would make. Where was Miguel now? What must he be thinking, feeling, now? Oh, dear little Miguel. When Miguel cried, which was rare, he had a way of holding his arms up, crossing his elbows in front of his eyes, to hide his tears. Was he crying now?

Miguel was a good boy, soft-spoken, a bit slow but a hard worker. Soldiers always leered and guffawed, carried guns. Miguel's only toys were a hoop of wire and a worn forked stick that made the hoop spin as he trotted along beside it. They might never be used again, those toys, for he would become a soldier now, brandish a rifle, chortle and kill. Josefina thought of the wire hoop and the polished stick, both still resting against the outer wall of the adobe house amid chicken bones and dirt. For the first time, she felt the loss of her brother, like a

29

stab of pain. She had barely thought of him or his suffering until now. That was a sin, a sin of omission, a sin that could be confessed.

Josefina clattered across the square, desperate to confess and to atone. She was in luck. After being admitted to the presbytery, she found one of the Irish fathers, the thin red-haired one, the one named Father Patricio, who set down his fork, washed down his food with water from a glass, pushed back his chair, and took her outside and into the church through the side entrance. He went directly into the confessional to hear the telling of her sins, even though it was not the proper time of day for confessions.

But something was wrong. Josefina emerged from the confessional to kneel alone among the pews and to say her penance, just as the priest had told her, but she still felt burdened—not absolved or purified, as she usually felt. It was as though she had confessed only a portion of her sins, as though some part of her was still impure. But why? What part? She had told the priest of her failure to concern herself right away with the suffering of Miguel. Poor little Miguel. That, she told herself, had been a failure to love, a terrible sin, a sin of omission. A woman's sin. And she had confessed it, hadn't she?

Nonetheless, she felt something still seething inside her, like a fire in the pit of her stomach. That Colonel Guerrero! The commotion he made! As if she'd done something wrong. But what? She'd done nothing. She'd only tried to win freedom for Miguel. That was all. Colonel Guerrero—he was the evil one. He was the one who'd taken Miguel. What had she done? Nothing. Anyway that was what she told herself. She had her

30

dignity, after all, her pride. She felt her eyes turn to slits. She'd done nothing, and yet—the way he reacted! The very idea! It was outrageous! It was . . . !

Josefina didn't know what it was. She had to close her eyes. She tasted bile in her throat. It was too awful. That horrible man!

After saying her penance, Josefina settled back onto the pew, set her purse beside her, with the rosary back inside. She clutched her parasol in her lap, started to worry at the worn fabric with her hands. She huddled there, silent and muttering, her blood still hot. She gazed up at the altar, at the dim ambiguous figure on the Cross, with its ribs sticking out and its little pointed chin. For a moment, her gaze misted and she thought she saw Colonel Guerrero up there.

But no. It was just the shadows. It wasn't what she imagined. It was Christ, after all. It was Christ bleeding to death up there on the Cross, just as always. Why was that deemed beautiful? Why sublime? To suffer, to bleed, and to die.

Josefina felt another pain, like a stab of anger. Then . . . just emptiness. She wrestled with the fabric of her parasol, her fingers taut, wet with perspiration. She tore at the furled material—and suddenly it split apart, tore in her hands. Look at what he'd made her do!

She peered down at the broken parasol in her lap. Now when she opened the parasol outdoors, it would no longer provide a cool flowery barrier. It would no longer give proper shade from the sun.

Half an hour later, Josefina left the church, stepped out into the square, and the afternoon sunlight struck her full in the face, like a blow from a shovel. She nearly

31

lost her balance, almost fell back. She opened her parasol, but the rip in the fabric shot to the hub, the little metal spokes twisted, and the fabric tore apart. The sun burned into her eyes, so that she saw only vaguely the three army jeeps as they roared past. She thought she recognized Colonel Guerrero riding in the front of the first jeep, saw a clump of soldiers in the back, the gringos piled into the second vehicle, more soldiers following in the third. That was all she saw.

And, in a flash, Josefina realized where the jeeps were headed—towards the Osicala road to the north—and she remembered the landmine planted that morning by the guerrillas. She threw up her arms, meaning to wave her empty purse and her broken parasol, anything, anything to stop the jeeps, to warn them. The brightness of the sun bore into her eyes, the jeeps seemed to blur, and Josefina suddenly felt an unfamiliar but not unpleasant throbbing deep inside. She couldn't believe it was so easy. All she had to do was lower her arms.

Colonel Guerrero led Larry and the others from his office, through the gloomy twisting corridors. Larry wasn't sure about this. He wasn't sure what to make of it.

The colonel had already called for three jeeps to be fuelled and made ready. A pair of soldiers had been dispatched to rouse the little boy, Miguel. Larry turned a darkened corner, saw a shaft of light ahead, and followed Colonel Guerrero out into a covered bay, where the three vehicles waited.

Their drivers were smoking. The instant their

commanding officer appeared, the drivers flung down their cigarettes and ground them out with their boots. They saluted.

Colonel Guerrero flicked a salute back at them and pulled on his floppy canvas hat. He motioned to Larry and the others. Sally hurried over. She was knotting a lime-green scarf under her chin. Larry removed his tinted glasses from his left breast pocket and held them at the ready, prepared at any moment to put them on. He and the others gathered around the Salvadoran officer. "*Sí, mi coronel,*" Larry said, in Spanish. It was what he'd heard the orderly say. It seemed appropriate.

The colonel pointed at the second of the three vehicles, the middle one. He muttered something to Sally. Her eyes followed the direction of his hand, and she nodded. "Here," she said to the others. "He wants us to ride in that jeep."

Larry watched the others go over and climb in. Pete handed the TV equipment up to Daniel. Bob hauled himself up and then sagged into the back. Sally got into the front with the driver. Larry remained standing beside the colonel, near the first jeep, trying to think of a question to ask. He was the reporter, after all. He had grade-twelve Spanish too.

A door scraped open. Larry turned to see a couple of guards emerge into the covered bay. They escorted a slim young lad, about thirteen years of age. He was barefoot and wore a pair of torn brown pants and a grimy white T-shirt. He had a thick bush of shiny black hair and kept his arms raised in front of his face, crossed at the elbows.

The other little boy—the one named Carlitos—

marched just behind, prodding the barefoot child in the side with his rifle. "Bang," he said. "Bang."

The two boys climbed into the back of the first jeep, along with the pair of guards. Carlitos gestured at Colonel Guerrero with his rifle. "I want to drive," he whined. "I never get to drive."

"Maybe later, when we're out of town," Colonel Guerrero said. "Maybe then. Now just be quiet. And don't point that thing at me. I've told you and told you."

"You never let me do anything," Carlitos said. He shoved out his thick lower lip. "I never get any fun." He jabbed his rifle barrel into the other boy's side. "Bang."

The other boy wrapped his arms more tightly in front of his face but did not make a sound.

Larry turned and walked back to the middle jeep to join the others. He felt pleased with himself. He hadn't asked a question but he'd understood every word. Now he saw half a dozen teenage soldiers run up from nowhere and throw themselves into the last jeep, the trailing vehicle. Five of them carried rifles. The other lugged another thing, a bigger kind of gun with a sort of bulb at the end.

"Grenade-launcher," said Daniel. Larry turned and met the cameraman's grey inscrutable gaze. Above a red paisley ascot, Daniel flexed his long neck and sniffed the air. He nodded. He was always identifying guns like that. The guy was a walking arms manual, according to Bob Carling. "An M-79," the cameraman added. "Keep your head down."

"Thanks," said Larry. He climbed into the back of the jeep and squeezed in beside Bob, just behind Sally. Larry shifted his feet to the side, to give Daniel and the camera more room. This wasn't going to be bang-bang, he thought—thank God—but it was going to be something, some kind of human-interest angle. He wasn't quite sure how he was going to handle it.

Larry thought of the obvious approach, something like: SALVADORAN WITH A HEART—ARMY OFFICER CONSENTS TO LET YOUNG CONSCRIPT RETURN HOME FOR THE PLANTING. Something like that. It had been Colonel Guerrero's idea. The colonel was a much smaller man than Larry had expected, a sombre little man with bugged-out eyes and a wormy complexion. He had outlined his idea to the Canadians immediately after ushering them into his office. Sally had translated.

A young boy, Miguel Velásquez Ochoa, had been picked up in error the night before. It turned out the boy was actually too young for military service, and despite the lies and propaganda of the international Communist conspiracy, the Salvadoran army did not press under-age boys into combat, although it was well known that the Marxist subversives did precisely that. Girls, too.

As it happened, the colonel said, the boy's sister had reported the mistake that very day. She had complained that her brother was needed at home for the planting of the corn. So Miguel was going to be reunited with his family, right now, this afternoon. The army was taking him home.

He, Colonel Guerrero, would personally direct the great mission of mercy, as was his custom, and he would be pleased if the Canadians came along in order to record this act of humanitarianism for the television viewers of their country and to help counter the calumnies and distortions propagated by subversion's grip on so much of the Western media. All he asked in return, Colonel Guerrero said, was a copy, perhaps two, of the Canadian broadcast. He specified VHS.

In the colonel's office, the Canadians had pondered the proposal. Finally Bob said they might as well go along. It wasn't as though they had anything else in the hopper that afternoon. Larry pushed his hands back through his hair, then kneaded the bridge of his nose, and finally nodded his agreement. Sally had translated the gist of this exchange into Spanish, and the colonel had smiled a pinched smile and issued the relevant instructions to his orderly.

Larry and the others now waited for Colonel Guerrero to give the command to set off. He did so, raising his right hand and pushing it forward, just like a cavalry officer in a movie about the American Civil War. Off they went, a convoy of growling engines and moaning transmissions, bristling with guns. The jeeps made a circuit of the square, then peeled away past the entrance to the church, flashing out of the shadows and into a blinding bolt of the afternoon sun.

Something caught Larry's eye. He had turned in his seat to wave goodbye to William, the driver, who was going to wait for the crew back in the square. Just then, Larry saw the young woman, the woman with the parasol. She was all alone. She had stepped from the church out into the sunlight and she was unfurling her parasol. A tear suddenly shot through the floral fabric, the parasol flew apart, and the sun burst upon her open face like klieg lights. Larry saw her clearly, as if in close-up.

The woman's features widened in surprise, apparently at the passage of the jeeps. Larry saw the surprise turn to what seemed like alarm. The woman started to raise her arms, as if to wave at the jeeps. Then the expression on her face changed again. Her face solidified into hard lines—like the clenched face of a man. She seemed to hesitate. She lowered her arms and stood stock still.

The jeeps roared away, snarling in protest against the shifting down of their gears. They swung to the right past the blue plaster wall of a shuttered general store, bounced along the rutted dirt road that led north of San Francisco Gotera, heading for guerrilla country. The young woman was gone.

Larry debated telling Sally what he had just seen. Maybe they should turn back. Maybe there was something wrong. There had been something about the woman's manner, her expression, the way she had moved her arms. But he was probably over-reacting. He waited for someone else to say or do something, but no one did. The woman was just being friendly, he decided. Or perhaps it was a misunderstanding. Besides, it seemed so peaceful now. Everything glistened in the afternoon sun.

Green and iridescent, a duo of parrots swooped overhead, parted, converged, then shot away across the parched brown earth, disappeared to the south. Larry watched them vanish. He turned, raised his hand to shield his eyes. He felt the wind blow his hair back, and he peered ahead along the Osicala road.

Several kilometres north of Gotera, Colonel Guerrero ordered his driver to stop. "All right," he said to Carlitos. "Now you can drive."

"I knew it!" shouted Carlitos, who threw down his rifle and hopped into the front seat just as the driver gave way.

Colonel Guerrero directed the other little boy, Miguel, to ride in the passenger seat beside Carlitos. He himself got into the back with his regular driver and the two guards. The colonel glanced around at the Canadians, smiled, and waved. This would be good, he thought. A nice touch. Two young boys: one an orphan being raised by the army, the other being taken home to help his family with the planting of the corn. One of them drives the other safely home—while, he, Colonel Guerrero, rides in the back like a proud benevolent father. Not even that bastard Sigi Castañeda could have dreamed up an idea like this.

A public-relations coup—that was what the army high command would say when they saw the videotape that Colonel Guerrero planned to send them. In fact, he decided he should suggest the phrase. A public-relations coup. The videotape would vault him to fame, better even than fighting battles on American TV. Here was the army, victim of so many scurrilous lies in the past, finally portrayed on foreign TV in its true role, as defender of the people, their protector and provider. This was exploiting an opportunity, exploiting it to the hilt.

Colonel Guerrero prepared to give the order to continue, but Carlitos had already rammed the shift into first and now floored the accelerator. He popped the

38

clutch. The jeep fishtailed in the dirt, churning up clouds of dust along with Carlitos's reedy screeches of laughter. The two other drivers raced to keep up.

Colonel Guerrero rocked back, gripped his floppy canvas hat. On second thought, perhaps he wouldn't employ the word "coup" when describing the afternoon's events to his superiors in San Salvador. They were touchy about that word.

Sally Gillespie saw the whole thing. She saw even more than Daniel, who had to stay low and concentrate on his camera. She saw what happened when the front wheels of the lead jeep hit the contact pan above the landmine. The full blast of the explosion burst through the front section of the jeep's chassis, splitting the engine apart and hurling the vehicle into the air, instantly killing the two little boys.

Colonel Guerrero and his driver and the two guards survived the initial blast and were sent somersaulting through the shimmering air, as if in slow motion. However, according to the medical reports—summarized to Sally later, off the record, by a friend of hers in the army's press section—the driver and one of the two guards were both dead of shrapnel wounds by the time they hit the ground. The colonel and the other guard sustained injuries of considerable, but not fatal, severity.

From the overlooking hummock, a band of guerrillas snapped to its knees and opened fire. Pete McArthur was hit in the chest straight off, but survived. He later vowed never to return to Central America. Larry Pozniak lost his glasses in the first moments of panic and admitted to Sally the next day that he remembered nothing of what happened. Could she fill him in? One of the soldiers in the trailing vehicle was shot in the head and died within minutes. The other soldiers fanned out along the edge of the road, flopped down on their bellies, started shooting. They drove the guerrillas off after a brief but thrilling firefight.

During the shooting, Bob Carling kept well down and used his blue terrycloth hat to sop up some of the blood seeping from Pete McArthur's wound. In a loud voice, he kept promising God he would give up smoking. "That's weird," Bob said to Sally that night, back in the capital, where they'd all been flown by army helicopter. "I haven't had a cigarette in almost two years."

Sally herself had observed the firefight from a position on her knees behind the Canadians' jeep. Over several beers a couple of nights later, she described the entire scene to Larry, right down to intriguing little details such as the quite different sounds made by outgoing and incoming rifle fire. Larry scribbled it all down for use in his report. "Great stuff," he kept saying. "This is great stuff."

Immediately after the initial explosion, which he'd recorded on camera, Daniel Rivard—a veteran of Beirut and other foreign trouble spots—leapt from the Canadians' jeep. He groped for the sound equipment and scrambled forward, across the road, into the teeth of the bullets—camera in one hand, sound-machine in the other. He crawled into a shallow ditch and managed to get the whole battle on tape, although the quality of the sound was iffy. Daniel's only other substantial comment afterwards was that it would have been better if he could have shot from a higher angle.

Toronto was deeply impressed and congratulated everyone. The bang-bang clip aired in the United States on NBC and in Britain on the BBC. Two months later, Larry telephoned Sally in triumph to say that he was going to be posted to Washington to replace Gloria Reynolds, who was returning to Ottawa. Health reasons were cited.

Colonel Guerrero was in the army hospital in San Salvador with shrapnel wounds and so missed the NBC broadcast of the bomb blast and the ensuing firefight. He grumbled about that when Sally went in to visit him. He also complained that Larry and Bob seemed to have forgotten their promise to send him a VHS copy of the CBC tape. Sally said she'd see what she could do. On the bright side, the colonel said, he had received a nice consoling note from the Defence Minister and another from "that bastard Sigi Castañeda". Colonel Guerrero seemed to be mourning little Carlitos, in his way.

Meanwhile, on the afternoon of March twenty-fourth— the first anniversary of the conception of her son— Josefina Velásquez Ochoa folded her broken parasol beneath her arm and set out on foot from San Francisco Gotera for the long journey home. She walked quickly, eager, squinting through the sharp rays of the late-day sun, wondering what she would see.

So Far, She's Fine

Carmen Lukovic Gasteozoro returned from the dead at 8:25 last Thursday morning, riding in the back seat of a Santiago taxicab. The driver let Carmen off at the corner of the Alameda and Vicuña Mackenna and sped away without a word. He didn't even ask for the fare. Carmen used a public telephone in the Baquedano Metro station to call her mother and father, to tell them that she was back and that she was fine. Carmen's father said oh, God, don't move, he'd be there like a shot.

Carmen imagined her father waddling out of the house and thrusting himself into the family's brand-new Peugeot stationwagon, forest-green in colour because that was what Carmen's mother had said she preferred. As he drove, Señor Lukovic would be perspiring heavily, mopping his brow with a great white handkerchief, his chins nearly touching the wheel. He was unreliable with a car at the best of times and a threat to all on the road when he grew flustered. Carmen also thought about her mother, who would be hurrying upstairs even now, in a frenzy, to wash her hair. Later, trembling with excitement, she would greet Carmen from the landing, with her head wrapped in a towel. Carmen's mother never did anything important without first washing her hair.

To pass the time while waiting for her father, Carmen went outside and crossed the street. She balanced herself on a wrought-iron bench in the Parque Forestal, by the banks of the Mapocho River. The late-winter sunshine spilled over the wall of the Andes to the east, still snow-covered. The shade trees in the park were budding and now shifted to and fro in the cool morning breeze. Nearby, a pair of teenagers wrestled— a boy and a girl, both in blue jeans, bulky sweaters, and plaid scarves. They took turns throwing each other to the grass, where they rolled over and over, nuzzled their cheeks together, rubbed their noses back and forth, licked each other's ears. Then they laughed, got up, and did it all again. The traffic barked and grunted past along the Alameda.

Carmen clasped her hands in her lap, crossed her long legs at the ankles, shifted her feet a little to the side, and watched the day expand. Aside from a rather nasty bruise on her left thigh and a cigarette burn on the inside of her right breast, she bore no physical traces of her ordeal, or none that she could detect. What she felt was a certain numbness, a slight tingly sensation all over her body, rather like a ringing in the ears after a very loud explosion. She felt almost as though she were floating through the air. That was all.

And that was what everyone remarked on. "She seems—fine," the people whispered to each other. They were neighbours, relations, friends of the family who dropped by the house that morning after hearing the news that Carmen had returned from the dead. They gathered in the dining room.

"How are you, Carmen?" asked one of her aunts, who'd just arrived.

Everyone froze. Idiotic question.

But Carmen simply tossed back her hair and smiled. "Famished," she replied.

That was obvious. They all watched as the girl put away three slices of chocolate pie and two large glasses of apple cider. Carmen didn't say another word. She just drank and ate and occasionally looked up with an apologetic sort of grin. Then she picked the crumbs from the plate with her fingers. Señora Lukovic stood behind her daughter, gently massaging her shoulders.

When the older woman eased her grip, started to remove her hands in order to clear the dishes, Carmen reached up and pulled her mother's arms back. "Please don't stop," she whispered.

It was a powerful moment. The onlookers in the dining room exchanged glances, nodded at each other. This was such an occasion. Just think—returned from the dead. It started with your name going down on a secret list, with a late-night ride in an unmarked car. When people went missing, as Carmen had done, they never came back. Once you lost sight of them, they were gone.

But here was Carmen—a tall athletic girl of eighteen, splashed with freckles, and crowned by a great tangle of dark hair streaked with coppery highlights. She played centre on the women's field hockey team at the Universidad Católica and often, when she strode along a crowded street or hurried through the rooms of the family home, she looked as though she were stick-handling through a maze of opponents, her eyes fixed like twin beacons on the opposing goal. But then she would burst out laughing, over anything, anything at all, and the illusion would be shattered. She was just a girl of eighteen, straightforward, good-hearted, taking the world as it came.

They had a press conference at eleven o'clock, right in the living room. Carmen's father and her older brother pushed the furniture out of the way to make room for the television cameras. The journalists crowded inside, bickering and jostling for space. They fussed with their tape recorders and microphones, set up their cameras, and switched on the TV lights.

Carmen presided from a chair placed behind a refectory table. She crossed her arms in front of her, shook out her hair, pushed her caterpillar eyebrows together, and leaned towards the bouquet of microphones in front of her.

"How do you feel?"

At first Carmen said nothing. She seemed to be drawing a complete blank on this one. She gazed at the speaker and wrinkled her brow, as if she didn't quite understand his accent or hadn't anticipated that there would be questions.

At the back of the room, a man cleared his throat. Somewhere in front, a woman sighed loudly. Anything to fill the silence.

45

But all at once Carmen straightened her shoulders. She made a what-can-I-say sort of face. "Savage," she announced and smiled.

The journalists glanced at each other. She was feeling savage?

But it seemed Carmen didn't really mean that. Savage was a new slang expression that young people were using as an all-purpose superlative—tiptop. The journalists went on frowning for a few moments, still unsure, but then relaxed. The word was harmless. They understood now.

"Do you have any idea who abducted you?" someone asked.

"Yes," Carmen replied promptly. "In fact, I do. But I'm afraid I cannot go into that part right now. I'm sorry."

Off to the side, Carmen's older brother, Alejandro, nodded to himself. Before the press conference, he'd warned Carmen about just this sort of question. She had to be careful not to point any fingers—there could be reprisals. The Chilean police, it was well known, responded badly to criticism. Alejandro was a lawyer, and caution was his watchword.

"Were you tortured, or beaten?" asked a slim young man in a tweed jacket, a brown V-neck sweater, and a tie. He was from *La Tercera*. His collar was frayed.

Carmen shifted sideways in her chair, and a muscle started twitching beneath her left eye. She reached up to hold that muscle still.

Alejandro stepped forward. "I think that will be enough questions for—"

But Carmen put up her hand. "It's all right," she

46

said. She looked back at the reporter from *La Tercera*. "Was I tortured? Beaten?" She swallowed and pushed back her hair. "Yes. I was."

Another reporter, from somewhere in the rear: "Do you have any idea why you were abducted?"

"I think," Carmen said, more confident now, raising her voice to be heard, "it was because of Jaime Calderón." She meant a former boyfriend, with whom she had broken up more than a year ago, entirely for personal reasons. Jaime was one of four men who had been found in a field in Pudahuel out near the airport, five weeks earlier. They'd all had their throats slit from ear to ear. Jaime had been a member of the Communist Party—so that was the explanation for that. Everyone had been horrified, Carmen no less than the others. But Carmen herself was not active in politics, never had been.

"Can you," asked a blonde-haired woman, a reporter for the Universidad Católica TV station, "tell us a little bit about your ordeal, in general terms?"

And Carmen did exactly that. She didn't hesitate at all, and her voice remained steady. She described her abduction—the two men who had accosted her as she hurried home through the pouring rain after classes. Carmen recalled for the journalists the entangling of arms, the revealed gun, the waiting car, its motor running, the blindfold, the roundabout drive.

But she did not refer to the pawing in the car that night, or the crude jokes about the smallness of her breasts. "Shit, man, you could put these things in an egg cup," one of her assailants had scoffed. He pinned back her arms with a single hand. "If all I wanted was a couple

47

of eggs I could've stayed home and tickled my own balls. Throw her back, man. We want grapefruits. Big ones." Another of the men had been inspired by this to pluck at Carmen's cheek with his thumb and forefinger, wagging her face and breathing on her a dense fume of pisco and onions. "Where are the big ones, dear heart?"

Then Carmen felt the man slide down to place his mouth at the level of her bare left breast. For a moment, she even felt the rasp of his whiskered jaw. "Where are the big ones?" he growled at the nipple. Carmen could sense the sour heat of his breath on her skin. He started to slap at her breast—almost playfully, slap-slap, slap-slap—just the way you'd do across the face of a tongue-tied captive, very early on, to get his attention. "Talk, you! Where are the big ones? Talk, you! Talk. . . !"

Interrogating a breast! Ha-ha-ha!

They all laughed. One man belched, and another changed the subject to soccer. What was the outlook for Colo-Colo, those faggots, this year?

And so, blindfolded, her blouse yanked open, her arms locked behind her, through the night and the constant drumbeat of the rain, surrounded by invisible men, Carmen Lukovic Gasteozoro was carried off to her death.

"Were you raped?" another reporter asked.

And there were a few low whistles and moans of disapproval. People didn't look fondly on this sort of question. Abduction was one thing, but rape was more private somehow, a more intimate pain.

"Yes," Carmen said. She spoke in a whisper and lowered her eyes. "More than once." She hesitated before she looked back up. She started to say something else but stopped herself. She took a deep breath.

It was only then that someone—Emilio Jones, a regular columnist for *El Mercurio*—asked the one question everyone had really wanted to ask all along, but had hesitated to pose for fear of seeming morbid. "What did it feel like?" he asked. He was wearing a navy-blue jacket, a red ascot tie. "What did it really feel like—to be dead?" Apparently this was the angle he proposed to take in his column.

Carmen looked down at her hands. On her left wrist she still wore the beaded blue and red bracelet that she'd strung for herself when she was twelve years old. It was the one article her captors had not removed from her during five or six separate interrogations. Who cared about a stupid bracelet when they had an eighteen-year-old girl? Carmen looked at those familiar strung beads and remembered her greatest fear as a child. She'd had a horror of being buried in the mud beneath a river, a lake, or the sea.

Now she looked up and tried to explain to the journalists about that fear, what it meant. As a child, it had been her firm belief that all souls were known to God and could be restored unto Him, except those souls that were trapped in bodies buried under water. Those souls were lost for all eternity. "It felt," Carmen said, "just that way. That was how it felt." She was silent for a few moments, then looked up and smiled. "Are there any other questions?" She believed she could handle at least another one or two.

But the journalists had got what they needed. They packed up their equipment and filed out into the street, climbed into their cars and mini-vans. They headed back downtown to put together their reports for the evening news or the next editions. SANTIAGO STUDENT RETURNS FROM THE DEAD. As usual, they all hit upon the exact same angle.

Carmen's family were amazed at how well she had handled herself during the press conference. Alejandro had been against it from the start, arching his eyebrows and clucking his tongue, but Señor Lukovic had overruled him.

"If Carmen wants to do this," he had said, "then we have to let her. Besides, the people have a right to know."

It was a risk. Señor Lukovic had known it was a risk. He'd worried she might break down. But Carmen had conducted herself with surprising composure, as if she'd barely been through anything at all. What was holding the girl up? Señor Lukovic shook his head. He just didn't know, and that made him uneasy.

In the middle of the afternoon, Carmen and her mother went off to the Hospital El Salvador in a taxi, so that Carmen could be examined. But everything seemed to go smoothly there as well, as Señora Lukovic reported to her husband that evening. The couple were talking in their bedroom, while they dressed for a small celebration in Carmen's honour.

Señora Lukovic buckled the belt on her dress and twisted in front of the full-length mirror, eyeing her reflection over her shoulder. "I agree. It's a miracle," she told her husband. "But that's what the doctors said. On the whole, she's in good shape. Good shape physically." Señora Lukovic got out two pairs of shoes from the closet and went over to the bed. She said, "Gus."

"Yes?"

"Doesn't it seem strange?"

"What does?"

"That she seems so—normal. Or not normal, exactly. But she should be a wreck. She should be in bed, taking tranquillizers. She should be speechless."

Señor Lukovic nodded. It was true. It was what he thought himself.

"Instead, on the way home from the hospital, she wouldn't stop talking. She wants to go to Buenos Aires soon. There's some concert there. And she wondered, should she cut her hair? Maybe just a trim? Oh, and of course we had to stop for ice cream. She was perishing for ice cream. And she's not going to be a lawyer, after all. She's going to be a vet. And she plans to read more, too. One book a week. She's thinking of taking up French. And jazz singing. And horseback riding. On and on. I couldn't make her hush. Not that I tried very hard. I just went along. I was glad, of course. But. I mean. I don't know. It seems so odd. What do you think?"

Señor Lukovic ran the heel of one hand across his forehead. "I know," he said. "I've been wondering the same thing." He shifted his several chins, in order to get a good look at his collar in the mirror. He clutched the loose ends of his bow tie with large pudgy hands.

"She's not facing up to it," his wife went on. "She's not facing up to what happened. Except for the press conference this morning, she hasn't talked about it at all. Not one word. A couple of times I tried to mention it, but she just changed the subject. She started to talk about clothes."

"Clothes?"

51

His wife shrugged. "Well, she is eighteen, after all. She's bound to be concerned about clothes. But still. It was very strange. I'm worried. You can't just get over a thing like this. Gus?"

Señor Lukovic let out a long breath of air. He wanted to say something reassuring, but couldn't think of any words that wouldn't seem trite or false. "We'll just have to see," was what he said. "We'll just have to stay close to her and see what happens. Maybe she'll be all right. You never know."

He looked back at the mirror. He wasn't sure what else to say—the things they had done to his daughter! At first he'd been stunned by what he heard at the press conference, so horrified that he couldn't feel a thing. But later Carmen's words had sunk in. Started to. The images haunted him all afternoon, until he had to close his eyes to shut them out. Otherwise he'd go mad.

Yet Carmen had survived, and more than survived. She seemed almost unchanged on the surface, as if nothing had touched her, as if her life had been returned to her, not shattered but whole. Señor Lukovic stared at his reflection in the mirror. What was holding their daughter up? He couldn't say. He didn't know.

He turned to look at his wife, her slender figure and powdered face, her short waves of blue-rinsed hair. She sat on the bed with one knee beneath her, trying to choose between two pairs of black shoes. She looked up to hold her husband's gaze. Then they both smiled and shook their heads and quickly turned away because they both were crying. Who would have dreamed they'd be having a celebration tonight?

Señor Lukovic blinked several times and began to

fumble with his tie. In a minute he'd give it up, and his wife would do the knot for him. But he always liked to try.

Immediately after his daughter's disappearance, he had made the rounds of a number of his associates in the Christian Democratic Party—effectively banned, like all the old political parties—in order to organize support for her release. In his younger days, long before the coup, he had been an adviser to President Eduardo Frei, so he was pretty well connected. Almost everyone liked him, which had turned out to be of critical importance following Carmen's abduction.

Even senior military officers tempered their usual contempt for civilian politicians when they dealt with Gustavo Lukovic. He was a good church-going family man, they had to admit. There he went—always shuffling about, mopping his brow, seeking appointments with generals and colonels about the issues of the day. He tried to get things done in a reasonable manner. The officers respected that and briefly wondered if they weren't sometimes a bit too harsh in the way they ran the country.

But when Señor Lukovic had left their gloomy chambers, the officers promptly forgot him and everything he'd said, and went right back to ruling Chile in their usual fashion. This may explain why, when the low-level order went out to abduct Señor Lukovic's daughter, it slipped through the system. Carmen's name was jotted down, just like all the others. By the time the mistake was discovered and verified, it was too late. She was already gone.

When the news of Carmen's disappearance

became widely known, there was an outcry. Twice, the Archbishop of Santiago broadcast appeals for her release over the Catholic radio station. All the banned political parties used what little influence they had to get the government to act. Meanwhile, telegrams of protest poured in from outraged officials and solidarity organizations in other countries.

Señor Lukovic barely slept during this period. He talked to everyone he could, drove from one building to the next, called in long-standing political debts. He plodded from office to office, from meeting to meeting, cajoled and pleaded. Perspiration ran down his great jowly face, and his handkerchiefs got soaked. Alejandro worked the phones, and Señora Lukovic enlisted as many of her friends as she could, to use feminine suasion with the wives of the military officers.

In the end, the question ran right up the chain of command to the very top, to His Excellency General Augusto Pinochet Ugarte, Commander-in-Chief of the Armed Forces and President of the Republic. He was the one who had to decide. There were no witnesses to the discussion itself, apart from the small tight-lipped cluster of senior military men who were in the room at the time. But when the meeting was finally adjourned, the order that was issued and repeated in hushed tones along the dark carpeted corridors of La Moneda, the presidential palace, went something like this: "I don't care how you do it, but give the girl back to her family. Alive."

This was unprecedented. It went entirely against the grain. How to begin? Did anyone know where the girl had been taken? Was she even alive? If so, to what extent? In the end it all got sorted out. They had one of their undercover people drive Carmen back in a taxi.

At the dinner party that night in her honour, Carmen almost seemed to float. About two dozen people showed up for the celebration, including some aunts and uncles, Carmen's godparents—Señor and Señora Echeverría—and a few of her closest chums from school. Guests made speeches and proposed toasts. The room erupted in gales of laughter, and Carmen and her school friends linked arms to sing their school anthem. "Savage!" Carmen exclaimed. She shook out her hair and hugged her friends one by one, then all together. She was wearing a short black skirt, a black turtleneck jersey, and a lovely vest embroidered with an oriental floral pattern. In addition to that old string of beads, she had gold bracelets on both wrists. She looked beautiful. She seemed perfectly fine.

Everyone stood up together to sing "Gracias a la Vida", the Violeta Parra song. They all embraced, and there was no shortage of tears. Señor Lukovic sauntered about with a bottle of Napoleon brandy. He grew more subdued as the evening wore on. He kept turning to watch his daughter, as she circulated among the guests. He was struck by how tightly she held each person, how she let go, immediately reached out for someone else.

Señor Lukovic could feel a strange pressure in his temples. Carmen was, by her own admission, or boast, a demonstrative sort of girl. What was that appalling phrase she sometimes used? Kissy-face, pressy-body— that was it. Those were the words she often used herself, to describe her penchant for hugs and cuddles—shows of affection that were normal for Carmen, a necessity.

But this was different. These weren't embraces. Carmen was holding on.

He noticed that her arms and hands were never still, that she was always reaching—to push back a girlfriend's hair so that she could whisper something into her ear, or to clasp an older relative by the elbow, or to draw a pair of friends closer, or simply to hold somebody's, anybody's, hand. She was always clutching at something, as though she might otherwise fall.

And several times Señor Lukovic caught snatches of conversation—his daughter telling her friends about the courses she planned to enrol in, or the dance steps she wanted to learn, or the trips she hoped to take. Once, when he wandered close to Carmen and several of her friends, she slipped an arm around his back, and took his hand in one of hers.

"Here's the man who's going to have to pay for all this educating," she said and grinned up at him.

Señor Lukovic shrugged, held up the bottle of brandy. It was empty. He looked at Carmen's friends. "I may of course go broke."

Everyone laughed, and Carmen laughed too.

"More brandy," someone shouted, someone who must have overheard. "You can go broke tomorrow, Gustavo. Tonight we drink."

More laughter. The snap of cigarette lighters. Señor Lukovic kissed Carmen on the forehead, turned, and trudged out to the kitchen. He opened the liquor cabinet and caught sight of his pale reflection in the kitchen window. Nothing that had happened that night had made him any less fearful. He pulled a fresh bottle down from the shelf, ran his handkerchief across its dark green surface to clear the dust. He recalled an anecdote he'd once heard, about a man who fell from the top of a very tall building. The man hurtled towards the earth, faster and faster. Along the way, he called to horrified witnesses staring out through the windows, "I'm fine so far!" Those words began to echo and shift in Señor Lukovic's mind. He thought again of his daughter.

When he returned to the living room, everyone had risen to sing the Chilean national anthem—not for the military government, they sang for *la Patria*—and he lumbered over to plant himself beside his wife, who was alone with her arms crossed at her chest, near the simmering warmth of the fireplace. She touched her hand to her hair, then smiled at him, and held out her brandy snifter. "Perhaps just a smidgen," she whispered. Carmen hurried over, and then Alejandro, and they put their arms around each other. The guests all turned to watch and briefly lowered their voices, uncertain what to do. But Carmen and her family looked up, joined right in—and now there was no stopping anybody. They all sang out, loud as they could.

Despite her parents' pleading that she take things slowly, Carmen went straight back to school on Monday. A nice boy, Roberto Sepúlveda, has asked her out on a date for this Saturday, and she has said yes. The two of them plan to go to a movie and afterwards maybe meet some friends in one of the noisy outdoor cafés near the funicular station at the bottom of the Santa Lucía hill.

Yesterday, Carmen even turned out for the Universidad Católica game against the women's field-hockey team from Concepción. She scored one goal and had an assist in a winning effort. In the dying minutes, she was jostled by two opponents and went down hard. She gave her ankle an awful wrench. But she climbed back up and kept right on playing—and now she won't admit that she was hurt at all. The ankle has swollen up like a balloon, yet she refuses to rest it. "Never mind," she keeps saying. "It's nothing at all."

View of Guazapa

Javier Mena peered out his office window late on a Friday afternoon. He watched the sunlight break against the shining ridge of Guazapa, and he thought—guerrillas. There were guerrillas on that mountain, had been for years. When push came to shove, Mena would join them. He would have nowhere else to go.

He reached up to put on his tortoiseshell glasses, and Guazapa suddenly turned to a roiling smear, drifting upon a sea of mud. The metal jambs of his office window leapt back into view. Mena turned. "You know the ground rules?" he said.

"I'm sorry. Ground rules?"

Mena peered across his desk, across the stacks of papers neatly assembled, the reference books sprouting page markers like gravestones, all carefully annotated, the card-index file. "That's right," he said. "The ground rules. We have to lay out some ground rules."

The American reporter shifted in his chair. He had a big, round head, an even bigger, rounder behind. He flipped open his notepad. His face went bland as pancake batter, two little blueberries for the eyes. "You mean you don't want to be quoted by name?"

"No. That's not what I mean. I mean: I don't want to be quoted at all." Mena reached forward, pulled out his chair, shifted his weight, lowered himself carefully. Beneath his baggy mock-fatigue pants, the pain in his right leg flared up again. Arthritis? Could it be arthritis? At his age?

Mena gazed at the reporter, at his slack untested face. This was the danger—they didn't understand. "Here's how it works," he said in English, forming the words as if by rote. "First. This conversation is off the record. You can't quote me. You can't refer to me. Not by name. Not at all. This is just a bunch of information you picked up somewhere. That's it. Okay?"

The American frowned, hesitated. Then a ripple of assent played across his features, leaving them much as before. "Okay," he said. As they always did.

"Second. You can't mention my name to anyone— to anyone. Not to your friends. Not to your colleagues. I was not your source." Mena parted his hands, sat back. "I've got no wish to become famous."

"No wish to—?"

"Become famous. You realize what happens to famous people in this country?"

"No," the reporter said. "No, I don't. I don't live in this country. Look, can't we—"

"If they're lucky," Mena said, "they have funerals."

The reporter looked towards the window, sighed.

"It's very simple." Mena spoke quickly now, from memory. "If you break these ground rules, if you identify me in print, then I'll become famous. The death squads will know my name. And, then, if I'm lucky, I'll wind up lying by the road somewhere, with a bullet through my head and my cock stuck in my teeth. Do you understand? If I'm lucky. If I'm not lucky, I'll simply disappear. I'll never be heard from again. No funeral. No nothing. The death squads aren't fond of people like me. So don't make me famous. Okay?" Mena crossed his legs, grit his teeth against a simmer of pain. "Okay?"

"All right. I understand."

"Okay. We have fifty minutes. Go ahead."

The reporter hauled himself up in his seat. He gestured importantly with his pen. "Doctor Mena," he said. "What portion of the rural populace currently supports the left-wing guerrillas? In round numbers."

And Dr. Javier Mena—Ph.D., political science, Columbia University, 1979—put his hands behind his head, gazed towards the ceiling, and proceeded to explain that in El Salvador in 1982 there were no companies conducting public-opinion polls.

It was Mena's standard response to the standard first question in the occasional off-the-record briefings he conducted for foreign journalists passing through El Salvador. The sessions invariably proceeded along similar lines and always contained the seeds of his death. Sooner or later, someone would blunder. A reporter would forget, and mention Mena's name in print. Or perhaps it would be done deliberately—who knew why? Either way, he would become famous, and his name would go down on someone's list.

There were dozens of lists in town. Sometimes they were even published in *El Diario de Hoy* or *La Prensa Gráfica*. "The Maximiliano Hernández Martínez Brigade respectfully communicates to the public that the following individuals have been sentenced to die." And the names would follow, row upon row, often misspelled. But normally the names were not published until afterward, if ever.

Mena did not propose to die that way. Instead, when the time came, as it must, he would try to outwit the death squads. He would abandon doubt and join the guerrillas. The guerrillas on Guazapa. He still believed in them, in their cause.

But it was not safe to discuss rebels or rebellion, so Mena always limited his briefing sessions to one hour, no longer. When this hour was at an end and another Friday dusk had snaked through the capital, Mena rose and strolled to the door of his office with the reporter. He briefly held the man's cool, unmuscled hand. They said goodbye. Mena watched the American sag down the stairs. Would this reporter be the one?

He went back into his office, flicked off the light, and rounded his desk to stand by the window. He removed his glasses and fussed at the lenses with the tail of his denim workshirt. He peered off into the rising darkness, tried to discern the outline of Guazapa. One day he would escape to Guazapa. One day he would have to. He would have no choice.

Mena drove home in his second-hand Datsun 240-Z. Just before the first police roadblock, the car stalled. He cranked the ignition three, four times—but nothing. Just click, click, click. Oh, Christ. He had to climb out and push the damn thing off to the side. He shoved the car forward with his left arm, steered with his right hand. A stalled car—that was suspicious. The police would want to search him now. He jumped in, hit the brakes. He looked up. They were coming, two of them, strolling over through the darkness and the shafts of fuzzy light. Automatic rifles. They carried automatic rifles—the traffic police.

"Abre el baúl," one said, pointed with his rifle.

Mena went back and opened the trunk. He stood over on the curb and watched them search, his hands in his pockets. Cars, trucks, buses clanked and rattled past. Exhaust fumes swirled like snow in the glow of the headlights. Mena waited. They were going over every inch of the car. This was risky—being searched. The police could always find something, or plant something. They knew he came from the university—there was a parking sticker in the window. People at the university were Communists, all of them, according to the police. Mena reached up and rubbed his two-day beard. He decided he would shave it off. It wasn't safe, a beard. It was . . . Communist.

Now they were probing beneath the seats. One of them was down on his knees on the pavement, with his head craned sideways. They were taking their time. They laughed at something, and one tapped his rifle barrel several times against the side of the car. It raised the level of tension, this. Made people like Mena squirm.

The police had the idea that rebels—or people running weapons for the rebels—would be driving dilapidated cars. Only rich people drove cars that worked—Cherokees or Mercedes Benzes. Rich people could fly the spare parts in from Miami.

Mena worried about the state of his car. Someday he might need that car, need it urgently. It bothered him that the machine could not be trusted. He wanted order, predictability. But what could he do? On weekends, he sometimes spent hours beneath the car hood, but it made little difference. The problem was spares—it was so difficult to obtain spares. Things broke and could not be fixed.

Wherever Mena looked, it was the same. The country's economy was a disaster. Almost every day there were power blackouts—the rebels blowing up another pylon. Who would invest in El Salvador now, a republic at war with itself? The money was flying out of the country—to Miami, to Los Angeles—in U.S.-dollar cheques purchased on the black market, in wads of greenbacks hidden in suitcases. All the skilled people were fleeing or had fled. Peasants staggered over the borders into Honduras, by the thousands. The country was bleeding through every pore, falling apart, because of the war.

"*Está bien,*" one of the policeman said. He slammed the door on the driver's side and dismissed the car with a wave of his rifle. "*Puede ir.*"

Both of them turned and sauntered away, over to the roadblock. Mena watched them go—their rifles dangling from their shoulders, the barrels seeming to smoulder in the beams of the passing headlights.

He climbed back into the car. Sure enough, it wouldn't start. He had to push. It was on an incline, so he managed to get the thing rolling. He jumped in, popped the clutch and . . . thank God. He drove the rest of the way home—no trouble at the second roadblock—and parked in the enclosed lot adjoining his building in the Colonia Miramonte. He left the keys with Juan, the *portero*, who lived with his ever-burgeoning family in a little hut upon the roof.

Why were caretakers always named Juan? And why were they always frail little men with pointed chins and a terror of everything that moved? In a way, Mena knew the answer. In El Salvador there was a very large pool of such men to draw from. As always, this thought saddened him. But what could he do? What could anyone do? *"Gracias, Juan,"* he said and passed through the door. *"Buenas noches."*

Mena walked straight through to the front, to check his mailbox. Often, there were personal letters, sometimes from Miami (his mother), or from San José, Costa Rica (his father). Now, there was only a newsletter he subscribed to from Guatemala City, called *Central America: This Week*. Mena searched the box for another letter—a letter from New York—but of course there was none. Two years he'd been waiting. More than two years. He closed the little metal door.

Someone coughed.

Mena froze, consciously stopped breathing. He clutched the key, still inserted in the slot of his mailbox. The cough had been faint but unmistakable—not really a cough, perhaps, but the first muted rasp of a cough. It had come from somewhere upstairs, the third floor. He waited, motionless. He felt a tingling in his hands. Was he imagining these things, these sounds? Lately, he'd

65

heard them every day, or every night, late at night—a cough, perhaps, or a piece of furniture scraping across the floor overhead. A drawer being closed. A footstep on a section of tile. A voice. Muffled words. A groan. Outside, another wave of traffic bellowed past along the boulevard, hurrying home before the nightly curfew. Then—only silence. He pulled the key from its slot. He removed his glasses and started to mount the front stairs towards his second-floor flat, a two-bedroom condo where he lived alone. Perhaps it was nothing, that coughing sound. Perhaps it was all in his mind. Most of the building was vacant—twelve units, but only three were occupied. The other residents had all left the country for one reason or another, as so many had. Still, they continued to hold onto their homes. They thought they might return.

The stairwell was dark, and shadows darted up from the street through the metal louvers that formed the exterior wall. They cast swift corrugated patterns upon the stairs and the railing, like the blades of knives. Mena felt his way up through the riddling of light and dark—Juan had forgotten to replace the bulbs. The man was not only terrified but, frankly, incompetent. He seemed to be getting worse. His presence was intended to provide the building with some shred of security—a rare and much-prized commodity in El Salvador, but never one to be counted on. Like most people in the country, Mena now simply hoped for the best.

He took another step and felt the pain in his leg again, the right leg, a furtive ache behind the knee this time. Arthritis? Could it be arthritis? He was only thirty-four. He should see a doctor, but he kept putting it off.

He'd have to miss Sunday's baseball game, a weekly affair among the American community. Mena played shortstop and was batting over .350 for the season—or had been, before he started skipping the games. He continued up the stairs towards his apartment. He stopped. What? What was that?

A scraping sound. It scuttled down the stairwell—no mistaking it. A scraping sound, the sole of a shoe twisting against grit on a smooth tile floor. It had come from the third floor, where no one lived. Mena half turned to descend. He listened, gripping his letter and his keys. "¿Hola?" he called up the stairs. "¿Hola?"

He heard nothing, but still he waited. His heart was pounding. Just like that, his heart was pounding. Perhaps he should not go up at all. But that was crazy. He lived in this building. This was his home. Besides, if there was anything wrong, surely Juan would have told him. Surely Juan would know.

He started to climb the stairs again. It wasn't far. He reached his door, with his key already out, his hand extended. He stopped again to listen—not a sound, except the belch of traffic on the street below. The tip of his key rattled against the slot of the lock, refused to enter, balked and chattered, and finally slid through the tumblers. Mena twisted the key, the lock released, the dead bolt slid back, the handle turned, and the door opened.

He pushed inside, closed the door, and locked it behind him. He flicked on the hall light and then went from room to room, turning the lamps on everywhere, or trying to. Some of the bulbs had burnt out. He kept meaning to replace them, but always forgot. And it was all right. Those sounds he'd heard, they were probably nothing. He walked into the kitchen and got out a beer from the small fridge.

It was all right. He had made it home, safe, again. It was all right.

Fear was like a molecule. It got everywhere—into his clothes, his muscles, into his blood, his thoughts, into his sleep. It spread like a virus, worked its way into every cranny, and broke the tissue down. Nights were the worst. They were long, and Mena was alone, and he never knew what to expect. Days were better. There was less to be scared of by day. No. That wasn't true: a lot of killings were carried out in blaring daylight. But it seemed true. It felt true.

It felt true on Saturday afternoon when Mena dropped by the Hotel Camino Real to pick up a copy of *The Miami Herald* from the newsstand just off the lobby. He often did that. The *Herald* was the only U.S. newspaper that always showed up, same day, in El Salvador. On his way out, he poked his head into the coffee shop, on the chance he might see someone he recognized, some of the American hacks. He could join them for a coffee, a conversation. But there was no one. The restaurant was empty. There was only a waiter, fussing with the contents of a drawer.

"Can I help you?" the waiter asked.

"No," Mena said. He reached up to adjust his glasses. "No. It's all right." He tucked his copy of the *Herald* under his arm, put his hands in his pockets, and went out to his car. He drove home alone, in a pelting drizzle. Low grey clouds swallowed the surrounding hills and the great volcano, El Boquerón. Here and there, someone shuffled across the pavement through the vaporous heat. A man? A woman? It was hard to tell. Palm trees sagged. Pariah dogs slunk along the gutters, made Mena think of failed genetic experiments. He couldn't look. He squinted through the mist and the rain, kept his eyes on the road. This city. His home.

His home? It had been for two years. For two years, he had been living and working in San Salvador. He had a job, a good one, as an assistant professor in the political science department at the Central American University on the outskirts of the capital. The other university, the University of San Salvador, had of course been closed, following the marches, the demonstrations, and, ultimately, the killings.

Mena was not himself a Salvadoran. He had been born and raised in Costa Rica, the Switzerland of Central America, as it was sometimes called in the American press. He had gone to the United States to do his graduate work and had stayed on in New York to teach, for he had dual citizenship.

He'd been married once, in New York, but he and his wife had separated. That wasn't why he left New York and came to El Salvador, though. The two events were unrelated. That was what he told himself. What connection could there be? You only had to look at the timing. Mena's separation was already two months old—actually a little older: two months, one week— when the Roman Catholic archbishop of San Salvador, Monseñor Oscar Arnulfo Romero, was assassinated while celebrating mass one Sunday afternoon in March 1980.

After hearing of the assassination, Mena had taken two more days off work. He tramped the streets of Manhattan with his hands shoved deep in his pockets. For no special reason, he took the Circle Line ferry, the one that went around and around the island of Manhattan, never getting anywhere. Near the Brooklyn Bridge, with the Chrysler Tower drilling a precise metallic hole into the sky off the port bow, he decided that it was time to cast away uncertainty at last, to abandon doubt once and for all. To find something true. When he landed in San Salvador later that year, he already had his job lined up. He was travelling light. Two suitcases contained all he would need, all he wanted. Mena's doubts arrived quite a bit later, heavy as memory, delayed perhaps by poor weather at sea.

He soon began his briefings for foreign journalists. Through a mutual acquaintance, he had met and then become friends with Matt Burrell, the *New York Times* stringer in San Salvador. They often linked up over a beer, or for dinner, and tossed ideas around—the war, the increasing military role of the United States, the rebels' tactics, the economic injustices, the campaign of terror.

They talked women, too. But not women they knew. Even now, after almost two years, Mena still had no idea if Burrell was married or ever had been. They never talked about it. Mena had been married once, and he still was. He still carried her picture in his wallet, still waited for a letter or a telephone call. It was only a trial separation, after all. But he and Burrell didn't talk about that, either. They talked about women they didn't know. And they talked about politics. That was how the whole thing got going.

Before long, some of Mena's ideas began to show up in the pieces Burrell filed to the *Times*. The two men had come to an agreement about that. It suited them both. Whenever anything really big occurred—a major guerrilla attack, an important act of sabotage, a larger-than-usual peasant massacre, the rumblings of another coup—Burrell contacted Mena, among others, to sound him out. Mena's sympathy for the guerrillas helped to balance the articles Burrell filed to New York.

Burrell himself took a cynical view of the war, cursing all houses. "How many angels," he once asked Mena, "can dance on the corpse of a country?"

Mena rubbed his three-day growth of beard, the beard he kept starting and then shaving off after only a few days, never able to decide. He said, "That depends."

Burrell made a sour face. "You dog," he said. "Like hell it does." Burrell didn't oppose the guerril-las—he'd simply seen a lot of blood, maybe too much. He didn't believe there were any angels left.

But Burrell always took pains to disguise Mena in his articles. That was essential. Rebel sympathizers did not long survive in El Salvador, and Mena qualified. Mena was taking a calculated risk by even talking to Burrell, a measured injection of fear.

Now and then, Burrell brought along one or two other journalists for his talks with Mena. They were usually experienced Latin America hands on another swing through Salvador from their bases in Mexico City or Miami. They stayed at the Camino Real, spoke decent Spanish, and knew the names of the main players on the right and the left. The old hands understood the need to

71

protect Mena's anonymity in everything they wrote. They knew the score. Security must not be breached. This was Salvador, damn it, not some bloody picnic. But they were less careful in what they said.

It wasn't long before Mena began to receive telephone calls at his office from other American reporters, men and women he'd never heard of. They were passing through El Salvador on special assignment, and wanted briefings, background sessions. This was inevitable. Mena's name and phone number were now on the journalistic grapevine, beyond his control. In a way he had never intended, behind a papery veil of anonymity, Mena was becoming famous.

Always, he was afraid. That did not change. What changed was his resistance to fear. It increased by a small critical increment, formed a shell, and so, day by day, warily, he survived. When push came to shove, he would join the guerrillas. He would escape to Guazapa. He would have no choice.

Mena swung the wheel to the right and rolled into the lot behind his building. He parked and got out, ignored the rain. He left the keys for Juan and carried his copy of the *Herald* up to his apartment. He pulled a beer out of the fridge and flopped down in a chair in the living room. He started to read. Later he wandered out for a steak at La Ponderosa—none of the hacks was there, so he ate alone—and then he went home to bed.

That night he lay awake, stared at the shadows on the ceiling. He was waiting. He closed his eyes and wished that this would end. But it kept on happening. There it was, the first one. It sounded like something soft and heavy—a weight being dragged. What was it? Who was doing this? Then a sound like water, like water running onto the floor—water running onto the floor upstairs, in an empty apartment.

The phone rang late on Sunday afternoon, and Mena dragged himself from bed, stumbled into the living room, picked up the receiver. He could hardly open his eyes. Had he managed to sleep at all? "¿Aló . . . ?"

"Javier? Is that you?"

He tried to clear his throat. "Matt . . . ?"

There was a pause. "Javier? Are you all right?"

"I'm fine. What do you mean?"

"What do you think I mean? *Are you all right?* It's not a trick question. Sheesh. You're sounding like one of my editors." It was Matt Burrell, wanting a favour.

An old colleague of his, Steve Schroeder, now with *The Miami Herald*, would be coming through town in a few days, on his first visit. Would Mena be able to brief him? "Just the usual stuff," Burrell said. "Standard ground rules to apply."

"Fine," Mena said. "No problem." He tried to swallow but found he couldn't. A knot of phlegm had formed in his throat.

"How about Thursday? Thursday evening?" Burrell paused. "Javier? Are you there?"

"Fine. Thursday evening. Fine."

"Are you okay? You sound—"

"I'm fine. Just fine."

"Say, we missed you at the game today, you dog. We could have used you. We needed some batting. Where were—?"

"Working," Mena said. "Sorry. I had a lot of work to do. Thursday evening, then."

"Okay," Burrell said. He sounded doubtful. "Thursday evening. Schroeder's a good guy. You'll like him. He'll come alone. Unarmed. He'll be carrying a copy of *Pravda*. He'll—"

"Fine," Mena said. "Thursday's fine."

"Okay. Thanks, you dog. See you soon."

"Okay." Mena replaced the receiver. He wandered into the kitchen in his pyjamas, rooted in the fridge for a beer. He carried the bottle back to the living room, settled himself in the one large chair, a squat box covered in imitation brown leather. He took a swallow of the beer and crossed his legs—Javier Mena, alone in his living room in his pyjama bottoms on a Sunday afternoon, the first beer of the day in his hand. He hadn't always been like this.

In the first months following his arrival in the country, Mena had felt sure of things—sure that the government would fall, sure that it deserved to fall, sure that life would then improve. He would gaze out his office window towards the wall of Guazapa, glowing on the horizon. There, atop that mountain, among the rebels, he sensed the presence of something that was true.

It was a year after his arrival that the rebels blew up the Puente de Oro, the golden suspension bridge that spanned the Río Lempa east of the capital. Mena had gone out the following day to view the damage, along with Burrell. He said little. He could barely believe what he saw. He and Burrell strolled across a field of sunburnt cornstalks in the shadow of the wreckage.

"Man, oh, man," Burrell said. He rubbed his large loose jaw, then reached up and slapped at a fly. "This is not a bridge, you dog. This is a former bridge. Hell. I'm going to put this bridge on the tour. What do you think?"

"Sure," Mena said. "Good thinking. Good plan."

Burrell had the idea that when he quit journalism—"Soon, dear God, let it be soon"—he would make his first million by leading well-heeled Americans on guided tours of the world's combat zones. Fares would be determined according to the insurance risks set by Lloyd's of London. Lebanon would be a ten, as would El Salvador.

Burrell picked up a stick, narrowed one eye, and pointed off to the left. "We could put a little restaurant and souvenir shop over there," he said. "We could sell miniature pre-broken bridges for the kids to take home. We could have them made up in Hong Kong or Taiwan." Burrell tossed the stick down and raised his hands, as if beseeching a divine being. "Why should all the really profitable ruins be ancient?"

"No reason," Mena said. "None at all." He was stunned at what he saw. He was on the guerrillas' side— but what incredible destruction! It was as though some colossal creature had crushed the bridge in a fit of temper, for no purpose, seeking only to destroy.

The image of the crumpled bridge had remained with him a long time. A broken bridge. Something that had once been hard and certain but now would no longer support a man's weight, or might not. You never really knew.

Still in his pyjamas, Mena remained on the chair in his living room. That night, the sounds were worse.

They continued almost until morning. Scrapes and scuffles. A man swearing. Pieces of furniture knocking a wall. Something heavy, soft, slapping against the floor overhead. Mena stayed in the living room, in his pyjamas. He stared out the window, at the streetlights shifting in the darkness outside. He drank one long, slow beer after another.

He didn't sleep at all.

In the morning, Mena drove to work along the Boulevard Venezuela. He swung off onto a dirt road that traced the old Santa Tecla railway line. It was a long time since he'd taken this route to work. It wasn't really a route—a detour.

He skirted the edges of the ravine and the willowy groves of bamboo down into a gully near a place called the Montserrat Swamp. In the early days, he'd come down this way quite often, because of the bodies. There were always bodies down here. They made him think of diabolical plants the earth had thrown up overnight, terrible things with wounds like exotic blossoms. You looked at them, at those bodies, and you knew that there was evil.

Mena followed the road down to where it swerved to the right. He shifted into second gear, put his foot down on the brake, and—oh, Christ. The bodies were scattered everywhere, flopped on the side of the road, crumpled in the shallow ditches, propped up against the trunks of trees, the cypresses and palms. Some were bloated, some nearly skeletal. Most were stripped and torn, with howling stumps, their appendages cut off and laid out at their sides, or missing altogether.

Already, at seven in the morning, with the sharp-angled sunlight streaming down from a cloudless sky, the crowds were gathering—people who had come to search among the bodies for their husbands or their children.

Mena rolled up his window, crept forward in his car past the silent people who probed among the corpses, who shuffled with their heads down, squatted low, reached out to turn a head, inspect a fragment of clothing, a bit of hair, a piece of skin.

He pulled his car over to the edge of the track, partway into the ditch. He switched off the ignition and got out. Why was he doing this? He wasn't sure. He'd seen this all before, hadn't he? He didn't need to see it again, did he? Yes, he did. For some reason he did.

He slid his car keys into the pocket of his jeans and started to walk back the way he'd driven. He made for a sizable crowd of people, all gathered between a pair of low tattered palms. There had to be something interesting, something unusual. He eased his way through. *"Con permiso,"* he said. *"Con permiso, por favor."* Wordless, the people shifted aside.

On a patch of bare earth, two bodies sprawled. Not two bodies: three. One of them was a woman's. She was stretched on her back and was naked, her head twisted to the side, as though she were straining to catch sight of something that had just vanished over her shoulder. Her hair was streaked with dirt and blood, and fanned out from her face. Mena didn't look at her face. More blood splattered her body. Also: clumps of earth, blades of grass. Her ankles were bound with twine, like a pair of hands cupped in prayer.

She'd been pregnant, this woman had. A machete had rent her open. There was the gash. Someone's hands had gone right in to yank the thing out. The fetus lay curled in her arms now, wrapped in blood. They'd done that, ripped out the fetus. They'd been laughing, no doubt. They'd put it in her arms, almost as an offering, as if to thank her for their fun. *Here you go, little mother. Here's your little treasure.* Then stood back, laughed some more.

The other body, a man's, lay twisted in the dirt at her side, bound at the wrists and ankles. Her husband, probably. His genitals had been cut off—Mena had seen this before, it was common enough—and now the things were stuffed in the dead man's mouth. Like a cigar. That's what the killers had been thinking, after they'd raped his wife, one by one, and after they'd cut her open. The show was over, and they'd gone at him.

Here, proud daddy. Here, have a cigar. Whoops! Don't you spit it out, you fucker. It's yours. Here, have a kick in the head. Now—open your stupid mouth.

Mena rubbed his forehead with the heel of his palm, rubbed harder and harder. Think, he told himself. Imagine how it was. Feel. Who were these men? Off-duty policemen, soldiers—he knew that. But what were they like? What did they do afterward? Did they go home to shave, have breakfast, kiss the kids? Were they members of a different species? How did they get this way? What would it be like to live inside their heads?

He tried to make himself imagine, make himself feel. But it was no use. You saw these things over and over, and soon you stopped feeling, as though there'd been a cauterizing of your nerves, as though proud flesh had formed. Calluses. Walls. All you could think was, *God, oh God, don't let me end up like this. Not this way.*

Mena reached down to massage a spot at the back of his leg. It was getting worse. Now it hurt almost all the time.

Entropy. He thought of that word. What did it mean? Entropy. Things broke down.

The other people swayed from foot to foot. The men clutched their hats in front of them. The women held handkerchiefs to their mouths. Insects. He heard insects.

No one moved or said a word until at last a man stepped forward, a frail man in an old grey suit and a pair of rubber sandals. The man crouched down and set his upturned hat on the ground by the woman's ankles—and at last the people knew what to do. One by one, they stepped forward to put money in the hat, to pay for the burial. Coins only. It was all they had. They were giving money even though they did not know the woman's name. How could they know? Her face was gone.

Mena felt at his hip for his wallet . . . nothing. He had forgotten to bring his wallet. All he had in his pockets was a jangle of centavos. He pulled them out. He went over to the corpses, dropped his coins into the hat. He didn't know what else to do. It was next to nothing, next to nothing at all. But at least, these people would get a funeral. Lots of people didn't. Lots of people just . . . vanished.

Mena stepped back, tried not to breathe through his nose. The stench was rising now. Things rotted fast—the insects, the heat. He stayed where he was until the policemen came to herd the people away. Then he drifted with the rest, slowly, back towards his car. The policemen took their time. It was best to let everyone have a good long look.

Mena got into his car, turned the key. Nothing happened. He tried again. The starter merely clicked. Again and again. Click. Click.

He had to get out, call for help.

Immediately, the people understood—a few men, several women with babies tied in shawls upon their backs, some children, even. They tottered and waddled across the street, bent down and pushed. The car rolled ahead, picked up speed. Mena released the clutch, turned the ignition, and the engine fired. He waved but didn't stop.

"Javier," said Burrell. "Listen to this. Here's a good one." Burrell pushed his plate forward and crossed his arms on the table. It was Wednesday night, and the two men were having dinner at a restaurant. That morning, the rebels had blown up a train, killed everyone on board, but Mena didn't want to hear about it. So Burrell was telling jokes instead. He leaned over the table, spoke in a whisper.

He said the American agrarian advisers in Salvador were having trouble with the name they'd given to their land-reform project, in which large blocks of private property were to be broken up into smaller plots and distributed to the peasantry. The Americans called the project Land to the Tiller, a troublesome phrase. It was Maoist in origin, after all, which sent out a confusing message.

"But that isn't the real problem," Burrell said. He stroked his lips, hiding a grin. "The real problem is that some folks have taken to switching the name around. Now they call the body dumps—Tiller to the Land." Burrell sat back and smiled. "Tiller to the Land—get it?"

"Tiller to the Land." Mena took off his glasses, winced. His arthritis was acting up again, if that was what it was. He started to clean his glasses with the tail of his New York Yankees shirt. He looked up, shrugged. "Yeah . . . ?"

"That's right," Burrell said. "Tiller to the Land." He gazed at Mena, with his mouth open, his chin slack. He moved his jaw back and forth, from side to side. He was still having nicotine withdrawal. "Cute, huh?"

"Yeah. Really. Vintage stuff."

Burrell brought his fist down against the table. He said he couldn't stand it any more. It was driving him nuts. The hell with it. The hell with it all.

"What? What?"

Burrell got the waitress to bring him a pack of cigarettes and he promptly lit one up, his first in three months. "This is a tragedy," he said. "This is a tragedy you are seeing, unfolding right in front of your eyes."

Mena thought—El Salvador. El Salvador was a tragedy. But Burrell really meant the cigarette. Three months gone up in smoke, just like that.

"Javier," Burrell said. He sat up. He'd just remembered something. "Don't forget about Schroeder, okay? You know—Steve Schroeder? *The Miami Herald*? He gets in tomorrow sometime. Sometime late. He'll drop by your office. Did I say seven? Is that okay?"

"Sure," Mena said. "Okay. Right."

"Good. And thanks." Burrell hesitated. "So," he said. "Do you want to hear about the train?"

"Seven," Mena said. "I'll see him at seven. That's no problem. Fine."

Burrell shrugged. He obviously wanted to talk about the train, but Mena didn't want to hear.

They were eating at a Mexican restaurant called Los Antojitos, hidden behind the Camino Real in the shadow of El Boquerón. It was a place where he and Burrell often came after work, to stretch out their legs, plant their shoes on the gritty concrete floor, order mugs of cold beer, bolt down long cuts of *churrasco* with chili peppers. Normally they talked and talked. But not tonight.

Burrell had phoned Mena at his office that morning. He wanted to talk about the big ambush. That morning, the rebels had ambushed a passenger train between San Vicente and Zacatecoluca. Mena already knew. It was all over the radio. The radio stations were supposed to be barred from broadcasting any news about the war, but they'd been ordered to broadcast this. Burrell was going to drive out there. Did Mena want to come?

"I can't," Mena said. "Work. I have too much work." It wasn't true. He easily could have gone. But he didn't want to. He had a feeling this time.

"Okay," Burrell said. "I'll call you when I get back. How about dinner? Los Antojitos, okay? I'll give you a call. If I don't call, I've hit a landmine. Send out a search party. Send out men. I want an all-male search party. I

82

don't want the women to see me like that."

"No," Mena said. "I mean, yes. Right. I will." He hung up, went back to his desk, sat down. He opened a book, a dictionary. "Entropy," he read. "The ultimate result of the degradation of matter and energy in the universe."

All day long, he kept thinking: don't let it be this way. The rebels had blown up a train, a passenger train. Maybe it was a mistake. Maybe the army did it, not the guerrillas. It must have been the army.

Burrell got back to town late in the afternoon. He called Mena and they met as planned at Los Antojitos. But they didn't talk about the train, not at first. Whenever Burrell tried to talk about the train, Mena changed the subject. At first, he did. But it was no use. He really did want to know. Finally he looked down at his plate. "So," he said. "Zacatecoluca." He looked up.

"What can I say?" Burrell lit another cigarette, in his amateurish way, clutching the thing on the wrong side of his mouth, blowing out the match rather than shaking it. He frowned, peered at the end of his cigarette. "It was the worst. Just about the worst I've seen. They really nailed that sucker. I'm trying to think of a way to get it on the tour."

"How many?" Mena asked. He pushed his glasses back up the bridge of his nose. "How many dead?" But it wasn't the question he really wanted to ask.

Burrell ran his hand back through his hair, bristly and black. He scrunched up his sad-dog face, shrugged. "Seventy? At least? That's my guess. I counted fifty-seven before they made me get off the train."

Burrell described the train. The old diesel engine

derailed by the bomb, collapsed on its side, like a dead caterpillar's skull, if that was what caterpillars had. Burrell told Mena about the splintered panels of the wooden cars, blood still running through the floorboards onto the tracks, dripping almost audibly into the midday silence.

"Javier," he said. "It wasn't the bomb killed them. It was the bullets. The boys kept right on shooting—shooting and shooting. Hell. Those wagons only have wooden walls, Javier. No protection at all."

The passengers—all peasants, only peasants rode the trains—had crawled under the seats in their desperation. There they lay, busted hampers, tangled clothing, streaks of blood, gobs of brain, all jumbled up beneath the seats. Burrell had counted fourteen dead chickens. The chickens too had scurried beneath the seats, to drown in their blood.

"The seats," Burrell said, eyed his cigarette, shook his head. "The fucking wooden seats. What the fuck where they doing trying to hide under the seats?"

But Mena knew the answer to that—they had nowhere else to go. He took off his glasses, kneaded the bridge of his nose, looked up. Everything blurred. He asked the question, the one he wanted to ask. "There's no doubt," he said. "There's no doubt it was the guerrillas." It wasn't really a question. This was the way Mena had spoken to his wife in the end. Where were you. What's happening to us. Why did you do that. Don't you love me any more. Questions that weren't really questions. Either you couldn't expect an answer or you already knew what the answer would be.

"Doubt. . . ?" Burrell repeated. He stubbed out his

cigarette on his plate, in the grease, amid the remains of his *churrasco*. He rolled his lower lip over his upper lip, shook his head. "Doubt? Nope. No doubt at all. Plenty of witnesses, Javier. It was the boys, all right. The boys blew up that train, wasted all those good folk." Burrell looked up, the muscles pinched at the corner of his right eye, held there. "Why? Why'd they do it? Why do you think?"

But Mena didn't know. There was no explanation. It was just something that had happened. It wasn't hard truth, what he liked to think of as hard truth. It had no apparent reason, fit no logical pattern. The guerrillas had wrecked a train, killed almost all of the passengers. Why? They were angry? They were bored? They wanted to try out some new rifles? They didn't like trains?

Mena could think of nothing to say. He merely thought of Guazapa. One day, when push came to shove, Mena would get into his car, start the engine, and drive north to the foot of Guazapa, where he would start to climb. He would scale the hard sure slope of Guazapa and never come back down. He would. He knew he would. He would cast doubt aside.

He heard it again that night: a noise upstairs. He was climbing up to his apartment, and he heard it. A scraping on the floor. And then a sort of cough, a man clearing his throat. It came from somewhere upstairs, the third floor, the empty apartments. Mena stopped on the stairs to listen. He felt something rising in his chest. He gripped his key, waited.

He should go up there. He should go up there and

see. This was his building. This was where he lived. Or maybe he should go back down. Get back in his car, drive over to Matt's place, think up some kind of story. A bomb scare. Earthquake damage. Anything. It didn't matter.

He stood still, willed himself not to move. It was dark, all the bulbs burnt out. Goddamn that Juan. Mena remained on the second-floor landing and listened. This was his building. He should go up there.

He shoved his key back into his pocket and started to climb. He put his hand on the railing. His hand flinched. He'd heard it again—a shoe turning. The leather sole of a shoe. It was a man. Upstairs, a man. Mena paused at the landing, then continued to climb. One step. Another. Another step. Did he hear the sounds now? He could hear something. What?

His own shoes. His own shoes gripping the tiles of the stairs, gripping and giving way.

He got to the top of the stairs. It was even darker here, almost completely dark. The shadows moved like dangling sheets waving in a breeze. He could make out the shape of the hall, the doorways to the two apartments. That was all.

"¿Hola?" he whispered. "¿Hola?"

At first he heard nothing, what he thought was nothing. Then—like a slight shift in the pressure of the air, something he did not hear so much as feel upon his skin—he sensed it. And now he did hear it—a faint sound, the sound of someone breathing. It was so slow, so regular, it might have been there all the time, buried in the background. A slow deep breathing.

Someone was standing there, in the darkness.

Someone watching him. Someone breathing.

Now, without pausing to think, without considering what he was doing, with the muscles trembling in his back, Mena walked straight over to the doorway, the one on his right, the one that led to the unit directly above his own. The sounds—whatever they were—he couldn't hear them now. Now it was silent.

The door was already open, ajar by inches. Mena pushed the door, it swung back, and he walked inside. He left the door open, stood with his back against the jamb. Why was he doing this? He stood in the darkness, breathing. Why was he doing this? He had never come up here before, never had any reason. The unit was vacant, had always been vacant. The owner had left, packed up, gone away—Mena didn't know where, had never asked, had never cared to know. Just . . . gone. That was what he thought. It was what he'd been told.

"¿Hola?" Mena whispered. "¿Hola? ¿Hola?"

The lights from the street pulsed up, spilled into the apartment, spread over the floor, against the walls, shattered upon the ceiling. There wasn't a sound. But he knew. He could feel it. There was somebody in here, now.

He forced his back from the door. He walked right into the apartment. He knew exactly where to go. This could have been his own apartment. It had the same layout, identical. He knew every wall, every room, every closet. Only the furnishings were different, that was all, and there weren't many of those—some tube-metal chairs, a rolled-up carpet, a large girlie calendar pinned to the wall. Sheets of newspaper were bunched up and scattered across the floor, like small dead animals.

Carcasses.

Mena didn't turn the lights on, didn't need to. In the semi-darkness, he began to search. He did this methodically, from room to room. And sometimes he heard sounds—a man breathing, the turning of a shoe against the floor, a shoulder nudging against a wall, a drawer opening, closing, in another room, another part of the apartment. The man—the other man, the man who occupied this apartment—was letting Mena search, had left the door open, had wanted Mena to come up here. Had been waiting for this. He was here now. He was here, staying out of sight, listening, watching.

Mena went from room to room. He did not hurry. He found the dark blue policeman's uniform hanging in the bedroom closet, in the room directly above his own. It was shrouded in a clear plastic wrapping that shone like a ghost. Mena pushed the plastic up, to touch the uniform, to feel it. It slithered against his fingers, a kind of nylon, slippery and cool, almost damp. The jacket bore several stripes stitched upon its shoulders—an officer. An officer of some kind. Mena pulled the plastic down, slid shut the closet doors. He looked at his hand. He had the sense that something on the uniform, some substance, had rubbed off on his hand. But no. He didn't think so. Still, his hand felt sticky.

In the kitchen, he found everything—the knives, the other cutting instruments, a cleaver, a saw. They were laid out on newspapers, all assembled on the counter, beside the sink, near the taps, near a coiled hose, sponges, jars of cleaners. They were easy to find. Someone had left them out there for him to see.

Mena knew immediately what they were. His

heart was pounding, but he did not turn away. He pushed back the folds of the newspapers and examined all these instruments, these cutting devices. The blood on the handles and on the blades was dry, clotted. That was how it seemed in the faint light. But Mena touched them, the handles, the blades, just to be sure. Dry—yes. But tacky, glutinous. The blood—he knew it was blood—adhered to his fingers. And there was something else, strange bits of matter that clung to the blades and the folds of the newspapers. He knew what that was, too.

Mena felt something happen. He froze. He'd heard a sound—the same sound as before, only louder. Much louder. It was like a rustling. He could hear it, a man breathing just behind him. Just over there. Breathing out, breathing in, with a rasp, a deep rasp, almost metallic.

He turned—but there was nothing. Dim trickles of light dribbled through the window and onto the floor. The refrigerator clicked on and trembled. Its motor made the only sound. The man didn't want to be seen. But he was here. He could move around this apartment, invisible, almost silent, like a ghost. And he wanted Mena here. He wanted Mena to see. Death itself got boring. You needed things like this.

Mena left the cutting instruments where they were, on the counter. He wondered what else there was to see. He looked at the refrigerator, a new model, wider than a coffin, taller than a man. Its motor droned in the faint light, and the box itself seemed to shiver. If no one lived here, then why leave the refrigerator on? But Mena knew that someone lived here. Or came here. He looked at the refrigerator, and immediately its motor clicked off. The machinery shuddered. He heard a gurgling of liquid, then a clicking—every few seconds, a clicking. Just click. Click. Click.

A relay switch? It sounded like a faulty relay switch. It wouldn't be long before that fridge broke down, and everything inside would thaw, go bad, start to rot. Who lived here? Who was standing here now, breathing, just breathing, watching him?

"*¿Quién es?*" Mena hissed out loud. He pressed his back against the counter. "*¿Como se llama?*" He stared at the refrigerator. What was in the refrigerator? "*¡Déjame en paz!*" he shouted. "*¡Déjame solo!*"

Something clicked. And clicked. And clicked. And Mena thought his head would burst. He turned, stumbled out of the kitchen. A stab of pain shot up the back of one leg—another pain, another. He was limping now. He thought he'd fall. He tried to run. He ran.

A raft of books lay in a heap on the floor by the couch, beside a sheaf of papers filled with Mena's own scribbles—lines and arrows, long bits crossed out. It was Thursday evening, dark. Mena was in his office—alone in his office. He'd slept here the night before, on that couch. He'd barely gone out all day. Now, he was waiting for Steve Schroeder. They had an appointment, but Schroeder was late. Maybe he wouldn't come.

Mena sat at his desk with his back to the window. Somewhere out there, behind him, Guazapa rode upon the night, tall, immutable. But it was dark. Even if Mena turned around to look, he wouldn't be able to see. He winced at the pain in his leg. He had a book propped

90

open on the desk in front of him. He was trying to read. He read letter by letter, word by —

"Mena . . . ? Doctor Mena?"

Mena looked up. A young man swung into the office from the corridor, panting lightly, waving a yellow notebook.

"You Javier Mena?" He had angular features, wispy hair, and eyes too big for his head. He wore blue jeans, a blue shirt. "Steve Schroeder," he said. "Sorry I'm late. Damn taxi driver didn't know the way." He reached out his hand.

They shook hands. The visitor dropped himself into a chair in front of Mena's desk and announced that he had only a few days to spend in El Salvador. Then he was off to Belize.

"You better Belize it," he said, hesitated, grinned. He pulled out a pen, flipped his notepad open. He said, "I hear you're a friend of Matt's."

Mena sat up, started to answer.

"Right, right," Schroeder said. "Great guy." He didn't want to hear. He was in a rush. He pulled off the plastic top from his pen. "So," he said, "what I want to know is, who finances these damn death squads down here anyway? It can't be such a mystery. How's it all organized? That's what I want to know. The names."

And Mena told him who. He told him how.

The phone rang at one o'clock on Sunday. Mena was still at his office. He'd been sleeping each night on the couch. He got up, went over to his desk, hovered over the phone, unsure. He waited until the fifth ring. The sixth.

91

He picked up the receiver, held it to his ear.

"Javier? Is that you? Javier?"

"Yes," he said. "Matt . . . ?"

"What the fuck are you doing at your office on a Sunday?" Burrell shouted.

Why was he shouting? Mena tried to answer. "I just—"

"Tell me later," Burrell said. "I don't want to know. I want you to get in your car and drive over here. Now. I've got something to tell you. I want you to do it. Now."

"What?" Mena didn't understand. "What are you talking about?"

A brief pause. Then Burrell said. "Your name, goddamnit. It's all over the front page of *The Miami Herald*. I don't—"

"It is?" Mena shook his head. "It is?"

"Yeah. I just said it was. Now get over here, Javier. Come on. Now. And don't go by your apartment. It probably isn't safe. Come here. Now."

An hour later, Mena showed up at Burrell's house with his overnight bag, some left-over U.S. traveller's cheques, both his passports—Costa Rican and U.S.— and a collection of private letters held together with a red elastic band. He'd had all this stuff with him at his office.

Burrell met him at the door, told him what had happened. Schroeder had named Mena in an article that had run that morning on the front page of the *Herald* in Miami. "It'll be on the newsstands here tomorrow," Burrell said. He was calmer, a lot calmer, now that Mena had shown up.

Mena didn't understand. "What are you saying? It's in today's paper in Miami? But it won't be here till tomorrow? How does that work?" He climbed onto a stool by the counter in the kitchen. He wasn't sure what he felt, apart from excitement. He thought he was excited. He ought to be—this was it.

"I thought you knew," Burrell said. "The *Herald*'s Latin American edition, the one it sends down here, is actually yesterday's paper with the dates changed." Burrell went over to the fridge and got out a couple of beers. "That's really the half of what's wrong with people in this damn country," he said. He opened the beers, handed one to Mena. "All this time, they've been following day-old horoscopes—and they don't even know."

Burrell took a swig of his beer. He said he'd got a phone call that morning from Ron Blake in Miami. Blake was the *Washington Post* correspondent there and had read Steve Schroeder's article over breakfast. It was in the metro edition of *The Miami Herald*. Blake had known right away that Mena was in serious trouble.

The article ran across the bottom of the front page of the *Herald* under the headline "Strangers in the Night: Rightist Death Squads Haunt El Salvador. By Steven K. Schroeder." Mena's name appeared three times, once on the front page and twice more where the article turned onto page six. Leftist university professor Javier Mena alleged. According to Mena. Mena charged.

Burrell had written it all down. He looked up from his notes. He shook his head. "I just don't understand this," he said. "Schroeder's no dummy. He wouldn't do this."

That evening, Burrell tried to phone Steve Schroeder in Miami, but his paper said he was on assignment somewhere in Belize. On a small island off the coast, they said. There were no phones. Burrell lit a cigarette. "Damn that jerk," he said. "He's not on assignment. He's snorkelling." Burrell couldn't explain what had happened with the article, the references to Mena by name. "I just don't understand it. I know Schroeder. He just wouldn't do this." Burrell blew a tattered smoke ring into the air and looked at Mena.

Mena didn't say anything. He thought of Guazapa. Now he had to decide. Now he had no choice.

Mena didn't bother phoning in sick the next morning. He just didn't show up at work. He stayed indoors all day, at Burrell's house. That afternoon, Burrell came in, lugging ten copies of the *Herald* that he'd got from the newsstand at the Camino Real.

"I bought them all," Burrell said. "Just in case."

But they both knew it made no difference. The *Herald* was also delivered to the newsstands at the Sheraton, the Presidente, and about a dozen other locations around town. Besides, most wealthy Salvadorans had friends or relatives in Miami, who would read the paper, clip the article out, and mail it back home. Mena's name would end up on somebody's list, probably already had.

"I've checked tomorrow's flights," Burrell said. He and Mena were sitting out on the terrace beneath a green-striped awning, overlooking the garden, awash with hibiscus and roses. The sun was setting. "There's a flight at noon to San José, another at four o'clock to Miami. I can lend you some money, as much as you

94

need. I'll drive you to the airport. Goddamn that jerk. I just can't believe this."

Mena eased off his glasses, rubbed his eyes, looked at Burrell. "I'm not going," he said. "I've decided."

"You're not what?"

"Going. I'm not going. I'm staying in Salvador. I'm going to Guazapa. I've decided."

Burrell nodded. "Sure you are. They're just dying for another myopic, U.S.-educated political scientist on Guazapa. You're just what they need." Burrell put out his cigarette, got up. "I'm going to book both flights. You decide." He went in to use the phone.

That night, Mena lay on his back in the spare bedroom in Burrell's house. He stared at the wall, at the shifting illuminated patterns flooding in from the garden lights outside. He divined the shape of a fortress, a cathedral—the outline of Guazapa. Mena fought to hold that image in his mind, to make it hard and sure, but suddenly it vanished—the lights had gone out. Somewhere, miles and miles from the city, along some dark and thinly forested slope, the rebels had blown up an electrical pylon. It toppled silently to the ground, in a whirlwind of sparks and flames, and the lights went out. The pattern on the wall disappeared. Mena closed his eyes and saw nothing, just darkness. Had he known this all along?

"What's the scoop?" Burrell said at breakfast the next morning. He was pouring coffee. "Miami or San José? Or is it still Guazapa?"

Mena took his coffee black. He had slept badly. He

95

let the first mouthful of coffee work its way down his throat. He felt the main effects of the caffeine at the front of his skull, like styrofoam being transformed back into brain cells. "Miami," he said. "Then New York." Burrell nodded. "Okay. I'll cancel San José. You'll be flying TACA." He grinned. "Take A Chance Airlines."

"Okay," Mena said. "Thanks."

"So. What's in New York?"

Mena shrugged. "I don't know."

It wasn't safe to go back to the apartment, so Mena would have to leave with just his overnight bag. He didn't have much else anyway. Burrell went out in his Toyota coupé to pick up Mena's ticket for the TACA flight to Miami and to get some money.

At two o'clock, Mena and Burrell left for the airport. Burrell drove. The airport was out on the coast, an hour's drive away on a not very secure road. Mena felt dazed. Could this be happening? Everything seemed so normal—normal for El Salvador. The bustle of people departing, always departing.

At the airport, he saw bulging suitcases cross-tied with twine, heard the clatter of high heels on the tile floor, a child's whine. Outside, beyond the plate-glass windows, beyond a palisade of palm trees, a crop-dusting biplane turned short looping figure-eights over a canefield, as though it were riding a trapeze. Back and forth. Back and forth. Spraying against infection. Never getting anywhere. Mena could not seem to focus, could not seem to get his mind to work. He stared and stared.

The coastal hills rose in the distance, shimmered in the clear Salvadoran light—light so pure it suddenly seemed to be shining through a vacuum—but he couldn't see Guazapa from here. It was hidden from view. Soldiers patrolled the terminal with their G-3 automatic rifles. Were they eyeing him strangely? Sometimes it seemed they were. Sometimes not. It was hard to tell.

He checked in at the TACA counter. The flight to Miami was on time. He got his boarding pass, paid the airport tax. He walked with Burrell to the immigration post. It was better to go straight through, right now, just in case. Mena said goodbye. Thanks. Yes. He'd phone when he got to Miami. He gave Burrell the keys to his apartment, so that later, when things cooled down, Burrell could go around, pick up some of his gear, send it to the States. Burrell said he'd try to do something about Mena's car.

Mena shrugged. "It's just a junk heap, anyway."

Burrell nodded. "That dumb jerk," he said. He lit another cigarette. "I still can't believe it. I swear to God. I know Schroeder. He wouldn't do this. I just don't understand."

"Never mind. It's done now." Mena pushed his glasses back up the bridge of his nose. He wanted to change the subject. "And thanks, Matt. Thanks again. Thanks for everything."

"Have fun, you dog," Burrell said. His long cigarette dangled from his lips. He narrowed his eyes, removed his cigarette, lowered his voice. He said, "You arranged this on purpose, didn't you?"

"What?"

"This was no accident, Javier—your name in the *Herald*. You did it on purpose, didn't you?"

"I don't know what—"

"That's what I think. I think you told Schroeder to identify you—or else you didn't tell him not to. Isn't that right? It is, isn't it?" Burrell turned his head, peered at Mena sideways, waited.

Mena looked down at his watch. He didn't say anything. He felt his heart, his heart beating.

Finally, Burrell shrugged. "Yeah. Okay. Just kidding. Only kidding." He dragged on his cigarette. "It would have been a neat trick, though. I sure wish I could do something like that. I'd give my right arm to get out of this dump." He blew smoke out through his nose, looked around, raised his voice. "No, I wouldn't! No, I wouldn't! Just kidding!" He lowered his voice once more. "Someone might take me seriously." Burrell examined his cigarette, shrugged again. "We'll have to find a new shortstop is all, I guess. So . . . what did you say was in New York again?"

"I don't know." Mena closed his eyes, opened them. "My wife. My wife lives there." It was true, as far as it went. As far as anything went. It might be true. There was a chance.

"Wife . . . ? Oh . . . ? Oh—wife. Oh, yeah. I used to have one of those. So, that's the ticket, huh? Wife. Is that it?"

"I don't know." Mena felt only the pulsing of his heart, each beat uncertain until its moment, and then it was past and gone. He had cast away everything now, everything but doubt. He looked at Burrell, shrugged. "I don't know."

Burrell glanced out the plate-glass windows, then looked back at Mena. "So . . . don't forget to write."

"No," Mena said. "I won't. You, too—either, I mean."

Burrell dragged on his cigarette. "So . . . ," he said, exhaled. He dropped his cigarette, ground it out with his shoe. His long arms hung free, uncertain.

"So . . . ," Mena said. He turned, stepped across the yellow line, handed his U.S. passport to the immigration officer, along with his Salvadoran temporary-residence permit. His legs felt weak, wobbly.

"How long will you be out of the country?" the official asked. As they always did.

This question was for the record. Mena was on the record now. He said, "I don't know."

The official nodded, stamped the permit and the passport, gave them both back to Mena. He turned to motion towards the next person in line, the next person who was leaving El Salvador.

Guerrilla Beach

It was a little thing—the dropping of the final "s" from the word "premises"—that made Jeff Oliphant decide to murder his editor.

"The word is *premises*," Jeff hissed into the telephone mouthpiece. "The shooting took place on the *premises* of the Spanish embassy."

"It's only one building," said E. He was at the other end of the telephone connection, more than a continent away. "Just one building. Isn't that right, Jeffrey?"

"I know," Jeff said. He took a deep breath. He couldn't believe he was having this conversation. Government soldiers in the Guatemalan capital had just stormed the premises of the Spanish embassy, where thirteen political dissidents had been holding out. He glanced at his watch and recalculated the time difference to Toronto. Damn—it was already five minutes past deadline for the first edition. "The building is singular," he explained again, through gritted teeth, "but the word is still *premises*. Plural."

"I'm afraid I can't accept that, Jeffrey. I'm going to drop the 's'. There. It's done."

"You dropped the 's'? You've got to be kidding. You actually dropped the 's'?"

"Yes, Jeffrey. I'm giving the story back to Tom now. It looks like we've missed the first edition on this one, though. Too bad, Jeffrey. Maybe we should start filing a little earlier in future? Take care."

That did it. That bloody well did it. It was a small thing, just a single letter, one twenty-sixth of the alphabet, but Jeff decided that the only answer was to kill his editor. Very slowly.

Motive he had. The dropping of the final "s" in "premises" was only the latest of many provocations. Jeff had kept track of them all. There had been, for example, the time he'd wanted to know whether his paper had printed any of his photographs.

He'd spent a week slogging through the Honduran hills, gathering information for a story about Salvadoran refugees. They'd fled the fighting in their own country, crossed the border into Honduras. They were living in scrap-wood shanties covered with bits of plastic. They had no land and almost no food, except for the little that the Honduran peasants could spare. Some of them were starving. Most nights and sometimes even by day, soldiers were marauding in from Salvador to terrorize them. And guess who'd suddenly shown up, out of the sub-tropical blue, on a humanitarian mission?

Bianca Jagger—that was who. The rock star's

former wife and a Nicaraguan by birth. Glamour. Conflict. Pathos. Squalor. The story had everything. Incredible stuff.

Jeff rode a succession of chicken- and goat-infested country buses back to Tegucigalpa, the Honduran capital. He checked into a hotel, showered and shaved, dined in the hotel restaurant, downed about a quarter-bottle of scotch, and then stayed up most of the night knocking the story out on his portable typewriter that was missing the little plastic keys on the "e" and the "k". He jabbed at the metal rods until his fingers bled. He dug out his Band-Aids and kept on typing. More scotch.

The next morning his brain felt like a roll of cotton batten soaked in horse liniment, but he got up early, staggered downstairs, and punched out a ticker tape of his article on the hotel telex machine, one of those dinosaurs that went chonka-chonka-chonka, and then he fed the tape through to Toronto. He caught a taxi to the airport and a plane to Salvador and filed three of his photographs from the AP office at the Camino Real, all well before his paper's evening deadline.

Next morning, he called up E. just to find out if any of the pix had been used. There was one he especially liked—Bianca in jeans and a tank top. She was holding a little Salvadoran boy, gun barrels bristling all around her, and she was staring grim-faced at the camera. Jeff knew by now not to ask how the story itself had played. E. refused to say how or where any given story had appeared in the paper. It was a point of principle with him, apparently. In E.'s book, editors were not supposed to tell their reporters anything.

"So," said Jeff. "Did you get my story?"

"Story?" said E.

"Yes. The one about the Salvadoran refugees living in hovels in Honduras. I filed it yesterday. You know. It had Bianca Jagger in it. She was trying single-handedly to stop the soldiers from dragging young refugees away and executing them. It—"

"Oh, yes. Oh, right. I remember now. That one."

"Good," said Jeff. "I was wondering about the pix."

"Pix? You sent pix?"

"Yes. I was wondering, did you get them?"

"I'm not sure."

"Oh. . . .? Well, did you use the story?" Dangerous territory.

"This morning?"

"Yes. In this morning's paper. Did you use my story?" It had been a long time since Jeff had asked this sort of question. He was on shaky ground now.

"I'm not too sure," said E. "I left early yesterday. Tom was in late. He would have taken care of it."

"Yes. But we're talking *today's paper*. The story would be in *today's paper*." Jeff hesitated. "Is it?"

There was a long silence on the line. "I don't recall."

Jeff counted to five. "Could—you—*look*?"

Another silence. A muffled voice: "I don't see any papers around here." Then louder: "I don't have any copies of today's paper around here, Jeffrey. Right now."

Jeff nodded, swallowed, slowed himself down. He said, "E. Look. I'm in Salvador. You're in Toronto. It would be a hell of a lot easier for you than it would be for me to get up and walk over to some place where there *is* a copy of today's paper, and just—"

"Jeffrey," said E. "Can I be honest with you? I'm running late for the morning news conference right now. Can I get back to you on this? Let's pick this up another time, shall we? There you go, Jeffrey. Take care."

Three weeks later, back in Mexico City where he lived, Jeff got his copy of that day's paper in the mail. And guess what. His story about Bianca Jagger and the Salvadoran refugees? Front-bloody-page. That great pic of Bianca? Above the fold. Another pic ran inside. Christ Almighty. Couldn't E. have told him that before? Was he being punished for something? What?

Of course, Jeff was not alone in having to deal with an editor whose motives and designs were beyond the understanding of ordinary men. In Buenos Aires to cover the war over the Falkland Islands, he had often spent evenings of misery and lamentation with the other hacks living in his hotel on the Calle Tucumán. They headed out to dinner at La Mosca Blanca or Los Años Locos. They ordered fried potatoes and walloping hunks of beef—all anybody ever ate in Buenos Aires, arteriosclerosis capital of the universe. They quaffed glass after glass of Mendoza wine. They shook their heads and railed against their editors.

A few of them had devised strategies of survival and even revenge. Correale kept a written record of every Personal Indignity inflicted on him by his editor. During years spent living out of a suitcase, roaming the world for his Los Angeles newspaper, he had developed a formula for the conversion of Personal Indignities—or

104

PIDs, as he called them—into numerical values. He then charted them on a ten-point scale.

If Correale was required, for example, to catch an airplane before twelve o'clock noon—which, in much of the Third World, entailed hauling himself out of bed before six a.m. in order to handle the bribes, the red tape, and the traffic—he immediately jotted it down in his record book as a two-point PID.

If his editor assigned him a story for which Correale had no enthusiasm but which he grudgingly agreed to produce, only to find that his work was later butchered, bloodied, and slashed in half before being shoehorned in somewhere near the back of the paper, between the bridge column and the funnies, then four more points were jotted down in the book.

Whenever the tally of Correale's PIDs reached ten points, he promptly took an afternoon off work, went out for a stroll in whatever city he happened to be in, and treated himself to a new pair of shoes. Later, on his expense account, the shoes appeared as PIDs. The shoe-store receipts were stapled in with all the rest.

Correale said that not once had such an entry been questioned. Editors never doubted anything that was backed by a credible receipt. Besides, no editor he'd ever met could understand a foreign language. Correale looked around at the other hacks assembled at the table. He smooched the tip of his cigar, then called to the waiter, "*Joven, más vino por aquí.*"

But Jeff did not want to go the shoe-buying route. Revenge, he thought, should really be more direct, more immediate, than a closetful of footwear. He hadn't yet considered the word "murder". He was not by nature a homicidal man. But bitter feelings were starting to stew and churn somewhere down there, deep within him. They would work their way to the surface eventually. He just wasn't ready yet. First, he had to go missing in eastern Nicaragua.

He'd gone over there to write stories about conflict and hostility between the Mosquito Indians on the Atlantic coast and the revolutionary Sandinistas who were ruling the country. He flew to Puerto Cabezas on a rattling old DC-3 twin-prop whose wings had muddy shoe-prints on all the places where it said Do Not Stand. Before leaving, Jeff had told E. that he would phone on arrival.

When he got to Puerto Cabezas, Jeff discovered there were no phones. No telex. No electricity. He slept on a hammock in the yard behind someone's house, right beside the cooking fire. He ate at the town's only restaurant, a Chinese joint where dog-like creatures copulated on the concrete floor. When it was over, the females dragged the still erect and now locked and whimpering males from table to table, begging for scraps. Jeff looked down at his plate. Chow mein. He headed up-country, to see about the fighting.

He bounced along dusty roads in the beds of ancient trucks. He slept beneath the stars or with squeaking choirs of rats in damp and murky granaries. He found a makeshift school for Mosquito Indians, where the principal was a fifteen-year-old Indian girl who had thick black hair, huge eyes, and nothing but a primary-school education herself. She put out her hands, smiled, and told him she just tried to do her best. He found people without homes, clinics without medicine, wives without husbands, children without parents, and village defence patrols without guns. Instead, the wizened, barefoot men carried lengths of wood whittled down to resemble guns. They were terrified of being attacked.

He hooked up with a column of Sandinista soldiers advancing into the north. He spent three days with them, mucking along dirt trails, traipsing through acacia scrub, staggering across gushing rainy-season rivers. They were ambushed six hellish times. Finally, Jeff rode down to Puerto Cabezas in the bed of a commandeered lumber truck, along with the wounded. It was time to fly back to Managua. He'd been gone long enough. Toronto would be frantic by now. They probably thought he was dead.

But Jeff kept getting bumped off the DC-3. The army needed the space for injured soldiers. Jeff spent five more days in Puerto Cabezas, avoiding the dogs, picking at his Chinese food, and making daily treks in vain out to the landing field.

Finally, on a Friday afternoon, Jeff got on the DC-3 and flew back to Managua. He'd been gone for ten days. Ten bloody days he'd been out of touch with his paper—in a war zone. That was no joke. Toronto had probably called in the Mounties by now. Or Interpol. They were probably wretched with worry. He threw himself into a taxi and raced back to the Intercontinental Hotel overlooking Lake Managua. He jogged inside, checked in at reception, rode the elevator upstairs, tossed his bag down on the floor, took a quick look at himself in the mirror—what a wreck—and booked a phone call to Toronto.

Half an hour later—miraculously fast—the call went through.

"Hello? Hello?" It was E.

"It's me," said Jeff. "I'm back at my hotel. It's all right. I'm safe."

"Safe?"

"Yes. It's all right. Everything's okay. There were no phones over there, so I couldn't call. Sorry. But I've got loads and loads of stories."

"Stories?"

"Yes. I've got . . . well, I'll tell you later. I just wanted—"

"Uh, who is this? Is that you, Jeffrey?"

"Yes. I'm all right. I'm back now."

"Oh. That's nice. Uh, back where? What country are you in . . . ?"

Jeff sat up straight, stared at the telephone receiver. What country was he in . . . ? Had he heard this right?

What *country* was he in?

Ten days, incommunicado, in a Nicaraguan war zone—and E. hadn't even noticed that Jeff was gone. Jeff could have been killed—and nothing in Toronto would have happened. Not a finger would have been lifted. He might have been wiped off the face of this planet, and up there in Toronto his absence would have gone unremarked. They'd have kept sending his paycheque to his bank in Mexico City. They'd have kept telexing story assignments to him and then crossing them out as Not Completed. They'd have looked up at each other and muttered, "Hmm. Haven't heard much from Oliphant lately," and then turned their attention to other things.

Meanwhile, his corpse would be decomposing somewhere beneath a light forest cover in eastern Nicaragua.

Jeff slammed down the phone, tore off his dirty, sweat-caked clothes, showered and shaved. He headed downstairs to the hotel bar for a Flor de Caña rum. Then another, and another, and another after that. Ten days he'd been gone.

Homicidal thoughts began to stir in the back of his mind—but vaguely, vaguely. Jeff still needed more provocation before those thoughts would turn to action. Several weeks later, in Guatemala, it happened. The dropping of the final "s" from the word "premises". That did it. That bloody well did it.

"I'm giving the story back to Tom now," said E. "It looks like we've missed the first edition on this one, though. Too bad, Jeffrey. Maybe we should start filing a little earlier in future? Take care."

Jeff hurled down the phone. He hated that phrase. *Take care.* As if care were a commodity you could fold into a little ball and tuck into your suitcase among your socks. Or as if care were something that E. had ever had the remotest interest in, at least insofar as it applied to Jeff.

And the word "premise"! It was unbelievable. As in "Guatemalan soldiers attacked the *premise* of the Spanish embassy." What . . . ? They were opposed on principle to the idea of a Spanish embassy? Good God. What was E. thinking? Jeff didn't know, and frankly he no longer cared. He'd kill E.—with his own hands. How difficult could it be? Down here, people killed people all the time. Motive he most certainly had. All he needed was a decent opportunity, a fair shake.

And, as luck would have it, one soon presented itself.

E., it turned out, was coming down to the region on a familiarization tour, part of a whirlwind trip that would take him to each of the five foreign bureaux maintained by the paper, whimsically scattered across the globe. First, E. would grace Washington with his presence. Then—Mexico.

"Mexico...?" said Jeff. He was on the phone in his hotel room, in San Salvador now. He'd just got back from a trip north to Suchitoto, to cover the fighting there. "Why Mexico? There's nothing going on in Mexico."

"Uh, Jeffrey?" said E. "I think the office is located in Mexico? Last time I looked it was." A silence on the line, then E.'s voice again. "Yes, Jeffrey. I've just checked the map. Mexico City. That's where our Latin American bureau is located, in case you didn't know."

Kill him. Kill him. Jeff couldn't stand this superior air, this sarcasm and condescension. "Yes," he said. "I know. But I think it would be better if you came down here to Salvador."

"*El* Salvador?"

Jeff grunted in the affirmative. He glanced down at the earth that was splattered on his canvas hiking boots and caked to the cuffs of his blue jeans. He'd spent most of the afternoon rolling around in the dirt to avoid being shot. It was a miracle that he hadn't been killed. It was a miracle that anyone who set foot in Salvador wasn't immediately tossed on a mortuary slab, there were so many guns.

"You think I should come to *El* Salvador?" repeated E.

110

"That's right," Jeff said. "*El* Salvador." He reached up and scratched his forehead. He felt a smile nip at the corners of his mouth—suddenly, in his mind, a tantalizing plan was beginning to take shape. He said, "You know, E., there's a lot more stuff going on down here than in Mexico. You'll get a better picture of how things operate. I really think—"

"Yes, yes. All right, Jeffrey. You may be right. I'll take this under advisement. Let's see what the word is from the powers that be."

And a week later, the word was—Salvador!

Oh, excellent. Oh, divine. It was perfect. It was . . . delicious. After he learned the news, Jeff almost had to physically restrain himself from scuttling around his hotel room, cackling to himself and rubbing his hands together in a kind of psychotic glee. He was jubilant, elated. What better location could there possibly be for a homicide than *El* Salvador! What was one more death amid the forty or fifty thousand civilian deaths that the country had already suffered in its civil war? An afterthought. A prick of the pin. Who would care? Who would even notice?

Jeff sauntered over to his window and gazed out at the rising darkness. He hummed to himself. He felt a thrilling in his chest, a sensation he'd never known before—or not like this. His blood was roiling. His heart sang. There were a dozen ways he could arrange E.'s death in Salvador and never be caught. He could—why, he could hire someone else to do it. A hit man. A death squad. No muss, no fuss. Assassination for hire was one of Salvador's leading economic activities.

Once, while having lunch in the coffee shop at the

Salvador Sheraton, Jeff had overheard two women at the adjoining table chattering about the high cost of *this*, the dismal quality of *that*. From their dress and their manner, he could tell they were members of the Salvadoran oligarchy, the fabled Fourteen Families who controlled the entire land.

It was terrible, one of the women complained. To have a man killed nowadays was something you could hardly afford. The cost had gone up to one hundred *colones*. It was a scandal, an outrage.

"Tsk, tsk." The other woman shrugged. "You see what this country's coming to?"

They both shook their heads sadly and spilled dressing onto their salads. They jabbed their forks into their lettuce. On the marble tabletop between them rested a video cassette—Jane Fonda's workout program.

Now, in his room at the Camino Real, Jeff did a quick calculation in his head. One hundred *colones*? It was about forty dollars. It was nothing. He could write off the cost of assassinating E. as a single business lunch.

But still. To hire someone else for the job—it robbed the whole enterprise of much of its visceral appeal. Jeff did not simply wish to have E. disposed of. He wanted to do the deed himself. He could buy a gun, maybe, take E. out to the countryside, and. . . .

No. No. He wasn't thinking properly. This had to be done with panache, cleverly, with an ingenious twist. On the other hand, Jeff had an idea that E. was not a man who would be immensely difficult to kill. Salvador was a scary place. With any luck, at the first sign of trouble, E. would simply keel over from a heart attack—out of plain, unadorned fear. Jeff didn't doubt it. He'd never met E. in person, but he imagined him as a stout old fellow, draped in tweed and drooling with sweat, his wizened arteries positively calcified from bad diet and neglect. Who needed fear? A stiff dose of cholesterol would likely do the trick. One more plate of charred roast beef, a little *salsa picante* on the side—and poof! He'd be out. Finished. Done. They could send him home in a bag.

It was a pity, really. Jeff had been hoping for more of a challenge.

Well, he had some time to think about it—and think he did. He was still thinking, two weeks later, as he paced the airport arrivals area up and down. The plane from Miami was predictably late. As usual, half the Salvadoran oligarchy was on hand to greet it. The men all sported dark glasses, white shirts, pot bellies, walkie-talkies, and black pants. They'd left their guns back in their armour-plated Cherokee Chiefs. Didn't matter—their bodyguards were armed. Impatient, the wealthy men wolfed down their cigarettes and growled at the kids. Their slender wives tapped their high heels against the faux-marble floor or stole glances at their svelte reflections in the plate-glass windows overlooking the Customs area. A platoon of blank-eyed soldiers patrolled the parking lot.

Finally, as darkness strangled the coastal mountains to the north, Jeff heard the arrival announcement for TACA flight 049. Soon, the first of the Miami passengers traipsed out into the arrivals area. Jeff waited impatiently for E., whom he imagined as resembling a Colonel Blimp in mufti, someone who would be melting

113

like an ice-cream cone in the inky sub-tropical heat, mopping himself with a handkerchief the size of Rhode Island, red-faced, groaning for breath.

What a pushover. All Jeff would have to do to ensure this fellow's demise would be to tamper with the air-conditioning unit in his hotel room, remove the thermos of purified water that stood on the desk, and wait for fate to take its inevitable course. Sometime after midnight, E. would grope his way into the bathroom, agog with thirst, and drink of the water there. Ha-ha! The trusty Salvadoran microbes would begin their evil work at once.

E. would collapse, naked and gasping, on the floor. It would all be over in a roar of dyspepsia, a flurry of flailing arms, and a last, pathetic gagging for breath. Not a pretty way to go. In the morning, the attending physician would merely shrug and shake his head. A sad thing, but no one could be blamed.

"Excuse me. Is that you, Jeffrey?"

Jeff swung around on his heels. He found himself facing a tall, angular man not much older than himself. The man had longish brown hair swept down over his ears, and slightly cavernous features, quite handsome in their way. He wore a dark polo shirt, weathered blue jeans, and canvas hiking boots—the foreign reporter's uniform, exact. Jeff glanced down at his own clothes—polo shirt, blue jeans, hiking boots. He looked back up.

The new arrival carried a plump haversack that he now dropped down at his feet. He extended his hand. "I'm Evan," he said. "Sorry I'm late."

Evan . . . ? Who was Evan? Oh—Evan. Of course, he would have a name. Jeff had spent so many months thinking of E. as simply E. that he'd almost forgotten that it must stand for something. Besides Editor. So—it was Evan. Jeff pushed the palm of his right hand down the side of his jeans to rub it dry and then reached up to shake hands. He was suddenly perspiring. "Oh, uh. Hi. *Bienvenido a El Salvador.*"

"*Gracias,*" said E. "*Estoy muy contento estar aquí.*" His accent was perfect.

They walked out to Jeff's car, threw E.'s bag in the back seat, climbed in themselves.

"I didn't know you spoke Spanish," said Jeff. He turned the ignition switch and briefly raced the engine. "You never spoke Spanish on the phone."

E. shrugged. "Never had to." He rolled down his window, and rested his arm on the frame.

Jeff pulled out of the parking lot and accelerated along the darkened, two-lane road that ran up into the mountains towards the capital. E. lit a cigarette—a Marlboro, the same brand all the hacks smoked. He started asking questions about the country. How were the restaurants? Were the women friendly? Was the place as dangerous as people said? How was the rum? The beer? Was a coup expected soon? What did a pound of coffee cost? Did Jeff think there was much chance the two of them would be able to hike up into a rebel camp?

Important questions. The kind of questions hacks always asked whenever they needed some basic dope on a new country. Jeff answered as best he could and glared ahead into the long pale wedge of the headlights. It was starting to look as if killing E. was going to be more complicated than he had thought.

A lot more complicated. The main problem was,

115

all the other hacks took a liking to the guy straight off. He was actually a hell of a guy. No one could believe it.

"This guy's your editor?" said Shirl Gordon, a few nights later, when E. had nipped out of the bar in order to make a quick phone call to the office in Toronto. "I can't believe it. He's like—I don't know what."

"A regular human being," said Grant Lovsted. He shook his head. "Fuck."

Jeff just shrugged and sipped his beer. He didn't know what to say. He couldn't believe it himself.

The next day, the four of them—Shirl, Grant, E. and Jeff—drove out to a place on the coast in Usulután. It was a long, deserted beach. This was E.'s idea. He said he'd heard about the spot from some old surfer friend of his, a California wacko who used to catch the waves in that part of Salvador many years ago, long before the war. E. said he had an idea it would be an interesting place to visit. He didn't say why.

Jeff knew why. He already knew about the place—the broadest, longest plain of sand you ever saw, with the Pacific surf rolling in like the very wings of joy. The sun beat down all day, scattering against the waxy sea-grape trees. Several rundown little places were dotted out on the beach where you could rent a cabaña for a few *colones* a night, but almost no one ever did.

There was the war to consider, after all. Besides, Jeff had heard that this was where the rebels came for R & R. They were only human. They needed a little down-time too. At least, that was the word in San Salvador. The rumour was, the rebels sometimes hung out here. It was known as Guerrilla Beach. It was the newspaper story that Jeff most wanted to write. But Jeff had come out here a couple of times before, looking for beach-combing guerrillas, and he'd never found any. The place was always deserted. He decided the whole notion was a myth or maybe a hoax. Guerrilla Beach? What an idiotic idea.

And yet, when Jeff and the others showed up this time, there was a whole platoon of them out on the beach—left-wing rebels on the lam. Jeff stood and stared, couldn't believe his eyes. There they were, lounging on the sand in their bathing suits, with their FN automatic rifles dangling from some branches by a cluster of rocks and palms and hyacinth. One of the rebels had stayed back to guard the rifles. When the four gringos approached along the beach, the sentry leapt to his feet, but he wasn't hostile. He just wanted to know their names and their business.

"We're friendlies," said E., "and we want to party."

Grant immediately turned his baseball cap around so that it faced backwards. He stuck out his fist with his thumb upraised, and growled, "Awright!"

Before long, the other rebels strolled over in their bathing suits and bare feet, a dozen of them—eight men and four women. They all seemed to be in their twenties. Jeff was impressed. He'd seen a lot of things down here, but he'd never seen a Communist guerrilla in a bathing suit before.

It seemed that E. was serious. He really wanted to party, and he took charge of the entire operation. As far as he was concerned, nothing else mattered from here on in—no other commitments, no deadlines, no nonsense about needing to be someplace other than right here, right now. For four days, they hung out on the beach with the rebels. And the rebels were delighted. They'd never met any gringo hacks before, but they'd always wanted to. By day, they all swam out to a small rocky islet not far offshore. Behind them, on a long rope, they towed a burlap sack full of bottles of Suprema beer. They stripped down and sunbathed in the nude. Grant got a thing going with one of the women guerrillas, and Shirl did the same with one of the men. Those two lovestruck couples would wander off at the strangest times, on the spur of the moment, and be gone for an hour or so—leaving the others to exchange glances and knowing grins. When the lovebirds returned, they were always shy but laughing. They looked ruddy and content.

Jeff astonished himself by striking up a woozy kind of friendship with another of the women rebels. Her name was Marisol, and she had curly black hair, a turned-up nose, and a voice as sweet as cantaloup. She could break down and reassemble her FN rifle in twenty-five seconds flat, blindfolded, and she let him watch her do it.

"Now, you show me something," she said.

And Jeff did. "It's called french-kissing," he said.

"I knew that already. So, now, you have to show me something else." She batted her eyes. "Something I don't know."

One afternoon, Jeff stayed back on the beach with Marisol while the others splashed and sunbathed on the islet. The two of them ate ripe mangoes sprinkled with hot ground chili—the finest meal known to man—and drank fresh coconut milk. They read to each other from a dog-eared book of poetry that Marisol carried with her everywhere. Rubén Darío. Pablo Neruda. Gabriela Mistral. She'd been studying Spanish literature at the Central American University before the revolution intervened.

She put down the book. "Show me that one again," she said, "*por favor.*"

"Show you what?"

"You remember. The one I didn't know." She smiled and slid off the shoulder straps of her suit.

Later, in the shade of the palm fronds, surrounded by hyacinth blossoms, she peered at her pretty brown feet and announced to Jeff that the main problem with being a rebel was not ideological or moral. No, it was the trouble with boots.

"Boots . . . ?"

"Yes, boots." She explained that the rebel life included a tremendous amount of marching, and she was always going through the soles of her boots. They wore out every three months, and there were always difficulties and delays in getting them replaced. "Just think," she said. "There are eight thousand rebels in this country. At four pairs of boots a year per, that makes thirty-two thousand pairs of boots. A year." She shook her head. "It's a lot. We're always running out."

"You mean you sometimes have to march with holes in your boots?" Jeff felt a rising pang of sympathy. To think of all the privations Marisol must have had to endure in her hard, lean life—and holes in the soles of her boots as well. It was too much. He frowned. "You must be kidding."

"No." She shook her head. "I'm not."

He thought of this young woman, high in the

Salvadoran mountains, fighting for the liberation of her people, risking her very life—all the while, with holes in her boots. Jeff couldn't stop thinking about it, or at least not until she suddenly rolled over onto his chest and covered his eyes with her hands. "What is it?" he said. "What are you doing?" "Blindfolded," she said. "I want you to show me that one—blindfolded."

Each evening, a portly woman named Señora López strolled down from the nearby village to prepare dinner all around. She cooked plump cornmeal *pupusas* on a wood fire. She boiled piquant chicken-and-chili soup, grilled freshly caught sea bass and lobster, along with banana fritters. She served it all up on cracked china plates with thick, gushing slices of tomato on the side, and peppery salsa.

Everyone cheered, with their mouths full. They washed the nightly feast down with shots of cheap Salvadoran rum, chased by swigs of Coca Cola. Then they lounged out on the veranda of one of the cabañas and told war stories as the sun exploded above the Pacific and sank towards Hong Kong. One of the guerrillas had a guitar, and he played it—everything from Guatemalan traditional songs to plaintive Cuban pop tunes by Silvio Rodríguez or Pablo Milanés.

Evan—everyone thought of him as Evan now—took the guitar over after a while and strummed a medley of folk songs from Andalusia, where he had apparently lived—lovely, haunting stuff that seemed to melt into the melody of the night, the throaty growl of the breaking waves, the mother's hush of the wind in the sea-grapes.

Jeff could hardly believe the transformation in that man, how different he now seemed from his disembodied presence on the telephone from Toronto. When you thought about it, there were just two kinds of people in the world. You had editors—people who stayed cooped up in an office somewhere, issuing orders, imposing constraints, making up rules, and destroying things that had been composed by others. And you had reporters. Reporters were out in the field, in touch with the earth. They were immersed in the process of creation, keeping themselves alive.

And now, all of a sudden, E. had come down to earth, to walk amid sunshine, green plants, the ebb and flow of life. And the changed surroundings had transformed him into a regular human being. People were like chameleons, it seemed. They adjusted to their surroundings. They could change—for the better. When Jeff closed his eyes and thought about Evan now, he found that all thoughts of homicide had vanished from his mind. Why would he want to kill Evan? Evan was one of them, a friend, someone you could count on.

The third night on Guerrilla Beach, Evan dug out his Sony shortwave radio and tuned in a big-band show on the BBC World Service. Everyone jumped up and started to jitterbug in the sand. The gees knew every move, even the most complicated steps. They tossed each other into the air like acrobats, the best dancers Jeff had ever seen. But then Evan got out there—and he showed them what real jitterbugging was. Marisol ran over and dragged Jeff out into the whirl. They danced all night, all of them, by the glow of a single hurricane lantern and a lofty, gibbous moon.

On their last night together, the whole crew—rebels and hacks alike—climbed up into the nearby village, called San Jacinto. It was a Saturday, and Evan had found out from talking to Señora López that there was a movie showing that night. "Come on," he said. "We can't miss this."

At first, no one had wanted to go. They were too comfortable. Too tired. Too content. But Evan insisted. "It's Saturday night. Time to do something special."

"What?" said Grant. "This isn't special enough? Hanging out on a Salvadoran beach with a bunch of Communist rebels?"

But Evan was not to be resisted. He harangued them until they all gave in. And a good thing, too. The whole village was out for the event—men, women, and shrieking kids. The movie was to be projected onto the outside wall of the village's whitewashed stucco church. There was no electricity in this part of the country, but someone had jerry-rigged a power supply for the ancient, whirring projector by hooking it up to a twelve-volt truck battery. The people had hauled the pews from the church and set them out on the stubbly grass in two tidy rows. Jeff and the others found a good place to sit, over on the left side—the rebels were adamant about that—and about halfway back.

The movie was *Elvira Madigan*, in Swedish with Serbo-Croatian subtitles. No one could understand a word, but it was the only movie the villagers had. During a reel change, they said they'd been watching it once a week for the past seven years. True, they couldn't make out any of the dialogue, but they didn't care. They looked forward to it all week long. They couldn't remember where the movie came from or how it fell into their hands. They just set it up and let it roll, every Saturday night. Once a week, for seven years.

And no wonder. The copy was scratchy, of course, and chattered on the reel. The Swedish dialogue and the Slavic subtitles were equally incomprehensible. But it didn't matter. The story sang for itself—the lyrical tale of a handsome Swedish soldier and a beautiful circus performer, their doomed love for one another, their flight together, and their poignant, tragic end. The melancholy strains of Mozart's piano concertos lilted through the salt air and the humid, Salvadoran night. As the final credits rolled, everybody started to cry—the villagers, the hacks, the guerrillas too. Jeff and Marisol huddled arm in arm, sharing his handkerchief. Everybody sobbed. No one could help it. And they didn't bother to hide their tears, either. What would be the point? They were human, after all—why deny it?

After the movie, the hacks and the dozen rebels strolled back down to the beach, wordless, each of them listening only to the murmurings of his or her own thoughts. Later, Marisol and Jeff and Evan stayed up long into the night, just the three of them, long after the others had gone off to sleep. They sprawled on a pair of palm mats set out on the veranda, gazed off towards the darkness and the sea. They passed around a bottle of Centenario rum and smoked Marlboros, one after another. They marvelled at the wonder of the previous four days.

Jeff shook his head, to clear a space in the warm, rum-soaked fuminess of his brain. "I've got to write all this down," he said. "I've got to write a piece for the paper about all this. What a great, weird piece. It'll go on the front page for sure."

Evan swallowed another mouthful of that fine dark rum. He was silent for a few moments. Then he too shook his head. He said no, that Jeff was wrong. He shouldn't write a word about any of this. There were some things you didn't tell. You kept them for yourself or passed them along to your friends, little by little, by word of mouth. He stretched out his arms. "This isn't about war," he said. "None of this is. It's just about being alive. Keep it a secret. It's yours. It isn't to share."

"Ours," said Marisol. She sat up, to swallow another mouthful of rum.

"Eh?"

"You said, 'Yours.' You mean, 'Ours.' All of ours."

Evan nodded and took the bottle as she passed it to him. "True," he said. For some reason, he suddenly seemed distracted, brooding. "That's quite true."

None of them said a word after that. A moon was up, and they simply gazed off into the velvet and shimmer of the ocean until they began to yawn. At last, they dragged themselves off to bed.

Before he fell asleep, with Marisol cuddled at his side, Jeff recalled that he still hadn't talked to Evan about this wonderful change of personality he'd undergone, about how different he seemed down here. Somehow, the moment hadn't seemed right. He thought—maybe tomorrow. He'd talk to Evan about it then. He turned to mould his body to Marisol's snuggled frame, and sleep enfolded him like an embrace.

The following morning was a headlong rush. There wasn't time to ask Evan about anything—anything

124

important, anyway. Everyone had to pack up. The hacks had to leave, head back to the capital. And the gees had come to the end of their holiday, too. They were going to hike back up into the hills, back to the war. There was much clasping of arms and throaty laughter, and more than a smattering of tears. Marisol told Jeff that he must write to her. There was a post-office box kept by the rebels in Tegucigalpa. He could send letters to her there.

"It takes some time," she said. "But I'll get the mail eventually. It's how my mother stays in touch."

Jeff scribbled the address down. He looked up. "Maybe I could come to visit you sometime, in your camp."

She shrugged. She wasn't too sure about that. Then she smiled. "Or maybe, someday, back here." She spread out her arms to contain the whole of Guerrilla Beach. "Think of me," she said, "whenever you have mangoes and chili."

"Or holes in my boots."

She seemed sad at that, but then they kissed, hugged, and whispered goodbye.

Jeff and the others piled into his car for the drive to San Salvador. They were silent during the trip. No one said a word. There was too much to think about. Besides, Evan was heading back to Miami the following day. From there, he was supposed to fly to London, to visit another of the paper's foreign bureaux.

That night, the entire assembly of foreign hacks in San Salvador trooped out to dinner at Siete Mares for a *despedida*, something they did whenever anyone important had to leave the country for a long time. In only a week, Evan had earned himself that honour. The Last

125

Supper, they called it. The evening was raucous and liquid and, by the time it was over, everyone was more than ready for bed.

Jeff was up early in the morning, though, in order to get downstairs in good time. He wanted to drive Evan out to the airport. But Evan shook his head. He said no. "I always like to leave a place by myself," he said. He and Jeff were standing in the hotel lobby. Evan had just paid the bill with his gold American Express card. His haversack slumped at his feet. "Really. I'd prefer it."

Jeff nodded. He sort of understood. Still, he felt there was something he wanted to say, maybe ask Evan some trenchant questions about himself, or apologize in some way for all the difficult conversations they'd had on the phone. Or maybe say something more, say something significant, something that would last. Maybe even confess all those terrible thoughts he'd had, those homicidal urges. He ought to say something about those. Jeff had the feeling that an important moment had come. He didn't want to waste it.

But, of course, he did waste it. In the end, he didn't really manage to say anything. All he did was shake Evan's hand and mutter, "Thanks." He hesitated before adding, "Evan."

Evan smiled. "Thank *you*," he said. He shouldered his haversack and strode outside. A taxi was waiting, and he climbed in the front.

Jeff closed the taxi door for his editor. He waved as the car rumbled away. He watched it merge with the fumes and clamour of the early-morning traffic. He suddenly had a sensation of terminus, of things coming to an end. He felt a wave of foreboding, a feeling that this

126

was the last time he would see Evan alive. Something terrible was about to happen. He could feel it in his bones. Maybe there'd be a firefight between rebels and the army out along the road to the airport—it had happened before—and Evan would be killed in the crossfire. Or something about the plane. The plane would crash.

But there was no firefight, and the plane landed safely. A month later, at the end of his global tour, Evan was ensconced once again at his desk in Toronto, and he was back to his old hateful self—supercilious, cold, patronizing. He was E. all over again, the sort of man who would remove the final "s" from the word "premises" without so much as a twinge of remorse.

Yet Jeff felt he understood. He thought he could see how it was. If he too had to spend all his days in a windowless office in the grey drear of Toronto, jabbering with foreign correspondents all the time on the phone—responsible for their every move, their regular debacles and occasional small triumphs—maybe he'd be condescending too. It was hard to say for sure, but he couldn't rule it out.

And what did it matter? He wasn't in Toronto. He was here, in Latin America, and that was what really counted. Now, whenever gloom descended, all he had to do was look back on those four luminous days on Guerrilla Beach. Those memories always cheered him up. Every two weeks, he wrote to Marisol, and dutifully she wrote back. She said she was confident of the rebels' eventual victory. Her faith never wavered—though sometimes, she confessed, she tired of the mountains and longed for the throb and rush and solace of the sea.

And there were times—especially after another of those maddening conversations with E.—when Jeff found that he too encountered an emptiness in his soul, a hollow place he could not fill. The truth was, he still wanted revenge. A part of him did. He couldn't help it. One afternoon in Guatemala City, after an especially gruelling exchange on the phone with E., Jeff walked out into the sunshine, past the pillars of cypress trees and the frothing bougainvillea sprays that sloshed over the tall stucco walls of Zone Ten. Such beauty—yet he barely noticed it. Instead, he railed at E. He swore under his breath at the wilful ignorance, the brute callousness, the sheer spitefulness, of that man. He felt a tremor of his old, raw hate. Kill him. Kill him.

Jeff paced for several blocks in a blur of rage, until he lurched to a halt at a street-corner just outside an Argentine restaurant. Suddenly he remembered old Correale, from those long-ago days in Buenos Aires during the Malvinas war. He remembered—and now he saw what he had to do. He hurried back to the taxi stand near the Camino Real, climbed into a clattering old cab, and asked to be driven to a leather-goods store, the best there was. Amazing how he'd never thought of this before.

When he got to the shop, Jeff leapt from the car, marched straight in, and asked the woman what they had in the way of leather hiking boots. He wanted the best she had. The woman showed him a selection of Italian imports. Of course, he knew the size. He had all the dimensions off by heart, could assemble them in his mind in an instant. He made a selection, paid in cash, and pocketed the receipt.

At the end of the month, Jeff put the bill through on his expense claim as a PID. A Personal Indignity. He worried at first that he might get an angry phone call from accounting or, worse, from E. himself. E. spoke Spanish, after all—he was sure to recognize the bill for what it was. But no. No one said a word. The claim went through without a hitch. Damn thing worked like a charm, as it was to do again and again—every three months. A parade of PIDs.

Jeff smiled to himself, sat back at his desk in the small fifth-floor office he rented on the Paseo de la Reforma in Mexico City. He was back at home base for a time. He banished from his mind all traces of homicide. Instead, he gazed out the window and thought of Marisol. He saw her high on a mountain ridge in Central America, her FN rifle glinting in the afternoon sun, and her shiny new Italian hiking boots gripping the red Salvadoran earth. He closed his eyes and forgot about E. He remembered mangoes and chili powder, a voice like cantaloup, and the long, proud arc of Guerrilla Beach.

Dangerland

That day in Dangerland?

When Curtis Rice got shot in the back of the head?

With a slug from an M-16?

And just sat there, for the next hour, reading a novel in the middle of the goddamn war?

Take it from me. You would not have believed the look on that guy's face.

This is what happened.

The three of us—Theresa DeLazzari, me, and that little worm Curtis Rice—drove south from San Salvador at about noon on a Sunday, headed for Dangerland.

We were in my car, a rented Toyota with a busted fender and both of the brake lights gone. I was driving, of course. To be honest, we didn't know where we were going exactly. Dangerland is not that kind of place. We were just out on a little reconnaissance mission, I guess you could say. A little look-see in the countryside.

We hadn't really expected to make a foray into Dangerland that day, but we'd gone to the mass at the Metropolitan Cathedral in the morning, hoping that the acting archbishop would say something peppy in his homily, as he often did. Denounce the ogres on the right. Deplore yet another horrendous peasant massacre up in Chalatenango that nobody but the Church knew about yet. Warn of a military coup in the offing that his office had gotten word of. Something like that. Something we could write about.

Two Sundays out of three you'd get excellent quote from the acting archbishop's homily, but not this time. This time it wasn't even the acting archbishop who gave the homily—the real archbishop being dead, of course—but just the auxiliary archbishop, and all he did was pray for peace.

Nice, but no story.

So there we were, empty-handed on a Sunday in Salvador, just the three of us—Theresa DeLazzari, or la Teresa, as she liked to call herself, me, and that little creep Curtis Rice. The only reason we'd even brought the little jerk along was we thought we were only going to the mass, and he asked to come, and what the hell? He was a hack too, so my informants told me. If you cut him, would he not bleed? So I figured, give the little turkey a break.

But take him into the countryside on a recon?

No way. Believe you me—I wouldn't be caught dead in the same car with the guy. . . .

Right. I know. Bad choice of words.

"I'll tell you what," said la Teresa. The two of us were sweating in the sunshine on the broad front steps of the Cathedral after the mass, poor people streaming out past us on all sides. "Let's take a run east along the coastal highway. Elaine and Rich said yesterday they ran into a roadblock around El Rosario on their way back from Zacatecoluca. We could go there."

It was down to just la Teresa and me at that point. The disarming Mr. Rice had wandered off to look for a washroom. He was having trouble with his bladder, he said, though the truth may have been a sight more gory.

"Army or guerrilla?" I said. I meant the roadblock.

"The gees, of course," said la Teresa. She was fiddling with her hair—black and very thick—fixing it into a ponytail with one of those little red plastic things. "Who cares about an army roadblock?"

I shrugged. "Okay," I said. "There's nothing else to do. Let's go."

"May I come?" said Curtis. He had reappeared from the battle zone of the innards, looking flushed, miserable, and close to surrender. As always, he carried a briefcase. Brown leather, possibly genuine. It contained—or so it was said—books. Printed works of fiction.

My advice to Mr. Rice at this point would have been, take a taxi back to the hotel, chico. Or, better yet, an airplane back to the States. In my view he did not belong in El Salvador. You just had to look at him. Too pudgy, for one thing. And all he did was read books— I swear to God. There was a war on down here, and the war was what demanded our attention. He was just taking up space that could have been better filled by somebody else. Anybody else. We needed people who knew what was what. I would have told the guy he couldn't come, but I didn't get the chance.

"Sure," la Teresa said to Curtis. "Come on." She started walking down towards the car.

"Terry," I said. "Hang on a sec. . . . "

But she wouldn't listen. She once told me that she quite liked the guy. Okay, not liked exactly. But she could tolerate him. Tolerate—her word, not mine. I dug out my keys and followed her across the square, over to where I'd parked the car. I unlocked the door on the passenger side and opened the door behind it. "You," I said to Curtis. "In the back."

And that was how all three of us got headed south along the airport road, down the mountain ravines towards the dried brown coastal flats. At the wheel, I lit a cigarette and listened to that metallic screech of the cicadas. I booted past the limping country buses even on blind turns, just the way the Salvadorans do. It's an acquired taste, but no big deal. If you do meet an oncoming car or truck—just don't panic. He's the one that's gotta move.

"Hey! Hey!" came a shout from the back when I started to pull out for the fifth or sixth time. It was Curtis, sounding none too pleased. "Don't! Don't do that! You—!"

"Goddamnit, Grant," said la Teresa, siding with the underdog as always. Normally, she liked a little unnecessary risk. "Damn you. Will you take it easy on the curves? Save it for the track."

"All right, all right," I said. I braked and eased back in behind this absurdly overloaded country bus, all crates and baskets and chickens and waving limbs. It looked like a mechanized pack mule. We could have passed it, no problem, but I didn't want dissension in the car. "There," I said. "Better?"

But la Teresa didn't answer. She just shifted around in her seat and went on talking to old Curt in the back. They were talking about books. Books they'd read in college. *Fine*, I thought. *Don't worry about me, folks. I'm just the driver. This is just a war—perhaps you didn't notice. May I draw your attention to the scene on our left? Those former electrical pylons now standing on their heads? Or, over there, in the ditch? That charred and gutted truck? Scenes of war, ladies and gentlemen.*

And we weren't even in Dangerland yet.

Books. . . .

I lit another cigarette, and stared at the butt end of that bus still wobbling through the curves in front of us. *"Dulce nombre de Jesús,"* it said on the rear panel above the tailpipe. Sweet name of Jesus.

Finally, we crept out beyond the wall of a ravine, and the fuzzy brown landscape of the Pacific coast gaped off to the left, the flats broken here and there by volcanic cones wearing clouds like little toupees, or by the bright green square of a canefield where there must have been irrigation ditches. You could just about infer the ocean too, that narrow band of hazy blueness that ran like a moat against the sky. . . .

Quick. Get me rewrite, Gertrude. I'm feeling metaphorical. I'm feeling inspired.

The road ran on straight for a bit, so I pulled out and roared past that old bus, and from there on it was pretty clear sailing down to the coastal highway, where I headed east. In the seat to my right, la Teresa was still twisted around, fiddling with her hair again and talking

134

to our mutual friend in the back about Charlotte Brontë. Seems they'd both studied Charlotte Brontë in university.

Charlotte Brontë . . . .

Like the man said, *Dulce nombre de Jesús.*

We got to El Rosario in good time. But there was no guerrilla roadblock here—not now, anyway.

"So," said Curtis. "I guess we turn back?"

I could have predicted he'd say something like that. He'd gone pretty silent a little earlier when he finally figured out that we were bound for Dangerland. Until then he probably thought we really were just out for a drive, the kind of thing you might do somewhere in Connecticut. Well, guess again, amigo. When he finally got it all sorted out, he seemed to lose interest in the pleasures of literary debate. He hadn't said another word except now and then, "Stop! Stop the car! I've got—I've got to go!"

Not: gotta go. But: got to go. As in: Oi've goht tew goh. As if elocution mattered at a time like that. I'd stop just the same, though, and let him out, and I'd light a smoke, and la Teresa and I would wait for as long as it took, until he dragged himself back up to the car.

But here we were, at the remains of a guerrilla roadblock, and Mr. Rice didn't seem to have to go at this point. Now he just said, "So. I guess we turn back?"

"Grant?" said la Teresa. She shifted in her seat. "What do you think?"

I looked at my watch. It was almost one o'clock. I looked up. The gees were gone, but it was pretty clear they'd been here recently. The poles and power lines were freshly toppled by the side of the road, and someone had pushed what must have been a barricade of rocks off onto the shoulders. About fifty yards ahead of us the bridge was gone, where the road ran across a dried-up stream bed. There'd been a bridge there only a week earlier. Now, just some slabs of concrete, steel rods, and rubble. If we did keep going, we'd have to drive off the road, down through the stream bed, and back up onto the road. It didn't look too bad.

A little beyond the road on our right a couple of adobe huts slouched in the sun, with their walls caved in from what must have been some pretty heavy fighting. Obviously the army had shown up too.

A smattering of peasant women shambled towards us along the road, and I got out to ask them what was what. La Teresa joined me. Old Curt stayed where he was. Guarding the car, I guess.

"*Buenas tardes,*" I said to the women.

They all had pottish bellies beneath their short, bright dresses and had babies tied to their backs with shawls. They had kerchiefs around their hair, and one carried an enamel bowl on her head, with a plucked chicken inside. They shielded their eyes from the sun. "*Buenas* tar*des,*" they crowed back, as if even the time of day were some kind of joyous revelation.

I asked them if there'd been any fighting along this stretch of road, although the answer was obvious.

"Of course!" they said. "Why not?"

"When?" said la Teresa.

"Yesterday?" they replied. "This morning?" They weren't too sure, or didn't want to be pinned down. The latter, probably.

Out of the corner of my eye, I saw something move—the car door. It was opening. Curtis Rice had decided to venture out into Dangerland after all. Not Dangerland proper. This was border country now. The rebels were evidently gone. This wasn't true Dangerland any longer. I looked back at the women. "The guerrillas," I said. "They're gone now?"

The women nodded.

"You're sure?" I said.

They nodded more vigorously. "Definitely," said one.

"They ruined our bridge," said another, the one with the enamel bowl. She made a miserable face and waved her hand.

Curtis ambled over to stand beside la Teresa. He was carrying, I noticed, a book. That meant he'd been reading, in the car. This was quaint. I tried to make out the title of his book. *Wide Sargasso Sea*? Jean something. It looked like Rhys. Curtis had on his tortoiseshell eyeglasses with the snap-on shades, and he kept slapping the cover of that book against his thigh. He was wearing a pair of wrinkled cotton pants, too tight. He stood with his knees locked.

Sweet name of Jesus.

I told him what was what. "The guerrillas have gone," I said. "As you can see."

He nodded. "Oh well," he said. "So I guess we head back?"

"Not necessarily." I turned to the women again. "The road up ahead—it's clear now?"

They pushed up their lips and eyebrows, as if my

question had unlocked whole new galaxies for enquiry and contemplation. They exchanged glances, looked back at me, and shrugged. One of them said, "If only we knew."

"Sorry?" Curtis said. "I didn't catch that. What did she say?"

La Teresa said, "He asked them—"

"I heard what he asked them. I speak Spanish, you know. I just didn't hear what the woman said."

"*A saber, pues,*" I told him. I pronounced the words slowly and clearly, so a moron could make them out. "It means something like—"

"I know what it means. Thank you. I just didn't hear her, that's all."

I shook my head. What a turkey. It was well known he spoke not a word of Spanish. That wasn't surprising—he'd only been down here a couple of weeks. But why pretend?

I looked at Curtis Rice again, from the bottom up—his goofy, thick-soled shoes, his bulging beige pants, his pale and pasty skin, his plaid shirt with the buttons near to popping.

Jesus. Why wear such ridiculous clothes? Why carry a briefcase? What on earth did this guy normally write about anyway, back in the States? Education? Book-publishing? *Bridge?* What had his editors been thinking, assigning him to foreign news? What had possessed them to send Curtis Rice, education reporter, down to this of all countries?

This was El Salvador. There was a war on, for Christ's sake.

I shoved my hands in the pockets of my jeans and

drew an arrow in the dirt with the toe of my boot. It pointed east. I said, "Let's keep going."

La Teresa shrugged. "Sure," she said. "Why not?" She took off her sunglasses and breathed on the lenses and started rubbing them with the tail of her denim shirt. "Okay," she said. She squinted up at me. "Let's go."

That was the spirit. She was famous for that. I could have hugged her then. She'd give anything a try.

"I've got a feeling," I said. "There might be something good up ahead. You notice—we haven't seen any oncoming traffic along this whole stretch of road."

It was true. It had caught my attention before, but I'd thought it was because of the guerrilla roadblock that was supposed to be here, at El Rosario. Now it looked like there might be something up ahead, some other obstruction.

"Hey, you're right," said la Teresa. She put her sunglasses back on and checked her hip pocket for her notepad. "Good for you. I must have been napping. I didn't notice."

Damn right she didn't. Too busy talking about the uses of metaphor with Mr. Scholar. What I wanted to know was, did Mr. Scholar carry a notepad? I hadn't seen one. Maybe he kept it in his briefcase, so he could spend about twenty minutes trying to find it when the bullets started to fly. Clever plan. I always kept my notepad in my hip pocket, just like all the other hacks did. You wanted a pad of just the right dimensions, too—so it would fit snugly in your hip pocket, so you could get at it fast when you needed it.

I thanked the women for their help and headed

back to the car.

This was the way I figured it. The gees had set up their roadblock near El Rosario a day earlier, to collect war taxes and just to wreak general havoc. The army had moved in that morning to chase them off. There'd been some fighting, and the rebels had withdrawn farther east. Now they were probably holed up in some village, to rest. They were blocking traffic again, just daring the army to do something about it—sheer bloody-mindedness, as usual. And they were waiting for dark. Then they'd vanish, sneak back into their camps in the hills.

But that part about holing up in a village—that was the key. It was a favourite guerrilla tactic. They calculated the army wouldn't attack them there. Too many civilian casualties. Too many headaches from the human-rights people. But the gees might be wrong about that. They sometimes were. So it could get interesting.

To la Teresa, I didn't need to explain a word of this. She'd have worked the same thing out exactly. She knew Salvador. She knew the way things operated. At least, she did when she wasn't sizing up the collected works of Charlotte Brontë with Our Egghead in Central America here.

And what of Mr. Rice? I didn't think he realized what was what. I doubted he'd had a clue from the word go.

So we all got in the car. I lit a cigarette, took pity on him, and mapped it out—what the gees were up to and what we proposed to do.

The little creep swallowed. He said, "But—what's

the point?"

I'd been expecting something like that. I looked up at the mirror, at the reflection of his face outlined by the shimmery light of the rear window. His features were too soft somehow—unfinished, as if moulded in a hurry from Plasticine. I removed my cigarette. "What's the what?"

"The point. Of this. What's the point of it?"

"*Sorry...?*" I said. "It's what we do, isn't it? We go. We see. We come back. We write about it. It doesn't have to have a point."

"That's not what he means," said la Teresa. "He means, what's the point of this in terms of the war? You know—what the gees are doing now." She turned to him. "Right?"

He nodded.

I thought, sure—that's exactly what he meant. I said, "Nothing, probably. No point at all. So what?"

Curtis didn't say anything. I kept watch on his face in the rearview mirror. White as plaster now, beneath those stucco whorls of short brownish hair. Because of his snap-on shades I couldn't see his eyes, but I could imagine what he was thinking. He was thinking, get me out of this bloody car.

I'd seen that look before. Dozens of times. They'd be thinking, get me out of the car—but they wouldn't have the nerve to say it. Trapped by fear on all sides. Surrounded. Desperately seeking salvation.

Dulce nombre de Jesús.

Take it from me. You don't want that kind of individual in your car, not when you're heading for Dangerland. You want people you can trust—exclusively.

People like Theresa DeLazzari. I shook my head. Maybe I should have just told him to leave. That was what I was thinking. That would have been for the best.

But la Teresa broke in. She said, "Come on. Let's just go. Nothing's going to happen."

And from the back came the wavery voice of Mr. Rice. "I don't know. . . . " he said. Then silence.

It was all he could manage.

I started the engine, put the car in gear, and eased back out onto the road. The peasant women, I noticed, were nowhere to be seen.

Rule number one: wave at the guys with the guns.

There were a couple of reasons for that. In the first place, it showed that you were cool, you didn't mind being noticed, you were just out for a drive in Dangerland. In the second place, it made you feel better—a whole lot better—when the guys with the guns waved back, their rifle barrels jostling at their sides.

So when we passed the second platoon of National Guardsmen, out skulking along the road, I waved and so did la Teresa—and a whole lot better was what I felt. They gave me the creeps, those guys. Just one glance and you knew that they could have no noble purpose. They looked like Prussian cavalry, or something worse, in their black steel helmets, tight green jackets, and riding breeches. What they were doing in those uniforms, out hoofing through the yellow grass in Central America, I swear to God I did not know.

Yes I did. Looking for things to kill.

"Soldiers?" said Curtis, about ten minutes later.

He hadn't spoken for quite a while. "Those guys back there, they were soldiers?"

"National Guard," said la Teresa. She sat up, peered ahead, and pointed. "*Those* guys are soldiers."

She was right. I'd peeled around a blind curve bordered by two black rock faces—and there, practically blocking the road in front of us, were three dark green army trucks jammed with soldiers. I hit the brakes.

It wasn't a formal roadblock, but I had to stop. Something was up. I could feel it in my chest. It wasn't that I was afraid—not yet, or not exactly—but something was definitely up. I could feel that quickening of the blood, that throbbing in the chest, that airy, almost porous feeling you got in the outer circles of Dangerland, as if some key element of your molecular structure had just dropped out of the picture, leaving a thousand little holes. They made you float.

It wasn't fear. Fear was different. This was just the beginning of fear. We were at the anything-can-happen stage, heading for the something-will.

We had to get out of the car so the soldiers could search it, which they did. Top to bottom. I lit a cigarette and handed out most of the pack to some of the soldiers, and even la Teresa decided it was a good time for a smoke. And then I noticed Curtis. He was over by the car, staying close to that familiar Japanese technology, and he was having a cigarette too, taking a smoke from one of the sol—

"Hey . . . ," I shouted. I couldn't help it. It was a reflex.

But I was too late. I was too late to do anything. I'd only have made it worse if I'd tried. The soldier—just a

kid with a shiny brown face—was lighting Curtis's
smoke for him and then his own and now waving out
the match. I saw him push his M-16 back up over his
shoulder and drag on his cigarette, breathe out through
his nose, stare at Curtis.

That little moron.

Rule number two: don't take smokes from the
soldiers.

It's hard to explain, that one. Maybe you can't
explain it. It was just bad karma to accept a cigarette
from a soldier. It was something you never did. We were
in Dangerland now. The rules were different. You didn't
take a smoke from a soldier.

I watched Curtis cope with his cigarette, watched
his scrunched-up face. He had the cigarette clamped in
the corner of his mouth and kept reaching for it with the
wrong hand and turning his head far to the side to blow
the smoke away without inhaling. He still had on those
idiotic clamp-on shades, and he stood with his knees
locked and with the beginnings of a pillow belly shoved
against the front of his short-sleeved plaid shirt. And he
had his brown-leather briefcase—possibly genuine—
resting on the dirt at his feet. Books, books, books.

I did not think that this was a time for books.

Curtis was nodding and wore a strange, nervous
smile and he listened to the soldier talking to him in a
low voice about things that the dumb twerp couldn't
possibly understand. . . .

And—sweet name of Jesus—it was then. I'm sure
it was then that I had this flash of insight, this vision.
Curtis Rice was going to get himself shot. I could almost
see it happening.

That scene with the cigarettes and the shiny-faced young soldier—it was like a communion or the administering of last rites. Something like that. I wasn't Catholic. I didn't know how all that hocus-pocus worked. But I suddenly had a vision. I saw what was going to happen. There was no possible way that someone so goofy, so unprepared, so doddering, could possibly survive in Dangerland.

And he'd just taken a smoke from a soldier—a thing you never did.

Maybe I should have decided then and there to call it quits for the day. Maybe I should have told la Teresa and Mr. Rice that we were heading back to San Salvador, no explanation. And maybe I would have. But just then the soldiers finished searching the car and pronounced it clean, and their lieutenant strolled up to la Teresa and me. He was a lean man, face dark as mahogany, skin pocked on both cheeks. He took one of my cigarettes and let me light it.

The lieutenant spit out a fleck of tobacco and probed his lips with his tongue. He looked at me. He said, "Where are you going?"

I must have hesitated, so la Teresa broke in. "Zacatecoluca," she said.

"Your purpose there?"

"We have some friends. The brother of the mayor."

"His name?"

"Juan Francisco Aldana." La Teresa took off her sunglasses but kept her hand up there, to shield her eyes from the sun.

The lieutenant pondered.

I waited, didn't say a word. I'd let la Teresa handle

this. This stuff about the mayor's brother—she was making most of it up. I knew that. And yet the essential bits were true—I would have bet on it. She really did know the mayor's brother. His name really was Aldana. That was rule number three: have an answer ready—and be sure that it will stand up. Don't hesitate, but don't tell an obvious lie.

La Teresa was a pro. She was the kind of person you needed with you in your car.

The lieutenant nodded. He blew out some smoke, peered back the way we'd come. "Subversives?" he said. "Did you see any subversives on your way?"

I shook my head. "No. Only some National Guard. Two platoons. That's all." No harm in telling him that.

He started chewing at his lip, looked at la Teresa and then at me, rocked back and forth on his boots. Now he nodded the other way, towards the road ahead. "That way is closed," he said. He waved off towards Zacatecoluca and shrugged. "There could be subversives over there. I don't know."

He did know. He knew just about exactly what was in front of us. La Teresa and I didn't say anything, though. We just waited for him to speak again.

"I cannot guarantee your safety," he said. He reached up with one hand and proceeded to stroke his moustache. His hands were as dark as his face. "The subversives—I don't know. They might mistake you for the CIA." He smiled. "And then your government would be blaming me"—his smile broadened—"for your deaths."

Funny guy. I didn't know what to say. It looked to me like we were going to be turned back after all. There didn't seem to be anything to say.

But la Teresa reached out with one hand and touched the lieutenant on his brown forearm just below where the dark green sleeve was rolled up. It was no more than that—a touch. It lasted a few seconds, no longer. But there it was: a white American woman touching a dark-skinned latino on his forearm. You could feel the air-pressure change. "We understand," she said. "It's not your responsibility. We'll take our chances." Slowly, with a sliding movement, she withdrew her hand.

He looked at her and then at me. He took another drag from his cigarette, only half smoked, and flicked it away. He waited a time before speaking, drew a thread of saliva through his teeth. You could tell he was thinking about what she'd just done, her putting her hand out like that, touching his skin. He was thinking, this pure-race American woman touched my skin.

He coughed and spat off to the side. "You may proceed," he said. He paused. "But I warn you about the subversives. They are very nasty. You must tell them you are Russian." He smiled again. "Maybe they will not shoot you then."

He walked away. "Russian . . . !" he repeated in a loud voice and started to laugh.

Then the other soldiers took it up. "Russian!" they all cheered and pointed at us. "Russian! Russian!" They swung their rifles up onto their shoulders, put back their heads, and laughed.

Now we were in between.

We had the army behind us, the gees somewhere

in front. I drove past the low adobe hovels with their mossy clay roofs, their clipped-cactus fences, past the scattered rock piles and the dead grey fields littered with corn husks, past the clacking starburst fronds of the palms. We and everything around us were trapped in Dangerland. It seemed peaceful now, almost deserted—but you never knew.

This was the essence of guerrilla war, its unpredictability. Dangerland was a place whose borders constantly shifted, never stood still. The peasants who lived here knew that. One day they could be out in the sunshine, ploughing their fields. The next day, dead. You just never—

"Stop! I've got to . . . stop! I've got to go!" It was Curtis. He had his hand up on the back of my seat, practically clawing at my shoulder.

I slowed the car and pulled over onto the edge of the road. By the time I got the car stopped, he was already out and running. He slid down the roadbed, clambered over a fence of black volcanic rocks, and then disappeared beyond some scrubby trees into the crook of a hill.

I shrugged, lit another cigarette. "Nature calls."

"I need to stretch my legs," said la Teresa. She got out of the car.

I did the same, went over to her side of the car. "Smoke?"

She shook her head. "No thanks." Then she shrugged. "What the hell."

I gave her a cigarette—I was on a new pack now—and lit it for her. We smoked in silence for a while, just watching the scenery—the way the banana fronds kept

148

still for so long and then would suddenly move. "Books," I said. "You sure read a lot of books."

She pushed out her lower lip and shrugged. "Used to."

"Not any more?"

"Nah. No time. All I read now is newspapers and death lists. Like you."

"Yeah."

She looked at her cigarette, nodded over towards the small barren hill where that little egghead, Curtis Rice, was battling his inner demons. "You think he's okay?"

"No. I don't. I think he's a total moron."

"I meant—"

"Yeah. I know. I know what you meant. I'm sure he's just got a normal case of the trots. He'll get over it."

"He's not really so bad, you know. He's damn smart, in fact. He's just insecure. That stuff about pretending to speak Spanish? It's just insecurity."

"Then he should see a therapist. He shouldn't come to El Salvador."

La Teresa nodded, and we both smoked in silence for a time. She looked up. "We shouldn't have brought him, should we?"

"No."

"Why not?"

"Because he's bad karma."

"Come on."

"I'm serious. He's bad luck. Those stupid shoes. That goddamn briefcase. Those fucking lenses on his glasses. He doesn't belong here."

"And we do?"

I dragged on my cigarette. I shrugged. "Maybe. I don't know." I blew out some smoke. In fact, it was a good question. I had to think about it. The thing was, did anybody really belong in Dangerland? Well, some people did. Some people were just made for the place. But me? Or la Teresa? Hard to say. I leaned back on my elbow against the hood of the car. I said, "It's like when you're walking alone at night, through some bad part of town where you don't want to be, and you've got all these tough guys hanging out in the shadows and you know they're just staring at you, cuz they're pretty sure you don't belong. . . . " I stopped. I had to think.

"Yeah?" said la Teresa. "Okay?" She meant, get on with it.

"Well, you just know they're waiting to hit on you, waiting for some excuse, some trigger. So what do you do?"

"I don't know," she said. "What?"

"Well, you don't wear goofy-looking shoes or carry a stupid briefcase, for one thing. What you do is, you square your shoulders, you put out your jaw, you look at them—just for an instant, a moment, just to let them see you know they're there—and then you walk past them like you know exactly what's what and who you are and where you're going. You send them a message. You say, 'Don't fuck with me.'"

"And that saves you?"

"Maybe. Sometimes." I shrugged again, tossed away my cigarette. "It's okay to be afraid. You just can't show it. That's bad karma. And that's what's bugging me about Mr. Got to Go." I looked up. "Speak of the devil."

Wan and tottering, Curtis Rice climbed over the

150

rock fence and hauled himself up the roadbed and back to the car.

La Teresa ground out her cigarette with the toe of her running shoe. "You all right?"

He grimaced. He looked terrible, white and sunken-faced with drooping eyes. "I need water," he said. "I think I'm dehydrating." He held up one hand, palm down, and pinched at the skin on top. The fold of skin just stood there. "Look. The elasticity's gone."

"We'll be able to get sodas in San Rafael," I said. "It's just up ahead. I wouldn't try the water. It's not—" I broke off because of the noise overhead. A helicopter.

La Teresa heard it too. We both peered up and back to the west. At first, I saw nothing.

"There it is," said la Teresa. She pointed. "One— no, two. Hueys."

We watched them throb past, high and a little to the north of us—a pair of olive-green helicopters churning out of the sunshine against the deepening blue of the afternoon sky.

And now I knew. We were near the centre of Dangerland now. "That's it," I said.

"What?" Curtis again. "What?"

"Those soldiers back there—that's what they were waiting for. The choppers. They're going to send the choppers in first, hit the gees from the air. Then the soldiers'll move up from behind. They must figure they've got the boys surrounded."

"What . . . ? What about us?"

"Got us surrounded, too. Come on. We can't stay here. Let's move." I started to go back around to my side of the car.

151

"Wait," said Curtis. "Wait."

"Come on," I said. I was getting anxious. We shouldn't have been standing around like this. "Come on. The army's going to be moving up behind us. We've gotta keep going. We're inside the loop now. They'll shoot at anything that— "

"No," said Curtis. "Wait. Wait." But he just stood there.

It was pathetic to see. I knew what was happening. He was trying to find a way out of this, trying to think of something to say to get us to turn back. "Come on," I said to him. "Get in the car."

"No."

"Get in the car."

He just stood there.

"Get in the fucking car, you moron."

"Curtis. . . . " This was la Teresa. "Grant is right. Just get in the car. Don't worry. Nothing's going to happen. Nothing will happen."

It was the right thing to say. Curtis clenched his teeth and got in the car. It was the right thing to say, all right. But it wasn't true. We were near the centre of Dangerland now. Something would happen. It would happen soon.

We drove three, maybe four more kliks before we got stopped again. At first I thought it was more soldiers. There were three of them, in almost full battledress— olive-green fatigues and elaborate web harness and black combat boots—and they were running almost full out along the road ahead of us.

When they noticed our car rattling along the road behind them, they suddenly pulled up, swung around on their heels, and started waving their rifles.

Their rifles. That was when I realized these guys weren't soldiers. They were rebels. One of them carried a G-3, another one had an FN, and the third, the tallest of the three, the one who started striding back along the road towards the car, he had an AK. He had it down in front, pointed at us. I saw his right hand drop to flick off the safety.

The car was stopped. I let it idle, kept both my hands high on the wheel, so the rebels could see them. La Teresa had her hands up on the dash. I didn't know what Curtis was doing, didn't have time to think about it.

It was obvious now that these guys didn't look anything like soldiers. Their hair was too unkempt, their faces too mobile, their uniforms too weathered and worn. They'd know by now that we were journalists, from the strips of tape on the windshield, the ones that spelled out "TV", a sort of international symbol for journalists. Usually we could expect a nice warm welcome from the rebels, but not this time.

The tall one pushed the barrel of his rifle right through the open window on my side of the car. The other two gathered on la Teresa's side.

"Journalists," the tall one said. "What are you doing here?" His voice should have been steady, but it wasn't. It trembled.

I realized he was scared. They all were. A bad sign. A very bad sign. I swallowed, fought to control the thudding in my chest. "We were looking for you.

153

We—"

"Open the door!" he shouted and wrenched at the handle of the back door.

I noticed that the hair had receded far from his brow, leaving only sparse wisps of black. I swung around in my seat. "It's okay," I said. "Get in. Get in." I didn't have much choice, so it was best to seem enthusiastic.

Besides, there was another rule. If there's going to be shooting, hitch up with one side or the other. Don't get caught in the middle. The balding one threw himself into the back seat, shoved Curtis into the centre. The other two gees clambered in the opposite side. Their rifles banged and clattered.

Curtis had his briefcase up on his knees, clutched the handles with both hands. His mouth was moving. He was trying to speak, but no sound was coming out. Those snap-on lenses were flipped up now, but still I couldn't see his eyes. The regular lenses were too thick.

"Drive," the balding one said. "Go on. Drive. But slowly. Just go slowly."

I got myself straightened out again and put the car in gear. I glanced at la Teresa. She was turned around, peering into the back seat, keeping an eye on Curtis. I started to drive ahead, just slowly, like he said. I kept the speed down to about fifty kliks.

"Soldiers?" the balding one asked. He had his voice a little steadier now. "You have seen them? Where?"

I looked up into the rearview mirror, met his reflected gaze. We both held that moment. His eyes were dark, slightly narrowed, but there was nothing threatening in them. These guys were okay, it seemed.

154

I thought I could count on that. They'd just been caught a little short on this particular day. Guerrillas got rattled too.

"Soldiers?" I repeated, and I didn't hesitate. You were a journalist, you were supposed to be neutral, not take sides—but you could forget that stuff now. "Yes," I said.

"How many?"

"Three trucks. Maybe a hundred troops." I kept glancing up into the mirror, meeting his eyes.

He reached up and ran the palm of one hand back and forth under his jaw, kind of a soothing motion, getting himself calmed down. "How far?"

"About fifteen kilometres back, when we passed them. They were stopped, waiting for something."

"The helicopters," he said. "They don't spit any more without those helicopters."

He did something with his eyes, and we both smiled. We were both thinking—what if the gees had choppers too?

I drove on for a while—not too fast, just steady—and no one said a word until my guy, the guy who was losing his hair, reached forward and slapped me on the shoulder.

"My name is Pablo," he said, although I knew it wasn't. They never gave their real names.

I nodded. "Grant," I said. "And this is Theresa. And that guy's Curtis." And then I realized he was speaking English. This guy knew English. "Where'd you learn English?"

"I studied at school," he said. "At university. I was going to be a teacher of English."

155

"And now you're a guerrilla?" said la Teresa. She shook her head. "I can't believe this country."

The other two gees weren't saying a word. They kept shooting glances out the windows, up, and all around. They weren't calming down.

The one named Pablo smiled and repeated our names. He put his lips together and pondered the sounds, as if he were testing some unfamiliar food. "American?" I nodded. "Chicago," I said. "Theresa here is—" "California," said la Teresa. "Los Angeles." "The Dodgers," said Pablo. "Very good."

Curtis said something, give him credit. It sounded like Hartford.

I drove on, and Pablo explained that he and the other two gees had deliberately dropped back behind the main group of rebels—he didn't say how many there were—to act as sentries, lookouts. The rest were going to hole up in a village farther east, San Rafael, wait until darkness fell. The usual thing. But then the helicopters came. They hadn't expected that. Pablo said he thought the other rebels were probably on the move again by now. There'd already been shooting up ahead, he said— the helicopters attacking the village.

There was silence again, no sound except the hollow whirring of our tires against the asphalt. Everything around us was still, as though we were in the eye of the storm. We were near the epicentre now—the army moving up on our tail, the rebels ahead, fanning out, trying to escape. Probably more soldiers were moving in from the east, from Zacatecoluca. The army wasn't usually this aggressive. Usually they'd just let the rebels go—it saved wear and tear on their own boots—but maybe they had some of the Yankee advisers up in those choppers today. Time to show off for the gringos.

"Tell me. . . . " This was Pablo. He leaned forward, pushed his elbow up against the back of my seat. "You and the Californian"—he nodded at la Teresa—"you have parents back at home?"

I kept my eyes on the road. "Yes," I said. "Why?"

"Just curious." More silence. Then he said, "Tell me, do they worry about you being down here?"

La Teresa laughed. "Of course. What do you think?"

In the rearview mirror, I caught sight of Pablo's face, creasing into a frown. He looked up. "And tell me," he said. "Life insurance. Do you have life insurance?" He slowed down on that phrase, as if the very idea fascinated him. Life insurance.

I couldn't believe this. Did we have life insurance? I didn't know what to say. I heard a snort from the back seat, a loud snort like a sneeze. Curtis. It was Curtis.

"Do *they* have life insurance?" Curtis exclaimed. There was a sharp edge to his voice, that edge of panic. He was fighting it down, struggling to stay in control. "Do *they* have life insurance! What are you talking about? What about you? Do *you* have life insurance?"

Not bad going, I thought. Not bad going to get a coherent sentence out right about now. I remember thinking, he's going to be okay. He's going to be okay after all. And it was as if Curtis had fed the rebel a deliberate set-up line, as if they'd both rehearsed this exchange a dozen times.

"Life insurance?" Pablo repeated. "Life insurance . . . ?" He cleared his throat. "A guerrilla has just two

157

forms of life insurance. One is tomorrow. And the other is the knowledge that—if we should die—after the triumph of the revolution, they'll name a road after—"

Just then we all ducked.

I hit the brakes. Out of nowhere—that pounding roar, like a hundred butcher's cleavers slamming straight into the roof of the car. The din widened, deepened, and a broad shadow shot across the road just ahead. The trees shook.

"Shit!" This was Pablo. "Shit! Shit! Shit! Drive on. Slowly. Drive on."

I did as he said. Up ahead, on the left, stood a thicket of scrubby trees, and the road curved around them. I followed the bend in the road, slowly, and where it straightened out, where I should have picked up a little more speed, was where I hit the brakes again.

More rebels. They burst out of the trees on the right, about thirty yards in front. They looked back at us, glanced upward—they were in the open now, worried about those helicopters—and suddenly started running our way. There were four or five of them, and they had their rifles out, barrels down.

"Christ." That was Curtis, muffled now, indistinct. "Oh Christ."

The rebels kept running towards us, then suddenly stopped. They brandished their rifles.

"Get out of the car," said Pablo. "They want us to get out."

"Okay," I said. "Fine. That's cool." My blood was racing, and now I heard that roar again—another helicopter. It pounded overhead, directly above the car. I fought off the urge to scream. I heard shooting.

Up ahead, the rebels scattered, flung themselves off the road. Moments later, they reappeared. They were shouting at us, still waving their rifles. I couldn't tell what they wanted. They seemed completely disoriented, probably just kids. There was no way of telling what they'd do.

"Come on," I shouted. "Everybody out. Out. Out. Curtis—that means you."

I threw myself out onto the road. La Teresa did the same. Like me, she was just concentrating on staying alive. Someone grabbed my arm—it was Pablo—and started hauling me over to the edge of the road, towards the grass and some low scraggly trees. And I could hear more shooting. We were down on our knees in the ditch, and I could hear shooting.

"Grant!" I heard la Teresa. "Grant! It's Curtis. He's back in the—"

"Move! Move!" Pablo kept shoving against me, pushing me ahead.

The other two gees ran off in front of us. And I couldn't help it. I had to keep going. We had no cover here. I could see where Pablo was aiming for—a small forested gully just ahead and off to the left. On the road in front of us more rebels appeared. I thought they were rebels. They were making for the same gully, scurrying across the road. They swung to the side as they ran, turned towards us, rifle barrels up, and the air began to crack.

"Down! Get down," Pablo shouted.

This was crossfire, we were caught in crossfire. I couldn't look back, but I knew there were soldiers behind us, moving up from behind. And I forgot all about Curtis or the car or even about la Teresa. I thought only about getting to that gully and down.

We didn't have to run far, just down that gully and through a thicket of trees. We found a clump of low adobe buildings in a clearing, and we banged on the door of the larger building, a house, until someone inside slid back the wooden bolt and let us in—la Teresa and me. Pablo kept right on going, and I never saw him again.

We stayed in that house with a family of peasants, all of us stretched out on the dirt floor as flat as we could. We didn't say a word. La Teresa and I both had our notebooks out, scribbling like mad.

It must have lasted an hour or so. Maybe more. The helicopters roared overhead, and now and then something heavy crashed with a report so deep and loud you thought it was going to bust your jaw. Those were grenades, rocket-propelled. It was just luck that we and that family weren't blown to bits. Those adobe walls wouldn't have stopped a direct shot from a pop-gun.

But somehow we came through it. And when it was over, everything silent again, we got back up on our feet, laughing, just about hysterical. We were okay. We all kept touching each other, as if we couldn't believe it. Solid. Whole. *Okay. Okay.* We laughed and laughed. That's what would happen afterwards, if you were lucky. You got this dose of adrenalin, long and slow, just pumping into your veins. And when you walked it was as if you were walking on an endless slab of foam rubber. You couldn't quite touch the ground, and the earth seemed to bob and weave. If you weren't careful you'd fall right down.

Then we had to go back to find Curtis.

And we did. There he was. He was still in the car. I could see him from a distance. He hadn't moved.

"He's dead," said la Teresa.

At first I thought she was right. But no. He was sitting up straight in the back of the car, and when we got to the car, it seemed there was very little damage—very little new damage—except for a couple of bullet holes through the rear window and one through the front. I opened the door beside Curtis and I said, "Jesus Christ. . . ."

He didn't move. He didn't turn his head or make a move. He was sitting up straight with that book, that *Wide Sargasso Sea*, held out in front of him, and he said, "I've been shot."

"What?" I said. "What are you talking about?" I thought he'd gone crazy.

But it turned out to be true. He had been shot. In the back of the head. With a slug, we later found out, from a goddamn M-16. Must have been a ricochet. It had entered at the base of his skull and pushed right up and lodged against the top of his spinal column, did no damage to his brain at all. A millimetre farther, and they'd have been weeping and mourning in Hartford, Conn. As it was, the guy should have been dead already, just from the shock.

I didn't know about that part then. All I knew was what I could see when I peered around to look at the back of Curtis's neck, and sure enough—a tidy little entrance wound. Hardly any blood to speak of.

Soon after that Curtis did go into shock. The car

was basically okay, so la Teresa and I got back in, and I drove like a shot back to the capital and straight to the Rosales hospital. Nobody spoke much along the way, certainly not Curtis.

They operated on him almost immediately, to remove the bullet. They kept him in for observation for a couple of days, on medication for the shock. The shock could have killed him, all on its own. But Curtis recovered. When he got out, he had eight stitches in the back of his head. That was it.

He remained in Salvador for two more days, spent most of the time at the lobby bar at the Camino Real, telling all the other hacks about his story. He was a big celebrity now.

"You mean you just sat there, in the middle of all that shooting, with a bullet in the back of your head, reading a goddamn book?" said Rich. He put down his beer with a thud and shook his head. "I don't believe it."

But it was true. I could vouch for that. So could la Teresa.

"What was the book?" said Rich. "I gotta get a copy."

"*Wide Sargasso Sea,*" said Curtis. He looked even goofier than usual, with most of his hair shaved off because of the operation. "By Jean Rhys."

"And you didn't go into shock?"

"Not till later."

"Incredible. A bullet in his head, and he doesn't go into shock. What chapter were you reading?"

Curtis shrugged. "The whole book, practically. I finished the book. So then I turned back to page one and started to read it again."

"I gotta get a copy."

"You can borrow mine from Grant. He's reading it now. Anyway it doesn't matter what book it was. That's not the point. It could have been anything. I'd just finished *The Comedians*, by Graham Greene. It could have been that. Now I'm reading *Burger's Daughter*, by Nadine Gordimer. Just as good."

"A book." Rich shook his head. "I can't believe it. Reading a book."

La Teresa and I drove Curtis to the airport the next day and waited with him for his plane. He said he was never going to come back to El Salvador, and I believed him. We didn't talk much, just sat out in the open, on the observation deck upstairs, while the air force flew in and out with its Cessna Dragonfly jets. It was a hot sunny morning, I recall, and you could see the ocean off in the distance, rolling inland, like a moat against the deep blue sky.

163

The Disappearance of Pepe Vásquez

So it is, lady gardener:
our love
is
earthly:
your lips are a flower of lights, a corolla;
my heart works deep in the roots.

Pablo Neruda, *Oda a la Jardinera*

Captain Gaspar Guzmán had never made anybody disappear before, so when the order came across his desk on Monday morning—fourteenth, August—he thought at first there was some mistake.

The order was from the Carabineros, regional command in Concepción, and the subject named in the document was one José (Pepe) Bartolomé Vásquez, an individual whom Captain Guzmán knew by name, by reputation, and by sight.

164

Pepe Vásquez was that harmless old coot who spent most of his afternoons down at the municipal cemetery tending the unmarked grave of Pablo Neruda's mother. He was a local eccentric, a crank, nothing more. People were always making fun of him.

But here in the crisp official document on Captain Guzmán's desk, the picture painted of Pepe Vásquez was of quite a different hue. The fellow was a suspected subversive, a merchant of seditious propaganda, and a misfit who engaged in dubious activities tending to undermine the stability of the fatherland (see Appendix A).

All this seemed a bit excessive. Pepe Vásquez was a small fellow with a narrow grizzled chin decorated most of the time with little scrapes and nicks from clumsy attempts at shaving. He sauntered about the town of Parral these bright winter days wearing a brown fedora, an old woollen overcoat with mismatched buttons, and a pair of tweed trousers, badly frayed. He worked weekday mornings as a custodian at the local library. He took his meals at the Little Flower café, a modest establishment operated in accordance with municipal regulations by the widow Zulueta. He lived alone in a sagging wooden house on Rivera Street, and he belonged to no known subversive organizations, which was not surprising. In Parral, there were none.

Captain Guzmán flipped to Appendix A in order to see what on earth this was all about, and almost immediately he understood. It was not a pleasant feeling.

Appendix A was a document he'd written himself almost a year earlier, one of his monthly reports on

165

Incidents of a Suspicious Nature. In it, he had identified Pepe Vásquez as a resident who bore further watching. He had noted this strange practice of Pepe's, this habit of planting flowers and tending the grass around one of the unmarked graves in the municipal cemetery, a grave alleged to be that of Pablo Neruda's mother.

Furthermore—as Captain Guzmán had observed in his report—the aforementioned José (Pepe) Bartolomé Vásquez was known to have published a series of six articles under his own name in the local weekly newspaper, *La Voz de Parral*. In them, he had agitated for the construction of a monument to honour Pablo Neruda—an illustrious poet but also a known Communist—in Parral, the poet's birthplace.

More than ten years had gone by since Pepe Vásquez had written those newspaper articles. They'd appeared prior to the great military salvage operation conducted by His Excellency General Augusto Pinochet Ugarte on eleventh, September, 1973. But Captain Guzmán had neglected to spell out this chronological factor in his report on Pepe Vásquez. He'd left the impression that the articles in question were of a more recent vintage—that they might have appeared, oh, just the other day. He regretted taking that liberty now, and wondered why he'd done it.

He removed his glasses, rubbed his eyes, put his glasses back on, and swallowed the dregs of his coffee. Ah, yes. Now he remembered the circumstances of that report. Even now, almost a year later, he could see why he'd sent it. Parral was such a quiet town. When the end of the month came around, he often had very little of a suspicious nature to forward to Concepción. Sometimes nothing at all. And what he did report—a group of children overheard in a school yard singing "Gracias a la Vida" (a seditious song), or rumours that certain women in the poorer parts of town were cooking their meagre daily stew in communal pots (a socialistic activity, from the sound of it)—invariably resulted in no more than a general admonition from Concepción to continue cracking down on all forms of dissent.

So last September, with no suspicious incidents of any kind to report, Captain Guzmán had decided there could be little harm in detailing his misgivings about the admittedly rather odd activities of Pepe Vásquez. At least it would give him something to put in his report. It was unwise to go a month without any evidence of subversion at all.

Captain Guzmán had pretty much forgotten about the affair after that. He hadn't expected anything to come of it. Certainly not this. To make disappear? This was the most drastic remedy in the police manual. It was something he had never previously attempted, except on laboratory corpses during his years of training long ago—and he hadn't been very good at it even then. It seemed to be an over-reaction in this case.

He got up from his desk, pulled on his heavy gabardine coat, and buckled on his Sam Browne belt with his service revolver in its leather holster. He donned his green peaked cap and told his secretary, Corporal Arias, that he was just going out to make some inquiries.

He strode onto Venezuela Avenue, where the late-winter sunshine splashed through the aspen trees and the air was cold and sharp. He turned left and promptly realized that he'd forgotten his polished brown truncheon, a common oversight on his part—he never seemed to need it. Would he need it now? Possibly. He wasn't sure. As far as he could recall, making someone disappear was a complicated affair, requiring several preparatory steps and quite a lot of equipment. He could no longer remember exactly what it was he might need. He clasped his arms behind his back and proceeded to walk in a westerly direction.

Captain Guzmán was not himself a native of Parral, this quiet community tucked in a wine-making region south of the capital. He'd been born and raised in Santiago itself and had received his police training up there. Those years of training had prepared him well for the evil and duplicity he was sure to encounter among those who threatened state security. His instructors had also instilled in him a cool professional willingness to inflict an array of harsh but unfortunately necessary and, in any case, thoroughly scientific responses.

On graduation, the young Lieutenant Guzmán had been given his first commission in Parral. When the time came, he was promoted to captain. He was never reassigned. And he had grown to like the place, its easy friendliness, its slow and natural rhythms. One season folded gently into the next, and hatred—while not un-known—seemed to lose its lethal edge. The occasional dispute cropped up, of course, and had to be dealt with. A man got drunk and locked his wife out of the house, or she locked him out, or their children locked them both out. Two farmers came to blows in a dispute over a cow. Incidents of that sort.

But political activity? Sedition? Subversion?

In truth, Captain Guzmán believed he had run up

against no such thing. He should never have written that report. Now he was going to have to make Pepe Vásquez disappear. And when he got right down to it, the prospect was not a thing he welcomed. It was not a duty he wanted to perform.

He turned right at Viña Street, and the bells at the church of Nuestra Señora de las Flores chimed out the quarter-hour. So it was just past eleven o'clock. He pondered what to do. Pepe Vásquez would finish work when the library closed for lunch a bit before noon. And what then? Captain Guzmán realized that his knowledge of the subject's activities was incomplete. The best thing to do initially might be to familiarize himself with the man's regular movements. He could pick up the trail at the library. But first he had three-quarters of an hour to kill, so he proceeded a little farther along Viña Street until he reached the Little Flower café. He turned and marched inside.

"Good morning, captain," said the widow Zulueta. She swayed down from her wooden stool by the counter, like a weight being lowered on a winch. "Coffee? Why don't you sit there by the window. Never mind the sun. Here. I'll lower the blind. A little carrot cake? You don't show up in my place nearly often enough. Perhaps you missed breakfast—I can fix you up some spicy eggs. Here. Read the paper. It's early, I know, but what about a little snort of pisco? You look sad. You could use some hard liquor. Or maybe a glass of wine?" She shuffled towards him.

"Coffee," said Captain Guzmán. He set his peaked cap down on the table and loosened his belt. "Just plain black coffee. That will be fine."

169

"In a shot." The widow Zulueta placed a newspaper before him and reached across the table to release the cord for the blind. The louvered shades rattled down and cracked against the bottom frame, releasing a swarm of dust motes that swirled in the horizontal bands of the sun. She turned and waddled back to the counter. Her fuzzy white slippers swished across the bowed wooden floor. In a voluminous blue skirt her large posterior seemed to drift behind her, like a prosthetic device not properly attached.

Captain Guzmán watched her recede towards the kitchen, then slipped on his glasses and peered down at the paper. *La Voz de Parral*. It was the current week's issue, and he'd read it already. Juancito Rosas, a ten-year-old student at the Escuela de la Santa Trinidad (shown in the accompanying photo accepting his award) had won first prize in the mayor's annual writing contest for his excellent little essay on this year's subject, The Dignity of Farming. Meanwhile, local señoritas between the ages of fifteen and eighteen were being called upon to enter the upcoming Princesita de la Uva pageant, to be judged by a panel of schoolteachers and clergy.

"Here you are, captain. A nice hot cup of coffee. And a slice of my best carrot cake, too. Don't worry. No charge." The widow Zulueta set the steaming mug down before him and beside it a fork, a spoon, and a slice of cake on a chipped china plate. She pulled out a chair and lowered herself into it. "Drink," she said. "Eat. You look exhausted. You look like you just saw a ghost." She put up her brown, pudgy hands and fluttered them in the air, like emanations of the spirit.

170

Captain Guzmán dug his fork into the cake. He was quite hungry, in fact, and the cake turned out to be particularly enjoyable. He sipped from his mug of coffee, and let the liquid bathe a trail down his throat. He undid the buttons of his coat, found he was still warm, and so—at the widow's urging—removed his coat entirely, along with his Sam Browne belt.

He wondered why he didn't drop by the Little Flower café more often. It was so pleasant to be relaxing here in the glow of the winter sunshine, eating some fine carrot cake and drinking this quite delicious coffee. The widow Zulueta was no bean-pole beauty queen—no one would accuse her of that—but she had a bluff chatty way about her that was really quite appealing. And all that extra weight she carried? Well, such a surfeit might be a comfort to a man on a cold winter night. He wondered why he'd never mused about such things before, or why he'd always held himself apart from the people of the town. His police training, he supposed. After all these years, its mark remained.

These thoughts reminded Captain Guzmán that he was on duty even now. He set down his coffee mug, ran his tongue across his upper teeth. He shifted forward. "Tell me. I gather that Pepe Vásquez often comes in here. Would that be . . . every day?"

As soon as the question was out, Captain Guzmán realized his error. He raised his fist to his mouth and feigned a cough, a ruse to deflect attention from what he'd just said. He was out of practice. That was what it was. He was being far too abrupt. "Excuse me. A bit of congestion in my throat. Nothing serious." His cough turned to a series of polite grunts. "Now, where was I?

171

Ah. About Pepe Vásquez. I'm just asking out of a mild curiosity, you understand. The fellow intrigues me, that's all. I don't really need to know."

"Every day." The widow Zulueta pushed back her hair. She didn't seem to find anything unusual about his question. "He's in here every day. Like clockwork, our Pepe. He comes in for breakfast, a big lunch, then dinner. Seven days a week. More coffee, Captain Guzmán? Perhaps another slice of that cake? There's plenty on hand."

"Well, perhaps just a drop more coffee. Excellent coffee. And the carrot cake is very good, too. But I've got to watch my. . . ." He patted his ribs beneath his starched beige shirt.

"Nonsense, captain." The widow got up and made her way back to the counter for the coffee pot. She returned and refilled his cup. "Your weight is just right. I've always said, we're lucky in Parral to have such a fine-looking police captain. It's an honour for our village. . . . " She looked up. The coffee pot floated above the table in her fleshy, dark hand. "Ah. Here comes our Pepe now."

Captain Guzmán reached out and opened a large peekhole in the horizontal gaps of the window blind. He saw Pepe Vásquez amble up the middle of the street— in clear violation of municipal regulations—with one hand shoved into the pocket of his old coat. In the other, he clutched a bouquet of flowers. Daffodils? They looked like daffodils. He had his fedora pushed back on his head, and he seemed to be whistling.

Captain Guzmán realized that his strategy was coming unstuck already. He must have lost track of the time. He'd planned to be waiting outside the library when Pepe Vásquez emerged. Or perhaps Pepe had left work early. But no—there were the church bells even now, tolling out their ponderous midday call.

The widow Zulueta set down the pot of coffee. "There. What did I tell you? Just like clockwork."

A bell rattled above the door, the hinges squawked, and Pepe Vásquez stomped inside the café, kicking his feet together for warmth. He removed his hat and made what Captain Guzmán interpreted as an almost flirtatious bow. "For you, Marga." He held out the bouquet.

"Ah, Pepe. . . . " The widow Zulueta clasped her hands. She dipped and twisted on her knees and shuffled over to accept the flowers. She sniffed them and shook back her soft, round face, her dark, bobbed hair. "How kind. Daffodils in winter. From the grave?"

"Yes. I had time to stop by. I—" Pepe Vásquez glanced over at Captain Guzmán. "Captain . . . ?" It was more a question than a greeting.

"Oh, yes." The widow Zulueta stepped back and pulled out a chair at Captain Guzmán's table. "The captain has been gorging himself on my carrot cake, and we've been gossiping about you. Here. Sit down. I see you've made a mess of shaving as usual. I'll have your lunch ready in a shot. Today, sausages. So delicious. First I'll put these beautiful flowers in a vase. Then I'll bring you a nice glass of wine. How's that?"

"*Wunderbar.*" Pepe Vásquez approached the table. "*Fantastique.*" He lowered himself into the chair held out by the widow, kitty-corner to Captain Guzmán. He set his fedora down beside the officer's peaked military cap. "About me . . . ?" he said loudly. He slowly

173

unfastened his coat, fumbling with each button. His fingers were short, stubby, callused. There was a trembling in his hands. He twisted out of his coat and frowned. "What could Captain Guzmán possibly have to say about me?"

The question was directed over his shoulder, addressed to the widow Zulueta, but she had gone off to the kitchen, clutching the coffee pot and her flowers. Captain Guzmán could hear her bustling in there now— a muffled clatter of dishes, the basso-profundo surge of a water faucet—and so the question posed by Pepe Vásquez dangled unanswered in the air. Captain Guzmán thought perhaps he should reply to the question himself, but he had no idea what to say. He had a sudden desire to study himself in a mirror, to devise an expression appropriate to this unexpected meeting.

"So, then. Captain." Pepe Vásquez straightened his arms until the joints cracked. He crossed them at the wrists and rested his elbows on the table. He was a small fellow, much smaller than Captain Guzmán. His hair was black, shot with grey, his skin leathery. Fans of wrinkles creased and uncreased at the corners of his eyes, as though his eyes were doing the talking. He leaned closer. "I trust you are well, captain. And I hope you have been bringing all our local malefactors to book. Show no mercy, that's my advice."

"Yes. Quite well. Thank you." Captain Guzmán felt cornered, as if he'd been trapped. He hadn't intended to place himself in such close proximity to his man, or not yet. He'd planned to follow him at a distance, study his movements, learn his habits, but yet remain undetected.

174

"Ah, thank you." Pepe Vásquez leaned back to allow the widow Zulueta to place a glass of dark red wine before him.

"Captain . . . ?" The widow held up the uncorked bottle and another glass. She coaxed him with her eyes. "A little gulp of wine for you? No charge."

"No. On duty, I'm afraid." As soon as the words were out, he realized his mistake. "No, wait. Please. Perhaps just a sip. This is an informal gathering, after all." He tried to laugh. There. That was better. *Assume a casual air.* He promptly raised his glass. "To Parral."

"Parral."

Both men drank, but it seemed to Captain Guzmán that it was no use. His presence here and his behaviour must already seem suspicious. Pepe Vásquez must already sense that something was out of the usual order. He set down his glass and peered at the dark circle of wine in his glass, superimposed upon the white tablecloth. Without his full uniform he felt almost naked. He wanted an excuse to put on his coat and his heavy belt— or even to get up and leave. But he couldn't think of a pretext for movement of any kind. Instead, he tried to come up with something to say, some words to lighten the mood. He glanced at Pepe Vásquez. "It was just idle talk, you know."

"Eh . . . ?" The other man was eyeing his glass of wine too, turning the tumbler around and around before him, studying the liquid's colour. He took another mouthful. "I'm sorry, captain? Idle talk?"

"The widow and I. It's true we were speaking of you, but just to pass the time." He paused. "Well, perhaps it was more than that. To be blunt—you interest me."

"I do?" Pepe Vásquez set down his glass, reached up and rubbed his ravaged chin. "I interest you? In what way?"

"Yes." Captain Guzmán felt that perhaps he was regaining the upper hand. "I am a student of human behaviour, you see. And I find it interesting, this practice of yours, the tending of this grave. You go there every day?"

"No. Not every day. But I try to go as often as I can." Pepe Vásquez tilted his head and arched his eyebrows. "You know, I find it quite flattering that you would take any note at all of what I do. Am I right?"

"Right . . . ?"

"Yes. To be flattered. Or should I be alarmed at this sudden interest?"

Captain Guzmán didn't know how to reply. He tapped his fingers against his wine glass, trying to think. Just then, the widow Zulueta set a large plate down on the table in front of Pepe Vásquez. It was heaped with grilled sausages and fried potatoes and a gushing fried egg. The sausages were twisted and intertwined. Their skins sprouted cracks, bursting with grease. The viscous fluid of the egg ran among them, like a glandular secretion. The plate sputtered and steamed.

"Would you care for a bit of sausage yourself, captain?" The widow hovered above him. "Ready in a shot."

But Captain Guzmán found he could not speak.

"Captain . . . ?" said Pepe Vásquez. He dug a fork into one of the sausages and it split in half, the grease and a dark fleshiness oozing out. "Are you all right?"

Captain Guzmán pushed his lips together, hard,

176

and tried not to breathe. He was staring at that plate. He sat back and put out his arms in what he intended to be an expansive gesture, a confirmation of well-being. Instead, he knocked over his glass of wine, sent the liquid frothing across his sleeve and over the table. It showered onto Pepe's plate, amid the tangle of sausages, the potatoes, the running egg.

Captain Guzmán looked in horror at what he'd done, at the blotches on his wrist and sleeve, the pools on the table, the red channels of wine on Pepe's plate.

"Oh, captain . . . such a clumsy old oaf. Like all men. There, there. Never mind." The widow Zulueta soon returned with a damp cloth. She dabbed at Captain Guzmán's forearm and shirt-sleeve. She set the glass upright and sponged the pools of wine from the table. "There we are. Good as new. It's all gone now. You'd never know anything was spilt. Except for your sleeve, captain. That might stain, I'm afraid." She whisked the plate away from Pepe. "I'll just toss this out and be back in a shot with more. Are you quite sure you won't eat, captain? I'll make you anything you like. You just say what—"

But Captain Guzmán had already donned his peaked cap and was buttoning up his coat and belt. He was on his feet and striding to the door. "No," he said. "No, thank you. I must go back on duty." He paused for an instant, gripping the handle. He turned to glance over his shoulder, nodded at them both. "Thank you for the coffee. Goodbye." He yanked open the door and struck out into the street, felt the winter air splash against his face like a spray of water. The air was what he needed. He'd felt almost faint in there. So stuffy.

That night, Captain Guzmán stayed up till late, trying to scrub the wine from his shirt. He tried every soap and detergent he could find, but it was no use. The widow had been right. It was stained for good. He tossed the shirt into the laundry hamper with the rest of his soiled clothing, and turned to leave the bathroom.

At the door he changed his mind. He went back to the hamper, reached inside for the discoloured shirt, pulled it out, ripped it in half, and carried it into the living room. He kicked open the hinged grate on the pot-bellied stove and threw the two halves of the shirt in there. He used the poker to work the bunched material onto the centre of the flaming logs. He squatted down on his haunches to watch. He didn't turn away until every thread had disappeared, up in smoke. All that remained were several small, round metal buttons.

When that was done, he felt a little better, oddly reassured. He set back his shoulders and strode to the bathroom to scrub his hands. It was dark outside, raining, and it was late, so he went right to bed.

The weather turned colder in the following days, and it rained most of the time, in slanted arrows. Captain Guzmán followed Pepe everywhere, to the municipal library in the morning, to the Little Flower café at noon, to the cemetery at two o'clock. There, Pepe slouched through the gates and disappeared beyond the tall brick walls that were crumbling in places, and mossy. He carried with him a bucket and a spade.

Captain Guzmán wanted to watch Pepe at work in the cemetery, but there was no way to manage it without risk of detection. So he slipped into an alley across Viña Street, lit a cigarette, and waited. An hour or so later,

Pepe would reappear, and the captain followed him to his home, careful to keep his distance, stay out of sight. He watched Pepe press the latch to his little house and vanish inside.

Captain Guzmán would continue to wait, down the street by a row of aspens. He kept watch, just in case the little man should show his head, but Pepe never did—not till it was almost dark. As he waited, the officer sometimes crept close to the house and put his ear up to each of the shuttered windows in turn, but he heard nothing. All would be silent until six-thirty, when Pepe re-emerged and shuffled along Rivera Street, turned onto Viña, and ducked into the Little Flower café for dinner. Perhaps, all that time, he'd been sleeping.

After dinner, Pepe Vásquez trudged home again, but now he did not go to sleep. Instead, a single light burned in a room at the rear of the house. Captain Guzmán huddled right beneath the window, out there in the steady rain. He blew on his hands to keep them warm, listened to the sounds within. They rattled on for hours, the clack-clack-clacking of a typewriter, the anguished slam of the carriage return, Pepe moaning aloud, and then a cracking, dull and rhythmical. It sounded like a man beating his head against a wooden wall, over and over. Once, Captain Guzmán raised himself to peer inside, above the window frame, through the cracks in the shutter, and it was just as he'd imagined. Partly swallowed in shadows, clutching a sheaf of papers, the man was banging his head against the wall. Captain Guzmán lowered himself back onto his haunches and swept away some of the rain that sluiced down through his hair. Inside, he heard more typing, low sobs, and finally silence. It was nearly dawn, and the only light in Pepe's old house at last went dark. This continued for two days. Perhaps it had already been going on for years.

Captain Guzmán slumped home, his joints stiff and sore, to wash up and change his clothes. He decided he wasn't yet ready to carry out the disappearance order. He needed to learn more about Pepe Vásquez before he could act. It was a delicate thing. The man was more complex, more mysterious, than he had previously supposed. What was Pepe up to in that room of his, banging away at that typewriter all night and crying all alone? Beating his head against the wall? That was very strange. And why did he tend the grave of Pablo Neruda's mother, anyway? Captain Guzmán felt he could not proceed until he had more information. He should not operate in ignorance. If he was going to make a man disappear—an entire life—then he had to understand what he was up against. He needed to learn more.

At two-thirty p.m.—seventeenth, August—Captain Guzmán was again smoking a cigarette in an alley across from the cemetery, with the collar of his coat turned up against the rain and cold. It was little help. The rain overflowed the eavestrough overhead and splattered down, splashed onto his peaked cap, ran across the epaulettes on his shoulders, slithered down his arms with their military braid, down his Sam Browne belt with its leather holster, down his pants and into the mud. It was almost impossible to smoke. The cigarettes kept getting sopped. Irritated and bored, he tossed another cigarette away—and he was aware of something, some movement. An instant later, he heard a voice.

"Why are you following me?"

Captain Guzmán started, shoved his hands into the pockets of his coat, as if he had something to hide. He looked up.

There was Pepe Vásquez, sodden with rain and mud, shuffling towards him along the alley. He carried his shovel.

"You've been following me for two, three days, ever since that time at the widow Zulueta's. Why?"

Captain Guzmán didn't answer, didn't know what to say. He felt as though he was the one being followed, and now he'd been caught.

"You think the whole town doesn't know?" Pepe stepped through the curtain of water that plummeted down from the eavestrough. He stood against the wall, maybe three feet from the captain. His fedora sagged upon his head, dripped long tassels of water from the brim. "Everybody knows you're following me. They think it's a hoot. *What's old Pepe done now? Cheated on his income tax?* I want to know why you're following me."

Captain Guzmán decided to ignore the question. It was he who should be asking the questions, not Pepe Vásquez. He nodded past Pepe, towards the cemetery walls. "What do you do in there every day? That's what I want to know."

Pepe looked up, as if to calculate the pace and trajectory of the rain. He gazed back at Captain Guzmán. "Do . . . ? Everybody knows what I do. You know perfectly well what I do. I tend the grave of Pablo Neruda's mother. It's no secret."

"I meant—why?"

"Because no one else will. Even Neruda himself,

when he was alive—he never came here. His mother died a pauper." Pepe nodded his head towards the cemetery. "She was buried over there, in an unmarked grave. Just a number."

"How do you know it's her grave, or that she was Neruda's mother?"

"Is this an interrogation?"

Captain Guzmán pondered his reply. It wasn't an interrogation, really. The order had already been issued. "No. Not an interrogation. I'm just curious."

Pepe Vásquez reached up and rubbed his chin. He wore a pair of woollen gloves, the fingers missing. He shrugged. "I did my research. The records are all there, at the municipal office. That's one thing about this country—the records. Nothing disappears."

Captain Guzmán shifted his weight in the mud. "So you tend the grave of this woman because no one else will. Why should you care?"

"I love Neruda. I'm not afraid to say it. He was a great poet, our greatest. But he neglected his mother."

"What about your own mother?"

"She's dead too. Buried over there. I tend her grave too. If I could write poetry, I'd write poetry. . . . " Pepe swallowed, grimaced, shook his head. "But I can't. So . . . instead . . . this."

For an instant he looked like a very small boy, just a boy hiding behind that grizzled jaw, the lines and creases of that tough, brown skin. He'd started out a hopeful lad—a poet maybe—but time and disappointment had chafed their way in.

More than ever, Captain Guzmán understood how little he wished to do this thing. But he was a

182

carabinero—that was all there was to it. Sooner or later it would have to be done, and all he'd managed these last few days was to put it off. He didn't need to learn anything more about Pepe than he already knew. He reached down and fingered the truncheon suspended at his side. He'd remembered to bring it this time.

Several blocks away, the bells at Nuestra Señora de las Flores rang out. It was three o'clock, and the rain gushed down.

Captain Guzmán looked back at Pepe Vásquez, this local figure of fun. For a moment he imagined he had the power to change his mind, to disobey. He could just turn around, walk back along this alley, the other way, and keep on walking. But instead he raised his military cap and ran his hand through his stiff brown hair. *Get it over with.* He stepped forward. "We've talked long enough. I want you to show me the grave of Pablo Neruda's mother. Your shovel—let me carry that."

An hour later, Captain Guzmán emerged from the cemetery. He was alone, carrying only the shovel. He took it home. He sawed the handle into four pieces, each a foot long, and burned them in the stove together with his clothes and his truncheon. He slipped into Pepe's house late that night—it wasn't locked—and gathered every scrap of paper he could find. This was an additional procedure in the case of writers—he remembered that now. He lugged the papers home in a bundle. He was tempted to read them, page after page of typewritten prose—a novel of some kind?—along with reams of verse, mostly crossed out. He resisted that urge, swallowed it back down. Why make this job worse? He burned one page carefully, then another, and another, then started cramming the papers into the stove. He shoved them onto the flames, first with the poker and finally with his boots. He didn't stop until every lick of paper was gone.

The shovel blade—he left that out in the rain for several days. Then he carried it down past the Rivas granary to the junkyard and threw it in there. That was all he could think of, so he went back to his regular duties. The work that had piled up.

No one ever saw Pepe Vásquez again. He'd just vanished, simply disappeared. And no one ever spoke of him after that, either, at least not as far as Captain Guzmán could tell—not even the widow Zulueta. It was as if someone had dug a hole in the ground and tossed something in. Before long, the earth settled back into place. Pretty soon, you wouldn't even know there was anything down there, beneath the surface, sinking through the rocks, the soil, the roots, the decaying plants, and the worms.

Captain Guzmán soon discovered an unexpected interest in gardening. It seemed to surprise everyone. Most afternoons, he'd be over at the cemetery, looking after that damn grave, the one they said belonged to Pablo Neruda's mother. But no one ever laughed at him or made fun. They wouldn't dare.

Welcome to the War

Only Cal was with him when it happened, both of them pinned down by crossfire in Suchitoto. It lasted no more than a minute or so, the dying part, but the shooting went on and on. "It was shit," Cal said that evening, when he got back to the capital, back to the hotel. "It was pure shit." Cal lit another Marlboro and breathed out a cloud of smoke. He asked Pedro for a beer.

Cal has this very lean face with blunt symmetrical features that look as though they were chipped out of stone. He's got freckles and a clipped wedge of dark brown hair. He's a laconic guy, like all the photographers. He doesn't say much or show much reaction. He just kind of rations it all out—the words, the emotions, the smoke from his cigarette. Just taking his time. Burning slow.

Shirl once said that's the only way they can do what they do. "Watch them," she said. "Watch the way they take their time. You think it's bravery, what they do? Yeah. Sure. That's part of it. But it's the slow burning that does it. They're all slow burners." She's probably right. It's like they're cold-blooded in a way. They have to be. They don't react the way the rest of us do, the print types, the hacks—cracking jokes, worrying about deadlines, running around in circles, and always getting into these incredible feuds that go on and on. They can't afford that, the photographers. Not with what they've got to do, out looking for firefights day after day. They've got to stay cool. They'd go crazy otherwise. They're cowboys, that's what they are. That's what the hacks call them.

That night at the lobby bar there were about half a dozen hacks, two or three cowboys, plus Pedro behind the bar, drying glasses, opening and closing the fridge, pretending not to listen. Everybody was drinking Supremas from those foggy glass mugs, smoking Marlboros, and eating banana chips. And talking, of course.

But not talking about him, because it was hard to believe what had happened. True, he was a cowboy, and they're the ones who take the risks, but you couldn't believe it could happen to him, even though you knew it could happen to anybody. Besides, nobody had been with him but Cal, so it was hard to imagine the precise instant—or the precise entire minute, really—and, because of that, everything else about him seemed to blur a little. Cal could have typed in the last few paragraphs for us—and would have and finally did—but it took a little time. Cal was Cal. Burning slow.

So everybody started talking about something

else. Not about him, but about not-him. Does that make sense? Started with Nate, who's been covering Central America for decades and who was in Nicaragua in '79 when they shot Bill Stewart in the head, they being Somoza's National Guard. Bill Stewart was a TV reporter who spoke possibly two words of Spanish—*cerveza, baño*—and all he could do was hold up his press ID and try to look intelligent when the Somoza guy made him get down on his knees, and then pow. In the head. Unbeknownst to the National Guard guy, Stewart's cameraman had been rolling tape the whole time, and so the whole thing got played and replayed at home on TV, and Carter pulled the plug on Somoza, and you know the rest. Now there's this little park in Managua, named after Bill Stewart but completely grown over.

"You should set up some kind of committee, raise some money for the maintenance of that park," Nate said. Notice: you, not we. "Damnit."

Nate gets into arguments with everybody, but the thing is, you always know it's just an act, he doesn't mean it. Out of the blue, he starts arguing with army officers even—well-known homicidal maniacs who'd happily disembowel a guy for whatever—and they just start laughing and clap him on the back and take him into town for a beer. Outdoors he always wears this huge panama hat. Smokes cigars, big bloody things.

"Stewart deserves a decent goddamn park," Nate said. "A death means something, damnit. Pedro—*otra más, por favor.*"

"Not always," said Shirl. "Not always it doesn't."

Shirl had a story to illustrate this point of hers, about death not always meaning something. She'd told this story before, to me, anyway, but not to the others, so off she went, first the background. Before she became a hack, Shirl was a nun and worked for a time as a missionary in Bolivia. She taught at a school, part of a combination school-hospital-agronomy project way up in the Bolivian altiplano near Potosí.

A word about Shirl. She's as thin as the thinnest girl you remember from your public-school graduating class. Her nose is a bit too long and a little bit crooked. It sounds unattractive but it isn't. You start to like it after a while. She always wears these crazy little blouses over her blue jeans, frilly little things with short sleeves. Weird, but you get used to it.

So one day this scabrous and rickety old peasant guy comes into the missionary place up there in the Andes, along with his wife, and he's carrying something in a green plastic garbage bag. First off, the old peasant guy goes right into the classroom, and all the little Bolivian children are there. But quickly Shirl and the other nuns take him into the hospital. It isn't a hospital in the normal sense, just one room. A clinic.

And the guy puts the garbage bag down on a stretcher or something and starts to open it up. His wife's just standing there, wearing about thirteen sweaters and six skirts and her little bowler hat, saying nothing, not a word, because she doesn't speak Spanish probably, the women don't as a rule. Quechua is what they speak. Or Aymará. One or the other. So what do you think's in the garbage bag?

Right. A little baby. No more than about six months old. Just a little Bolivian baby, a little girl. With her arm chewed off. Terrific, right?

Turns out the pig did it. The pig was hungry and so it started to eat the little baby. Now the baby's dead. The pig's perfectly fine. What does it all mean?

Shirl removed her cigarette and did that thing she does, that sideways look, looked at everybody in the room sideways all at once, which is impossible, but that was the effect. "They came to see us," she said, "the man and his wife did, because they didn't know what to do."

There was a pause.

"About the baby, you mean," said Cynthia.

And you could feel the tension go crackle-crackle around the bar because Shirl and Cynthia are Not the Best of Friends. They both work for the same newspaper, which should probably be grounds for homicide or something. Shirl's based here in Salvador, she's completely one of the guys, while Cynthia's the roving ace who jets from place to place and who suddenly just showed up down here, unannounced, with all this French-looking luggage and specially tailored safari outfits and monogrammed reporters' notebooks and so on, to do a special report on the war for the Sunday magazine, which Shirl could perfectly well have done herself. You can see the problem.

"You mean, about the baby," repeated Cynthia.

"No," said Shirl. "The baby's dead. They wanted to know what to do about the pig."

"The pig."

"Yeah. They had a feeling they should kill the pig. It had just eaten their daughter's arm, you see, and— well, the problem was, the pig was a boar. The only boar. If they killed it, where would they get another boar?"

"I don't see that it matters," said Cynthia. "I think

189

it's outrageous that they would even consider—"

"They're poor. They're poor. They're—"

"Hold on," said Nate, waving his cigar in the air like a referee, if that's what referees do. "Hold on." He turned to Shirl. "So what did you tell them?"

"To keep the pig. What do you think?"

"And?"

"They went away happy. First we buried the baby, and then they went away happy. They could keep the pig. That was what they wanted to hear. They just wanted someone else to decide, tell them it was okay. You see? The baby didn't matter. The pig mattered."

That was when I got into it. "Nope. I don't see it," I said. "I don't see how you can conclude from that story that death doesn't matter."

"Not doesn't matter," said Shirl. "Sometimes doesn't matter."

"Nope. Either death matters or it doesn't. Death doesn't come in sizes. One size fits all." I swallowed the last of my beer and gave Shirl a shrug, to show I was just making conversation, no offence intended, which I'm sure she knew anyway. "Death matters," I said. "That's my point."

"Example," said Shirl. Out went her chin. "Give me an example."

"Okay," I said. But first Pedro came through with another round of Supremas, and everybody signed on their rooms. And then it was Marlboro time again and then I told this story that I'd got from a Guatemalan Indian refugee woman. I was in southern Mexico at the time, checking out the Guatemalan Indians who were dragging themselves across the border because of all the

190

army counter-insurgency stuff that was going on in the Quiché, which is this part of northwestern Guatemala where everything is Indians and guerrillas and stuff. And army, of course.

They were in bad shape, these guys. What they didn't have crawling around on their outsides, they had crawling around on their insides. Parasites and insects and bacteria and you name it, not to mention all the junk that just dribbled from their noses, their eyes, and their ears. And their feet—! Christ, their feet. Never mind their feet. You don't want to know. The kids were even worse. These people'd lived for days, or weeks even, on just roots and bark and grass. Hiding out by day and walking through the hills at night. Trying to escape. And they were totally, you know, terrorized. A lot of them were completely insane. Honestly. Everybody at the bar had seen something like it, or worse. Plenty of times.

So this was the story, as told to me by the Guatemalan woman. She was an Ixil woman. Ixil. It's this little tribe of Indians, hardly any left. The women wear these thoroughly amazing costumes, all of them dressed up like royalty, all in red and white. Truly fabulous. You have to see it. When these people talk, it sounds like they're chewing gum or something. Just chewy, chewy, chewy, the way they talk. They mostly don't speak Spanish—the women don't. I had to use a translator, a Guatemalan Indian guy.

So one day the soldiers came into the village. They called all the people to come down to where the school was, which the people immediately started to do. "Now don't forget your machetes," the soldiers said to the men. And the soldiers made all the people stand over here, by the school itself, in the yard where you can probably imagine there was some scruffy grass and probably a section that was gravel and maybe an old basketball net on a wooden post with a backboard, or actually no net but just the rim. There'd be mountains all around, green and tangled. Blue skies, probably.

So here are all the people. Men, women, and kids. All over here by the school, all together. The soldiers come and take all the machetes away, put them in a pile a little distance off. Up comes the commanding officer, a young lieutenant, and he's going to read the riot act. That's what the people think, anyway. He probably doesn't speak Ixil, this young officer, so he uses a translator.

The lieutenant goes through all the usual stuff. Army good. Subversives bad. Blah. Blah. Blah. International Communism. Western Christian values. Et cetera. Et cetera. The people listen politely, with their heads tilted to the side, to show that they're really interested, hanging onto every word, though they've heard it all before and didn't understand it any better the first time. Now comes the surprise question.

The lieutenant asks one of the Indian guys, "Do you have any corn, señor?" And the guy he's chosen, he probably just kind of nods his head for a time, and sort of works his mouth from side to side, because he's so surprised he can't believe it. What's he asking me for? So they have to ask him again, only much louder this time. "Señor, do you have any corn?"

And the poor guy still hasn't got the foggiest notion what to say. He's thinking, what does this question mean? What am I doing here? What does he want me to say? Which is exactly the point. Corn or no corn—that's not the question. The question is, what's the answer? But there's no choice, he's got to say something. So the poor old guy just kind of mumbles it out. Some kind of answer. "No," he says. Which is probably true. Corn? He probably doesn't have any. Half the time they don't.

"No corn?" says the lieutenant, acting surprised. "If you have no corn, there is only one explanation: you have given it all to the subversives. You go and stand over there."

Oh, boy. Trouble now. The old guy does what he's been told, but his head's not shaking now. He can't even move his head. Wrong answer. Oh, boy. Trouble now.

And the lieutenant asks the next guy, same question. And this guy thinks he's got it worked out. Corn? Why, yes. Yes, I do. Got lots. But the lieutenant says, "Why would you have any corn, except to give it to the subversives?" And he tells this guy to go and stand in a different spot. The lieutenant works his way through the men, all of them, asking them the same question. Corn or no corn? And it roughly evens out. This many say yes. That many say no. These guys go over there. Those guys come over here. The women just stand where they are, here by the school, with the kids— thinking, thinking, thinking.

The lieutenant gives the order, and the soldiers hand machetes to one group of men and sort of push them across the yard, over to the second group of men. And the lieutenant goes over and looks at the group with the machetes. He nods towards the other guys.

193

"Kill them," he says.

What? What's he saying? Is he crazy? Nothing happens.

"Kill them," the lieutenant repeats, louder.

Still nothing.

A third time, the lieutenant yells it out. "Kill them!"

And a couple of guys do actually move their arms, but that's all. Nothing more than that. Little flinches. Reflexes.

"Shit," says the lieutenant. "You bunch of yellow shits." And he whispers something low to some of his soldiers.

Upon which the soldiers take one of the machete-guys off a little ways and shoot him through the head. Down he goes. The lieutenant nods. There. That should do the trick. He gives the word once more, and this time it works. Away they all go, stumbling around the yard, arms jerking like crazy, pumping up and down, machetes flashing in the sun, arms going up for protection, slash, slash, men falling down, getting up, screaming no, no, no, and all the women shrieking but not moving and the children falling down crying and the men falling down and trying to get up but nope there's an arm gone, slash, slash, slash, up, down, up, down, until it's all over. Blood everywhere.

And then the soldiers take the men with the machetes and herd them over to a clear wall of the school and shoot them all through the head, and after that the soldiers have their way with the women and plenty of the girls, and then they march off on foot back down to the south, and the women grab what they think they can

194

carry, collect the kids, and flee to the north. Days and days it took them to reach Mexico, and they were in a terrible state when they arrived, just awful. Their feet.

I lit another cigarette. I waited for someone to say something.

"I'm afraid I don't get it," said Josh, another hack, a kind of walrus-looking guy, paunchy, talks real slow in this deep Southern voice, but he's not so dumb, you just have to get to know him. "I just don't get the significance. What's your point there, Rich? I don't seem to get it."

"You don't get it?" I said.

"That's what he said." Nate held another match up to his cigar and puffed. "He said he doesn't get it. I heard him."

"Surprise. Surprise." Cynthia arched her little squiggly eyebrows and peered over at Josh, whom she detests. She says she can't abide fat men, but that's not it. Josh was not part of the press convoy that got stopped in a guerrilla roadblock on the way back from Suchitoto a few days earlier. Cynthia's decided this means Josh's an out-and-out coward—while of course she's anything but. She was there, after all. Imagine. There. In the thick of it.

"What do you mean, 'Surprise, surprise'?" I said. "What do you think's the point of the story then?"

"Well, I—I haven't really given it much thought," said Cynthia. "I—well, it was rather bloody and—"

"Exactly right," I said. "You get the prize. 'It was rather bloody.' That's the point. You're remarkably perceptive, did anyone ever tell you that?"

"Okay. Okay." Nate waded in, cigar aloft. "Why

don't you just tell us, Rich? Why don't you just tell us the point of the story?"

I turned my mug around in a small puddle of water. I shrugged. "I'm with Josh," I said. "I don't get it, either. It was just a story. What does it mean? Who the hell knows?"

"Maybe that's the point." This was Kev. He put down his beer and snapped his fingers. "Maybe it's not who dies that's so important in the end, but who doesn't. You see? Just the fact that there's somebody still around afterward to talk about it, to tell the story, and somebody else to listen—that's something, isn't it? You see what I'm saying? Maybe that's the point. Death is a tale told by the survivors. Get it? Maybe that's what's important."

And everybody looked at each other, as if to say: what's he talking about? But Kev started right in, telling the Jack Kennedy story, except that it had nothing whatever to do with Jack Kennedy.

Somebody once said, and this has nothing to do with Jack Kennedy either, that you can always tell a hack because he's the one—or she, of course—in the pressed blue jeans. Hacks always have to live in hotels, you see, and the hotel laundries always press your blue jeans, whether you want them to or not. So the hacks are always walking around in these beat-up old blue jeans with perfectly straight creases back and front, like a kind of uniform. It's not vanity. It's just the way things are. Kev is not a good example of this, however. He would probably press his blue jeans anyway.

So, the Jack Kennedy story. I call it that, not because it has anything to do with Jack Kennedy, which

196

it doesn't, but because it's the same kind of thing. Everybody remembers where they were when they found out about Jack Kennedy being shot and everybody's got a story to tell. For hacks down here it's the same thing with the time that Dan and Liz were blown up by a landmine on this little dirt road up around Chalate. That's short for Chalatenango. You just have to mention that incident, and everybody remembers where they were and what they were doing when they found out. Kev, it turns out, was in Mexico City, where he lives. He's the regional field producer for one of the big American nets.

"I'd been out late that evening," he said. "And I'd just got home and I'd poured myself a brandy, you know, and I turned on the TV to watch the news. Now, at this point, I had no idea about what had happened to Dan and Liz. Right? You're with me? Fine. So there I was, sipping my brandy, and all at once the announcer came on and reported that two American journalists had been killed in El Salvador. Killed, he said. Just like that. You know?" Kev crossed his legs, thigh over thigh, sat back in his chair, held up his hands. A cigarette burned between two fingers of his left hand. "And then the announcer said—he said: 'More details after these messages.'"

Kev slumped down in his chair and peered at the ceiling. He slapped his right hand against the top of his forehead, where there might have been hair once but not any more. "Well," he said. "You can just imagine. I had to sit there during all these commercials, and they go on and on for about five minutes or so. Right? And I didn't have the ghost of an idea who had died. And I was

197

thinking, who's in Salvador right now? And who isn't? Do you follow me? And I went through the names, everyone I could think of, all of you, everyone. You know?"

Kev put up his hands in front of him, as though he were pressing at a window. "And I was thinking, my God, what if it's him, or what if it's her, or him, or her? And on and on. Right? And then, you know what? Listen to this. When the announcer came back on and said that it was Dan and Liz, I—I wasn't even sad. I didn't feel any sadness at all. Do you see what I'm saying? I was happy. I was happy because it wasn't someone else. You see? And if it had been someone else, not Dan and Liz, but two of you—well, I don't know. Maybe I would have felt the same way. Not sad. Happy. Do you see what I mean? Do you see?"

So Kev sat back again and lit a new cigarette off his old one, and it was time for another round of Supremas, which Pedro quickly produced, and everyone was probably thinking, now what the hell does that mean?

"Gosh," said Cynthia. "I think that's very thought-provoking, Kevin."

"Thought-provoking, yeah," said Shirl. "But what does it mean?"

"That death is for the living," said Josh in this deep Southern voice of his, stentorian is the word you might think of to describe it. "Death weighs most heavily on those who live. That's where its true significance lies. On the living."

"Us, you mean," said Cal, who was the only guy who was with him when it happened and who had said approximately *nada* so far all evening, as photographers are inclined to do. He was biding his time. Burning slow.

Josh shrugged. "I guess you could say that." He pulled out this big handkerchief from the pocket of his jeans and slid off his glasses by their heavy black frames. He frowned and went to work on the lenses. "I've got me a story, too," he said. "One I'd like to tell."

And Josh started to tell this story about the Green Cross guy, from the independent Green Cross, who got plugged in the head by another Green Cross guy, from the pro-government Green Cross, one evening while he was taking a nap.

You may not know what the Green Cross is. It's this emergency-rescue outfit, all voluntary, supposedly, and it is, or was, the stuff of legend in Salvador. Heroes, these guys. When you think about it, there are only two kinds of civilians who, when shooting breaks out, actually voluntarily run towards the fighting rather than away from it. You've got journalists and you've got these Green Cross guys. And the Green Cross guys go all the way into the very smoke and clamour of it, to try to rescue the wounded. They go after the wounded on both sides. Completely impartial. These guys are the true heroes of the war. At least they were.

But then, somehow, the government got the idea that the Green Cross was favouring the guerrillas. How did they figure that? Who knows? It was just the conclusion that they reached. So the government set up its own Green Cross, such is the logic of the war. And they started putting the arm on people to contribute to their Green Cross and not the other one. And do you know what happened in the end? Of course you do. The two

Green Crosses started killing each other. *Bienvenido a la guerra*, as they say. Welcome to the war.

Josh was in on the first of these killings, or shortly after, when the guy's co-workers wheeled the body into their headquarters downtown.

"There he was, this poor fella," Josh said. "Good looking boy, about thirty-five or so. They'd shot him right between the eyes. You could see the powder burns there on his nose and on his cheeks. Not even a spot of blood on his face. The blood was all back there on the sheet, from the exit wound. And I thought, damnation."

Josh shook his head. "Damnation. I counted about a dozen of these young fellas in the room where they brought the body, and I'll be damned if they weren't all just sitting around there crying like damn-all. One of them was right down there on the floor. He had this bitty white towel that they must've used to soak up some of the blood, and he had it pressed to his face, all soaking with blood, and he was just crying into that damn towel like a little baby with a broken doll.

"And I thought, damn. I thought, now, these are the boys who have about seen all there is to see down here. Why, they've taken every damn risk you'd care to name. They've gone into shoot-outs that, hell, just about make my hair stand on end. There ain't nothing they ain't done. And here they are, and one of theirs is gone, and, hell, they can't endure it any better 'n you or I."

And Josh put his glasses back on and took one of Cal's Marlboros, and then everybody else lit up, too. And Nate blew out a match and puffed his cigar to get it going and called out to Pedro, "*Oye, Pedrito, la penultimatita, por favor,*" which reminded everyone that

200

they were going to have to get up early the next morning to go to the little memorial service that was planned just for the hacks and the cowboys and a few others, diplomats maybe, before they flew the body back to the States. So Pedro served up the *penultimatitas*, and that was when Cal finally started talking, trying to describe what it was like to have been with him when it happened.

It's hard to explain, the next part. For most hacks, you see, there's one rule: if you're close enough to hear the shooting, you're close enough to write about it. But with cowboys, it's different. They've got no choice. They go in there, over and over, on purpose—because they need the pictures. That's where the slow burning comes in. Either they burn slow or they go nuts. Either they're slow burners naturally, or they learn how.

Well, he was a natural slow burner, this one. Anyone could see that. Cowboys don't talk much, but he barely said anything at all. He'd ease a cigarette from his lips, chew a little at his moustache, and say, Fuck this, or, Like shit, like he was spitting out a bit of dirt that had got stuck in his teeth. And that was about the extent of his personality. He probably doesn't sound like a very charming guy, and he wasn't, but he'd been down here as long as anybody, year after year, and so he was one of the guys. That's all there was to it.

Almost.

Once, a year or so ago, a couple of cowboys and two or three hacks were hiking up into Morazán with some guerrillas, a half-dozen or so. Actually, we weren't just hiking, not at that point. We were on the run because all at once there were a hell of a lot of troops around, more than expected. Even the gees were rattled, which you just know has got to mean trouble. Gees. It's what hacks call the guerrillas.

Before long, one of the hacks started having trouble keeping up. He kept falling behind, because of the pace and the fear and the exhaustion. But there was no way the gees were going to slow down. Negative, Mr. Journalist. Finally this particular hack, he just went berserk. He went right out of control. He attacked one of the guerrillas, tried to wrestle the poor guy's rifle away, crying, "Stop! Stop! We've got to rest! Stop!"

Well, it's times like those when you suddenly wish you'd never left your hotel room, after all. You think: the guerrillas are going to shoot us all, they've got to, they're scared, they're not sure what's coming down, and we're just holding them back. This is war. They've been trained to do this. I could hear the safeties clicking off on about half a dozen FNs, and all I could think was, *adiós, mis muy estimados amigos.*

No one had the faintest idea what to do—except him. He threw down his camera bag and got himself between the screaming hack and the poor struggling gee and pushed them apart and got the hack to shut the fuck up and somehow managed to get the gees cooled down, all of them. He offered them all Marlboros. He handled the whole thing on his own, talked like crazy, like a goddamn diplomat, cracked jokes, these soothing little jokes—he who hardly ever said a word. He said all the right things, didn't put a foot wrong, got everybody back down to planet Earth.

Five minutes later, we were on our way again, with the pace just a bit slowed down from before, and everything turned out okay in the end. It could have been a catastrophe, though. Damn near was.

There were other stories, similar kinds of stories. In a scrape, when you got in too deep, when the shooting broke out all around, you'd depend on his word, you'd let him lead the way. And after that, you'd probably owe him your life. You wouldn't talk about it much, least of all to him. But there it was. He'd saved your life. And that was what you'd remember about him. He wasn't charming. But he had that knack, the knack for getting out of a place alive. At least, we thought he did, until he and Cal got caught in crossfire up in Suchitoto.

They had gone up there on their own that morning. All the hacks and the cowboys had already been out there, earlier in the week, to report on the big battle between the army and a huge force of guerrillas—and for the hacks the job was done. But he and Cal decided that the stuff they'd got the first day wasn't good enough, so they went back to Suchitoto that morning for more. And Cal leaned forward in his chair, to tell about it.

"We were trying to move in on foot at sort of right angles to the main shooting," Cal said. "Everything was closed up tight. The air was real still. No breeze. We had one of the towels from the hotel tied to a pole—you know, as a white flag. We were moving along, crouching down low, staying close to the edge of the street, trying to get closer to the shooting."

Cal took a swig of his beer. "We got to this, I don't know, this T-intersection. And the cross street ran up and down, and there was nothing opposite us but just a stucco wall, painted blue, and a bit of a bay, a little alcove. It looked like a good place to take shelter until we decided which way to go, left or right. All we had to do was cross the street and then just hunker down for a while. There was nothing to it."

Everybody at the bar was silent. The only sound was now and then somebody puffing on a cigarette. Even Pedro was standing still, with a towel in his hand, not even pretending to be drying glasses any more, or that he didn't understand English perfectly well.

"I went first," Cal said, "because I had the flag. The shooting sounded like it was at least one more street over. But it's confusing, you know. You know that. It's hard to tell. I got down low and went straight across. He was right behind me—I thought he was—and I didn't even hear it, the shot that got him. How can you pick out one shot from all the rest? I got across the street and pushed myself up tight against the wall in that little alcove, and I looked back to see how he was doing. He was down on his knees, just like he was praying or something, and he was looking straight at me, but he wasn't moving."

Cal pulled a Marlboro out of his pack, offered one to Josh, who accepted, and to Cynthia, who shook her head, no, then changed her mind and took one. A few others also lit up. Nobody said a word.

"I yelled to him," Cal went on, "'C'mon, man. C'mon.' But he didn't move, and I guess I knew what had happened. I was going to go back and get him—he was just a few feet away, hardly any distance at all—but then he went down on his stomach, just slow and easy, his face right down on the cobbles. And bang! The bullets started flying up and down the street right over his head. I tell you, it was shit. It was pure shit. I had about two feet of wall to protect me on two sides and I was wide open in front. All I could do was just get down low and wait. I couldn't budge. It went on for at least ten minutes before I could get out of there, get to him, get him back across the street."

Cal glanced up at the asbestos tiles on the ceiling, tightened his jaw, moved it from side to side. "It took about a minute for him to go. He only got hit the once. Maybe it was a stray bullet, maybe a sniper. There's no way to tell. He was conscious the whole time. He knew what had happened. He knew what was happening. Lying there in the dirt, sort of half on his side, looking at me. He knew I couldn't do anything, and he couldn't move. Paralysed, probably."

Cal flicked away a length of ash from his cigarette. "His lips moved, though. Every ten seconds or so, his lips moved. I couldn't hear him but I could tell what he was saying. He was lying there in the dirt, with all the bullets cracking over his head. He was looking at me, no expression, and every few seconds his lips moved, and they'd be saying, 'Goodbye.' That's what he was saying, over and over, five or six times before he died. Just 'Goodbye.'"

Cal blinked his eyes, took a long pull on his cigarette. "And then it was over. He stopped moving, he just lay there, and I stayed where I was, waiting. I couldn't do anything until the fighting moved off, and then I got out of there, and I dragged him away. But he was dead by then. And that's it. That's what happened." Cal shook his head. "It was shit," he said. "Pure shit."

Everyone in the bar stayed where they were, not moving. And no one said a word. Everyone was probably thinking something like, goodbye? How can it be good-bye? Jesus Christ, just this morning we were all having breakfast together in the coffee shop, and he was there, one of us, drinking coffee and eating these stale crescent rolls they always serve.

You know, there's always this kind of summer-camp atmosphere in the coffee shop at breakfast. Every-body moves around from table to table, cracks jokes, drinks gallons of coffee. The hacks pass around names of contacts or complain about how their stories are playing, and the cowboys clean their camera lenses or advance new rolls of film with that whirring sound, and then everyone heads out for the day, never alone but always in groups. It's hard to work alone in Salvador, you see—not for any reason you can put your finger on. It's just that you'd go crazy or something. Anybody would. So you work in groups. You have to.

And when Cal finished talking, everybody sat there, staring at their beers or smoking Marlboros and thinking about all this kind of stuff. And nobody said a word, not even Cyn for once. Crazy, right? Nobody said a word, which was crazy because hardly anybody even really liked the guy that much. But that wasn't the point. The point was, he was one of the guys—and, maybe, just maybe, on a hike up into Morazán one afternoon a year ago, he'd saved your life.

And nobody said anything until Nate held up his cigar and looked at the little of it that was left, and finally he was the one who spoke. "So . . . ," he said. He just kept staring at the smouldering end of his cigar. "So . . . ," he said. "Do we keep the pig?"

Fighting in Gotera

Fighting in Gotera! But who would go? There was just one plane. Room for three passengers.

Even as he prepared to scribble down his name on a lined sheet of paper in his notebook, R. Dale Wickham knew the fix was in. There was fighting in Gotera, his name would be chosen, and this day would be his last. He held his breath, tried not to breathe, for death was in the air, like a contagious infection. It was aiming straight for him. Did he often feel this way?

These days, nearly always.

They'd got the call that morning. It came in to one of the wire agencies on the second floor of the hotel in San Salvador. Fighting in Gotera! Or near Gotera. Something like that. The word went out, hit the coffee shop downstairs where everyone was eating breakfast, drinking coffee, and reading *El Diario de Hoy*. Fighting in Gotera!

Fighting near Gotera?

Anyway, fighting. And it was big. It was a big guerrilla attack on the town itself. Or a major guerrilla movement near the town. To the north, perhaps. Details were sketchy. But there was fighting in, or near, Gotera. That much was known. Apparently.

And the coffee shop erupted at the news.

R. Dale put down his coffee, which was too strong here anyway. It made his hands ball up into fists that he had to pry open with his chin. He'd also developed a nervous tic at the corner of his mouth. The caffeine was doing this. Today, as most days, he was wearing a white dress shirt, grey cotton slacks, and black leather loafers—but that was his choice. The coffee could not be blamed for his clothes.

All the other hacks and the photographers wore blue jeans and faded polo shirts and canvas hiking boots. They drank monumental amounts of coffee and should all have been quadriplegic as a result, but they weren't.

R. Dale watched them scramble up from their tables. They snuffed out their cigarettes, drained their coffee mugs. They grabbed their equipment and their knapsacks. And they all hurried out into the lobby, shouting, laughing. There was fighting in Gotera!

He debated what to do. He felt like a visitor here, not one of the guys at all. He'd been down here for two months and he had yet to venture out of the capital. "You can do this story from the capital," he'd told his editor on the phone after the first week. "Everybody does."

"Not *The New York Times*," his editor said. "A piece

just moved on the *Times* wire. It—"

"I mean the big picture," R. Dale said. "You can do the big picture from the capital."

"Yeah," his editor said. "But what about guns, shooting? You know—bang-bang. What about the war?"

What about it? It was out there, somewhere. In the countryside, in the villages, in the provincial garrison towns. But R. Dale didn't leave the capital. He stayed at the hotel or took a taxi over to one of the embassies for an interview. He wrote opinion pieces, speculated about political trends, assessed the economic variables. That kept him busy. How could he leave the capital? There was no time. Something always came up. That was what he told his editor.

Lately, R. Dale had been thinking about maybe phoning up his editor and simply asking to come home. The thing was, everybody down here was crazy. It was true. It was like a virus, a strain of sub-tropical insanity that got to everyone eventually. All the other journalists had it. Their eyes had gone glassy, and they sniggered when they spoke. They'd fallen in love with war.

R. Dale worried that it might happen to him. A few days ago, his nose had got plugged up, and he'd started suffering some irregularities in the functioning of his alimentary system. He'd gone to a doctor recommended by the embassy—an American, in fact—who diagnosed R. Dale's condition as BGR. That's what he wrote on the report. Then he gave R. Dale some sinus pills and something for his stomach.

"What's that?" R. Dale said. "BGR. What's that mean?"

The doctor looked up. No expression. He said,

"Bug Going Round."

"Oh," said R. Dale. "What should I do to prevent that?"

The doctor shrugged. "Only one thing you can do," he said. "Don't breathe."

Don't breathe . . . ? Great. Wonderful. That guy was crazy too. Was R. Dale the only sane one left? It seemed that way to him. He'd thought a lot about his idea of leaving. He'd thought about it yesterday, the day before, the day before that. And this morning he'd awakened once again with the metallic taste of doom lying thick upon his tongue. The medication wasn't working. Was it already too late?

And now—fighting in Gotera.

R. Dale reached for his notebook and realized he was standing up. It had happened to him without his knowledge, like a balloon inflating. Here he was—in the coffee shop, in his white shirt and his grey cotton trousers—and he was standing up. He was starting to walk forward, step by step. Was he going crazy too?

He made his way out through the lobby and into the morning sun, where the last of the hacks and photographers were lighting cigarettes and climbing into little yellow taxis with gaping holes and strips of electrician's tape where the upholstery was supposed to be.

R. Dale got into one of the taxis. He didn't want to. God, he didn't want to. But he got in.

They all rushed out to the Ilopango Airport, in a convoy of taxis and rented cars, some with the letters "TV" or "PRENSA" emblazoned in masking tape on their windshields and side windows. There was no point in trying to drive to Gotera itself. It was too far. By the time anyone got out there, the excitement was sure to be over. So everyone went to the old airport.

R. Dale sat in the front seat, with his knees jammed up against his chest, almost suffocating him. The meter rattled against his chin. Three hacks from the U.K. had squeezed themselves into the back. They all cracked jokes along the way, mostly Argie jokes. All the limey journalists in El Salvador had swarmed down to Buenos Aires the year before to cover the Falklands War, and they all said they remembered it fondly. Buenos Aires. The pedestrian malls. The lights of Corrientes. Nights of tango, steak, and wine.

"Ah, the Falklands War—"

"Malvinas War."

"Yeah, right. Malvinas. Say, how do you get fifty Argies into the same coffin?"

"You've got me. How?"

"Deflate them."

Deflate them! What an idea! They'd all heard it a dozen times before, but still they laughed and lit cigarettes and leaned their arms out the windows, and they rolled up to the little terminal at the Ilopango Airport to join all the other hacks and photographers who were already there, milling about in the sunshine.

It turned out that only one charter company was willing to fly to Gotera, and it had only one plane. Room for three passengers. That was when Fred Zeppelin—not his real name—had the idea of drawing lots, to form a press pool. R. Dale knew immediately that this day would be his last. It wasn't a question of odds or luck. It was simply a matter of fate. Death was in the air—his death. He just knew it. They all pulled out their notebooks, to jot down their names for the draw. R. Dale clutched his pen and looked upward for a sign.

Overhead, the dry-season sun beat down in vivid monotony. Scattered cumulus clouds turned slow cartwheels against the blue backdrop of the sky. A wind was blowing up there, making unpredictable shapes, patterns he could not foretell. But down here no breeze stirred the tatty flamboyant trees that lined the entrance to the Ilopango Airport. Down here, where R. Dale stood, fate seemed immutable, unwavering, like nausea. Down here, death had a sickening odour, similar to the smell of aircraft fuel. R. Dale tried to breathe only through his mouth. Then he tried not to breathe at all. He really did feel ill.

But he grit his teeth and somehow wrote down his name. He tore out the sheet. He couldn't believe he was doing this. He felt weak, that was all—too weak to resist. He folded the paper with his name on it and handed it to Fred Zeppelin, who jammed it with the rest into his inverted panama hat.

Fred Zeppelin went back to the stairs at the entrance to the terminal. He stroked his little beard and made a big production, but finally drew three names, and they were R. Dale Wickham—of course—Mary Blake, and Garth Arnold.

R. Dale closed his eyes. So this was how it was meant to be. He would go to his death with an American photographer who looked like Tom Selleck and thought he was Indiana Jones, and a pretty little librarian *manquée* who detested him for reasons he had never managed to discern.

"I have no respect for you," Mary Blake had told

him once, at dinner at a restaurant, when there was nowhere to sit but right beside him. "I just wanted you to know that." She hadn't bothered to explain, and he'd been too amazed to ask. She had ignored him for the remainder of the meal.

He opened his eyes. A few feet away stood Mary Blake. The very one. She squared her toes, narrowed her gaze, and looked at him. In her prim, powder-blue shirt-dress, her sensible flat-soled shoes, and with her straight blonde hair cupping her little face, she looked exactly like the mousy efficient mid-western librarian she was no doubt intended by God to become. Where had she gone wrong? How had she ended up down here? How had anyone? Well, at least she was wearing a dress. That mollified R. Dale a little. She wasn't prepared for this trip either. Both of them were dressed for church. They were meant to die like this.

The pilot's name was Raul. He wore aviator sunglasses and a yellow *guayabera*. His hair was a trim black wedge installed above a dark poker face and those two shiny green lenses. Raul reached up to open the throttle, all the while babbling something indecipherable into the microphone suspended an inch in front of his lips. It sounded like *war-war-war-war-war*.

The flimsy four-seater airplane began to tremble and moan. Raul released the brakes. The craft rolled forward, gathered speed, and soon it raced along the runway, alternately floating up and weighing down upon its undercarriage. The patched asphalt yawned ahead—and suddenly receded, dwindled, dropped away. The clusters of palms became little pinwheel shapes, bright green decorations against the baked brown earth. The plane banked to the right, coasted above the gnarled surface of the sierra, and clawed its way into the sky.

Garth Arnold peered back from the co-pilot's seat, winked at Mary, and gave a thumbs-up sign. He wore a baggy orange Hawaiian shirt and had a pair of sunglasses suspended from his neck on a red string. "Too much!" he shouted above the engine's roar, first at Mary, then at R. Dale. "Too fucking much!" Where did he get that moustache? Those curls? That tan? He turned to the front once again and began to root about in his camera bag.

He'd be getting a camera out now, a camera or two. He'd start snapping pictures pretty soon, even from way up here. Never mind that there was nothing much to see, nothing but the dry and sinewy surface of the land, broken here and there by the jumbled shapes of villages, like heaps of pottery shards that no one had bothered to sweep away. The bone-china glint of whitewashed churches.

Like the other photographers, Garth Arnold took pictures all the time. He snapped frames of everything that moved, and much that didn't. War was a gas. The visuals.

R. Dale glanced at Mary. She was hunched over in her seat with a set of earphones clamped to her head, frowning and muttering to herself. She had her tape recorder on her lap and fussed with the buttons. She played the machine forward, wound it back. Busy, busy, busy.

R. Dale crossed his arms at his chest and shoved himself into the corner of his seat. Why were they doing this? Why were they flying to Gotera? It didn't make any sense. They'd all be killed.

Mary looked up, slipped off her earphones. She leaned forward and tapped Garth on the shoulder. "Garth!" she shouted. "I vote we go straight into town and talk to Guerrero!"

Garth put down his camera and peered back. He scratched his moustache, nodded. "Good idea!" he shouted. He pulled a cigarette from the pack in his shirt pocket. "But what if we can't get through? You know, because of the fighting? In that case I vote we try to make contact straight off with the gees!"

At the sound of that word, the pilot turned his head, shot a glance at Garth, and quickly looked away. The gees. R. Dale knew what that word meant. The guerrillas. Maybe the pilot did too. Maybe he had connections to the air force. And now he was going to report them. R. Dale was almost sure of it. Right away, the pilot began to babble something into his microphone. His expression didn't change. Was he reporting them? Was he?

"Okay!" shouted Mary. "That's good, but. . . . " She frowned. She turned to look at R. Dale. She said to him, "Say, you don't have any contacts with the guerrillas in Morazán, do you?" Before he could answer, she drew her head back and sort of flicked at him with her hand. "No," she said. "Why am I asking you?" She turned back to Garth. "We'll have to see!" she shouted. "We'll just have to play it by ear!"

Garth nodded. His cigarette dangled, unlit, from

the corner of his mouth. He picked up one of his cameras and held it to his eye. He played with the focus. He started taking pictures of the pilot.

R. Dale slumped back into his seat. The roar of the airplane seemed almost palpable now, like a weight pressing down on his chest, smothering him, making it almost impossible to breathe. He didn't know what they were talking about. Play it by ear? Play what by ear? And now the plane began to bounce. The craft pitched forward, bucked, and yawed in a sudden storm of turbulence.

"¡Termas!" shouted the pilot. He fought to hold the airplane up.

Termas—what did that mean? Did that mean thermals? Columns of rising air? Or was it something else entirely, something they were all supposed to do? *Open the termas immediately or we'll all be killed!* R. Dale had no idea. He gripped the seat in front of him and held on. Maybe this was how he was meant to go. In an airplane crash. Somewhere in eastern El Salvador.

The bouts of turbulence lasted most of the way to Gotera, but finally subsided. The pilot flew the plane right over the town at a high altitude, then slowly circled down, in tight little twists, like a corkscrew. Down and down.

"Have to do this!" Garth shouted back at Mary. "If we flew low over the gees, they'd hit us with ground-to-air rockets for sure!"

"The boys don't have those!" Mary shouted back.

Garth shrugged. "Maybe not! But in this little plane? If we even got hit by rifle fire—shit! It could sure spoil our day!"

216

Down and down and down.

They went straight into Gotera. They had no choice. A bunch of soldiers made them get into a jeep and drove them there. R. Dale crouched in the back of the jeep and watched the little airplane. It turned around on the dirt landing strip, bobbed like an insect, raced away in the dust, and took off. He could be on that plane, flying back to San Salvador, back to his hotel room. He shook his head, put his head in his hands.

The jeep bumped over the rocks, raced between rows of scrubby trees towards the town of San Francisco Gotera. But there wasn't any fighting in Gotera or anywhere around Gotera. None at all.

Or not yet. That, it seemed, was the thing.

"*Sí, señores y señoras periodistas,*" said Colonel Guerrero, a thin little man with a glum defeated expression. He walked with a limp. He pulled a collapsible pointer from the breast pocket of his fatigues and extended it to its full length. He did this with an air of moment and drama, as though he were preparing to attempt a complex and unexpected manoeuvre—a pole vault, perhaps. Instead he aimed the pointer at a chart on the wall, a maze of lines and arrows in red and green. "*Vamos a desarticular la infraestructura militar de los subversivos comunistas,*" he said. "*Aquí e aquí e aquí.*" He stood back. "*Ustedes, estimados representantes de la prensa mundial, están invitados a acompañarnos.*" He pressed his lips together. A smile?

R. Dale didn't have the slightest idea what the officer was talking about. He couldn't understand Spanish,

217

hardly a word. "You'll pick it up in no time," his editor had said. "I took it in high school myself. Easy as pie. How did it go? 'Hey, garçon, *une cerveza por favor.*' *Cerveza*—that means beer. You'll get it."

But R. Dale's editor had been wrong. Two months down here, and R. Dale still barely understood a word. *Cerveza. Dos cervezas.* That was about it. He turned to Mary. "What?" he said. He no longer cared how humiliating this was. "What's he saying?"

Mary rolled her eyes. She put up her hand so that the officer would wait, and he did. "He says that the army is going to break up the military infrastructure of the Communist subversives." She narrowed her eyes. "In other words, they're going north to look for people to shoot. You with us?"

He nodded. Then he shook his head. He wasn't sure.

"He says we're invited to come along."

"Oh."

Colonel Guerrero looked at Mary, then at R. Dale, then at Mary again. "*Bien,*" he said. He collapsed his pointer between his hands and went over behind his desk. He peered down at some papers. "*Hasta entonces,*" he said. He seemed a shy sort of man.

An orderly came and took them away. He guided them into a dining room—the officers' mess, it seemed. They sat down, and a woman brought them water in yellow plastic cups, hot tortillas, lettuce, tomatoes, pieces of boiled chicken.

"Far out," Garth said. "Far fucking out." He dug in.

"What do you mean?" Mary said. She pulled a

little package from her navy-blue knapsack—a lemon-scented sterilized paper towelette. She peeled it open and began cleaning her hands, daintily, one finger at a time. "It'll just be a joke. I've seen this dozens of times before." She crumpled up the towelette, placed it on the table beside her, and started to eat. "Guerrero and his men will hike up the road, shooting at the trees. The gees will pull out and head north to Honduras. Guerrero will take a couple of towns, lecture the people on the merits of the free-enterprise system. Then he'll come back down here, and the gees will move back in. I've seen it a dozen times. It's a joke."

Garth nodded. He reached up to pick something out of his teeth. "Yeah," he said. "But still—great pix!"

R. Dale spent the rest of the day out in the square in front of the garrison, in a state of semi-slumber. He huddled in the shade with his back pressed against a faded stucco wall. The troops were assembling and now almost filled the plaza. He watched the lines of soldiers with their dark green backpacks and their rifles. He listened to the trucks outside the square, their groaning engines, their smooching brakes.

He felt almost exactly like a child—a child who is forever being picked up, packed into a car, and driven to mysterious destinations that no one tells him anything about. He was in a daze. His throat was sore, his sinuses were jammed, and he could feel the infection creeping down into his chest. His lungs made a rasping sound when he breathed. He had to struggle for air, and the air was infected. He needed a doctor.

Mary was up and doing, as usual. She went around the square in her trim blue dress, with her knapsack on her back and her tape recorder slung from her shoulder. She was interviewing young soldiers or groups of cringing peasant women, their hands pressed over their mouths. In the middle of the square, Garth hunched down on his knees, cupped one of his cameras in front of him, like something to eat, and took pictures of everything. He switched lenses, replaced rolls of film, scratched his moustache. A pack of barefoot little boys gathered around him, watched and imitated his every move. He let them look through the lenses.

R. Dale released a long sour breath. His ribs rattled, and he could taste the infection. But it didn't matter. He didn't care. How could he? His brains cells had turned to mucus. He wasn't capable of thought. He got out his notebook and started to draw pictures—crosses and coffins and angels. Angels with gilded wings. Fat little cherubim that floated on the air, like children's balloons. What else was there to do? He didn't understand Spanish, and soon he was going to die.

That night they made him take off his shirt. Colonel Guerrero gave the order, and the others all agreed. They were way out in the middle of God knew where, marching on a dirt road to somewhere in the almost utter darkness, and the colonel drove up in a jeep, stopped, and said, "Take off that shirt." That was what Mary said he said. A white shirt. It threw off too much light. Bare skin was better. Take it off.

"Take my shirt off?" R. Dale repeated. He couldn't believe this. "He wants me to take my shirt off?"

"Just do it," Mary said. She was wearing blue jeans now. She must have been carrying them in her knapsack—blue jeans, sneakers, and a sweater over a dark tanktop.

R. Dale wanted to protest, but he knew how it would sound. *Please. Please, no. I don't want to take my shirt off.* Pathetic. So he did as he was told. He unbuttoned his shirt, took it off, rolled it up, and stuffed it into Mary's knapsack. Goose-bumps rippled up and down his chest, his arms. He shivered. Christ—it was bloody freezing out. The altitude—that was what it was. And he was going to have to walk the rest of the night in just his shoes and his grey cotton pants. Why hadn't he worn blue jeans?

Mary shook her head in the dark. "A white shirt," she said. She pushed it down to the bottom of her bag. "Didn't anyone ever tell you not to go out on a march at night in a white shirt? It reflects everything. It's like you're a walking target. Do you actually want someone to shoot you? Shoot us all? A white shirt . . . my God." Again, she shook her head.

"Should've worn Hawaiian, man," said Garth. "Should've worn anything else but white, man. Out here, white sucks."

Colonel Guerrero nodded and got back into his jeep. Mission accomplished. He looked over at Sergeant Ungo, the platoon commander, and said something that included the word Ocotepeque. That was all R. Dale could make out. Colonel Guerrero put up his hand and then let it flop forward, the Salvadoran command for Go. His driver touched the gas, and the jeep rumbled away into the night with its headlights off.

"*Bien*," said Sergeant Ungo. He cleared his throat, spat, slapped the dust from his rump, and adjusted the rifle that dangled across his chest. He spat again. "*¡Vamanos!*"

In the faint moonlight, R. Dale watched several dozen shadows move, twist, rise—soldiers. The shadows bent down to pull on their bandoleers and backpacks, sling their rifles. Without a word, they started to trudge away through the darkness towards a ring of orange light that glowed in the distance. That was Ocotepeque, a mountain. Some soldiers were already up there, setting brush fires to flush out guerrilla snipers. That explained the orange light. That was what Mary had said, in a bored voice, as if this was something any idiot should know.

"Right," said Garth. "Let's go." He pulled his camera bag onto his shoulder and started to walk, right behind Sergeant Ungo.

Mary trotted ahead to keep up with him. "He said what? Did you hear Guerrero? He said we'll be on top of Ocotepeque by daybreak? I think he's full of it." She looked back at R. Dale. "Well . . . ?" she said. "Come on."

He couldn't move, couldn't breathe. His nasal passages were blocked, his lungs had ceased to function, and he was freezing. He had his arms crossed at his chest, and he was freezing. This he did not believe. Out here in the darkness, in the dry season, in his grey cotton pants, in bloody Central America, he was going to die of pneumonia. There was no way out.

"Come on," Mary hissed.

"All right," he said. Somehow he made himself get going, start breathing. He caught up.

Garth clapped him on his bare back, and he almost fell down. "Should've worn Hawaiian, man. Hawaiian's the way to go."

Mary was right. Guerrero had been wrong. They didn't get to the top of Ocotepeque by daybreak. And why not?

Guerrilla snipers.

"Some kinda brave," Garth said. He pulled out a cigarette. He clenched the cylinder between his teeth, flicked at a match with his thumbnail, and cupped his hands in front of him as though he were lighting a smoke on the deck of a boat in the middle of a force-ten gale. He waved the match out and tossed it away. "Ain't those guys something else?" he said. Smoke came out his nose.

"I'd like one of those," said Mary. She normally didn't smoke. She accepted the cigarette and held it the way a socialite would, at the very tips of her fingers. She let Garth light it, and then she started to smoke in quick little gasps. She blew the smoke away to the side. She didn't inhale.

"No thanks," R. Dale said. His breath came in whistles now, and his head clanged. He blew his nose into a handkerchief Garth had given him that morning. Already it was a sopping revolting mess. He stuffed it back into the pocket of his grey cotton pants. His eyes sagged. His chest wheezed. He didn't feel dead. He felt worse than dead. He felt like an extinct species. A cigarette? He couldn't bear the thought. It was hard enough just to breathe.

And this was war. Fires were burning all around,

and smoke rolled down the mountainside, clogged his throat. The din of gunshots cracked and echoed everywhere. Still, he found that the ruckus of war alarmed him less now than it had the night before or even that morning. They were out of range, supposedly. Plus he had a shirt on, not his own but an olive khaki shirt lent to him by Sergeant Ungo, a soldier's shirt.

Garth shrugged, tucked his pack of Marlboros into his breast pocket, and settled back against the trunk of a scraggly little tree. He examined his cigarette, nodded to himself. "Like I said—some kinda brave."

He meant the guerrillas. They were up there on top of the mountain—a handful of them, a dozen or so— raining sniper fire down on hundreds of government troops. The rebels were slowing the soldiers down so that the main guerrilla forces and their civilian supporters could retreat farther to the north, to escape the army's advance.

Mary had explained all this to him earlier that morning, above long bursts of rifle fire, the stutter of machine guns, and worse. Much worse. Every minute or so, a huge explosion had roared down the mountainside, smacked R. Dale's ears like a pair of hands.

"Oh, God!" he'd cried the first time. He was down on his knees. "I mean. . . . " He tried to straighten up. "I mean, what was that?"

"Mortar!" Mary shouted. She had her microphone out and was fiddling with the knobs on her tape recorder. She hurried up the dirt switchbacks, surrounded by smoke and marching soldiers. The sun beat down hard, and she had to yell to be heard above the commotion. "But don't worry!" she shouted. "Outgoing! Outgoing fire! That's us firing at them!"

Garth snorted. He put down his camera, looked at Mary. "Us?" he said. "Them? Who's us and who's them?"

Mary laughed. *"Touché!"* She looked over at R. Dale. She had her hair pulled back into a ponytail now, bound with an elastic band. Beads of perspiration clung to her brow, and she reached up to wipe them away. Her arms were tanned, and the muscles flexed near her shoulders. He'd never noticed before how slim she was, or how tall. "It's funny," she yelled to him, "how you always think of the people shooting at you as 'them'! Never fails!" She shrugged, pursed her lips, and blew into her microphone. She cleared her throat. "It is another day in El Salvador," she declared into the microphone, in her reporter's voice, "another day of—"

The earth seemed to shudder, and the air exploded. R. Dale felt the ground hit his knees. Rocks scraped against his elbows, gravel against his chest. He opened his eyes, looked up. That wasn't outgoing. No bloody way.

"Whoops!" said Garth. He was hunched down too. All around, the soldiers were running forward. Their boots twisted in the dirt. Their legs spun past. Garth snapped a new roll of film into one of his cameras and let out a wolf whistle. "I think one of those shells went off in someone's hands!" he said. "I think someone's got trouble!"

It was true. They passed the spot a couple of minutes later. A mortar shell had exploded on the ground, killing four or five men. It was hard to tell how many. Clumps of soldiers stood nearby and stared.

There was a hole in the earth and a terrible mess. No one seemed to be doing anything.

"*¡Seguimos adelante!*" Sergeant Ungo called out to his troops. "*¡No se preocupen! ¡Váyanse! ¡Váyanse!*" The platoon kept right on climbing, past the pit in the earth, the muddle of uniforms and blood.

Half an hour later, Sergeant Ungo called a halt. His men flopped down on the roadside, against the wall of the great smoking hill. It was late morning, and the sun burned down from almost directly overhead. The soldiers rummaged through their packs for hunks of bread, tins of meat. They seemed to pay no attention to the deep reports of rifle fire. They were used to this and, besides, they were out of range.

Garth and Mary went over to sit in the sparse shade of a haggard little tree, an aspen or a eucalyptus, almost the only tree in sight that wasn't on fire. R. Dale followed. Smoke and cinders swirled overhead and all around, like swarms of insects loosed by the burning grass and trees. The flames cracked and roared. There was nothing to breathe but smoke and fumes. For a few moments the shooting stopped, then started up again. *Crack-boom. Crack-boom. Crack-boom.* R. Dale coughed and coughed. It was something, though—a handful of guerrillas up there, pinning down at least a brigade of government troops.

"Yep," Garth said. "Some kinda brave." He flicked the remains of his cigarette over the edge of the road, lifted one of the two cameras slung around his neck, and went back to work, peering at everything through the lens, testing for things to shoot. "Too much," he said. "This is really too fucking much."

Mary blew out another wisp of smoke, held her cigarette away to the side. "You've never done this before, have you?" she said.

"Eh?" said R. Dale. Did she mean him? There was something wrong with his ears. Was it the noise, or the congestion in his head? "What?"

"This," she said. She extinguished her cigarette carefully, on a stone. She made a gesture with her hand that included everything. "You know—this. War. You've never been in this kind of thing before." Her voice sounded amused, as though they were engaged in cocktail patter, as though she were asking if he took his car to work or the train.

He looked down, shrugged. "No," he said, in a whisper. He suddenly felt shameful. How he wished he could answer yes. He started to cough.

"Are you afraid?"

"What?"

"All this—does it make you afraid?"

What kind of a question was that? Wasn't it obvious? In his voice? On his breath? Was he afraid? "Well," he said. He swallowed. "I guess. I mean . . . sort of."

She nodded. "Me too."

"What?" he said. "You are? But. . . . " He didn't know what to say. His head was throbbing. He felt weak, feverish. It was hard to breathe.

She smiled. "You'll learn." She reached up with both arms, to tuck in some loose strands of her hair. She drew in a breath and her breasts rose. The muscles quivered by the pits of her arms. "You're already doing not so badly," she said. "Pretty soon you'll be like Garth and me. Cool cats. Right, Garth?" She lowered her arms,

227

turned, and gave Garth a shove against one of his knees.

"Yeah," Garth said. His face was buried in his camera. He was taking a picture of something. "Sure thing. War's a high, man."

Mary looked back at R. Dale. "But everybody gets scared." She shrugged. "Everybody. You just learn to . . . cover it up. You get this veneer of bravado. And then, after you get into some scary situation—when you come out okay, when you're still alive, on your own two feet— you get this high. It's like a drug or something. It takes you over, it's addictive. And it's dangerous, too. The thing is, you've got to be scared. Being scared is what keeps you alive—maybe." She leaned back against Garth's knees. "Garth," she said. "What's that line from *Moby-Dick*? You know. It's Starbuck, I think. Something like 'I won't have anyone in my boat who is not afraid of —'"

"Shit!" Garth snapped onto his knees. "Did you see that? Come on. Move!" He jumped to his feet, crouched low, ran across the dirt track to throw himself against the nearly vertical surface of the mountainside.

What? What was he doing?

Mary followed, dragging her tape recorder. R. Dale must have run across too, because suddenly he was huddled beside the others, his face pressed against the rocks and gravel, the ashes and bits of dead grass. The mountainside.

Shots roared out all around him, and R. Dale saw that the soldiers had also taken cover, up and down the track. Now they were firing almost straight up, and there was a zinging sound right above his head, and something was spitting in the dirt right behind him, and

Mary had her microphone out, and Garth was down on his knees twisting from side to side with his camera pressed to his face, and R. Dale's heart was near to exploding, it was beating so hard, and his lungs were bursting, bursting with air, and he felt a revelation break upon him like a whirlwind. Shoes! That was it. He wasn't wearing shoes! He looked down, and it was true. He'd run right out of his shoes!

But he had his notebook out and his pen. And he realized what he was doing. His hands were shaking—he could barely control them—but he'd somehow got his notebook open and he was scribbling. He wanted to get this down. He wrote, "Ran right out of my shoes." Then he put down something else, and something else, on and on. What he heard. What he saw. He was—he really was—he was getting all this down.

They reached the top of Ocotepeque a little before sunset, after the rebel sharpshooters had withdrawn from their positions and fled. It had been a hard day for the army. At least a dozen more soldiers had been killed in sniper fire, in addition to those who'd been blown up by their own mortar shell. Many more had been wounded. They'd been flown out in helicopters or hauled away in trucks, the dead and the wounded. The rest of the soldiers were dog-tired, you could see that. And they were surly, too. So many of their comrades dead or dying. They groused and swore, stared at Mary, put their hands to their crotches, spat.

But R. Dale was elated. He couldn't believe it. His notebook was practically bulging. He'd written down everything. What a story! He couldn't believe what a great story. They'd splash it across the front page for sure—Our Man under Fire in El Salvador, by R. Dale Wickham! He was tired, caked with dirt and sweat, hungry and thirsty. But he was exultant. He hadn't died. He hadn't been shot. He wasn't meant to die, after all. He was meant to survive. And what a great fucking story he would write! He had come through with flying colours, his trial by fire. He would never be afraid again. He'd be like all the others, the other hacks, the photographers. He'd grow a moustache, damn it. He would. He really would.

He put his head back and stared at the sky. God. He'd never felt like this before. He'd never felt so—oh, Christ, he didn't know what. The blood was just pumping through his veins, just surging, like a river, a flood. And the air. Just taste that air. You could get drunk on that air. He felt great. His sinuses were spanking clean, his lungs, throat, head—everything. Sharp and tingling. Alive! Alive! The world seemed to float around him— the rich red earth, the shimmering trees, the bottomless blue of the sunset sky, the vivid golden shards in the west. The sunset! Would you look at that sunset? He turned to Mary. "What a great story, eh?" he said. "How was your tape? Did you get good tape?"

Mary just shrugged. "I guess," she said. She practically mumbled.

Well, she was tired.

"Garth," he said. "Just look at that sunset. The colours. Aren't you going to shoot that sunset?"

Garth held up his light-meter like a stop-watch. It was attached to a cord around his neck. He squinted down, then dropped the thing. He shook his head. "Nah," he said. He shook his head again.

Sheesh. Not taking pictures? What was the matter with the guy?

Mary said to Garth, in a low voice, "I'm feeling creepy. This is giving me the creeps. They took more than a dozen dead today. You know?"

Garth lit a cigarette. He sucked saliva through his teeth. He nodded. He looked around at the soldiers. "Yeah," he said. "So we just stay cool. That's all we can do."

Right. Fine. Stay cool. Suit yourselves. What did it matter? He had this fucking great story. Christ, what a story! He was wearing army boots, too—combat boots. He hadn't been able to find his own shoes again, so one of the soldiers had lent him these, an extra pair. Not a bad fit, either. So he had on an army shirt and combat boots. Weird.

The mountain was almost flat on top, like a table. Some old buildings slouched beneath the trees—the remains of a coffee plantation. The concrete yards, for the drying of beans, were chipped now and faded, riddled with moss. The tracks that wound through the trees were disused, overgrown. A wind was up, silent and nearly cold.

Here and there, across the cracked stucco walls of the buildings, revolutionary slogans were sloshed in red. "¡No pasarán!" "¡Revolución o muerte!" "¡Venceremos!"

R. Dale knew what this was, this old coffee plantation. The rebels had used it for a camp. It was now an abandoned rebel camp of some sort. This was great. They kept on walking. A battered flatbed truck sagged at the side of the main dirt track. How the hell did it get up here? It still had something chained onto the wooden bed—its cargo, what looked like an electrical generator. The generator just sat up there, rusty and old-looking. The rebels hadn't even unloaded it.

It was getting dark. Not dark, really. Just dusky. Gloomy. The light was seeping away. The air sharpened, grew cold. They kept on walking, around and around. First one track, then another. Why didn't they just sit down, put up their feet, have a rest? It had been a long tiring day—but what a day. What a glorious fucking day. And yet, the soldiers didn't rest. They walked, kept turning their heads from side to side, looking, looking.

It occurred to R. Dale that they were looking for something. This wasn't aimless walking, after all. It was a search. That was what it was. He realized that something serious was going on. The soldiers conferred with one another, pointed, broke up into groups, converged, waved their rifles this way and that, looked back at Mary, whistled low tuneless snatches of songs he did not recognize. They glanced at each other, nodded, peered around, patrolled the old buildings. They kept looking back at Mary.

The soldiers finally found what they apparently were after—a group of peasants, cowering behind one of the buildings, an old storage shed. They were mostly women—too sick to walk—or old men. They had a few children with them, mostly little girls, one a cripple. Her left leg stuck out at a strange angle below her skirt. They didn't say anything, these people, just huddled against the wall, waited. They didn't look well. They were dressed in rags. The men wore shoes made of strips of black rubber knotted together with twine. The women were barefoot, and so were the children. These were the ones who'd been left behind.

Sergeant Ungo got on the radio. The receiver crackled, and he started shouting something into the microphone. More crackling. More shouting. He was talking to Colonel Guerrero. R. Dale could tell that much—the sergeant kept saying, "*Sí, mi coronel. No, mi coronel. Sí, mi coronel.*" Then it was over. Everyone waited. Sergeant Ungo cleared his throat with a growl and spat off to the side. No one moved. No one spoke. No one smiled or did anything. Everyone just stood there, waiting.

R. Dale didn't like this. He turned to Mary. "What's—?"

"Quiet," she whispered. "Just be quiet. Don't do anything."

Garth turned and shook his head. "Stay cool, man," he whispered. "That's all we can do now. Just stay cool."

The light was grey now and darkening. Everyone looked ghostly. Everyone waited. It was about ten minutes before Colonel Guerrero arrived in his jeep. The driver stopped the vehicle some distance off, shone the headlights on the peasants, who slumped against the wall. They squinted into the light. The hand-brake made a cranking sound as the driver pulled it on, and the motor rumbled in the semi-darkness. Sergeant Ungo went over to talk to Guerrero.

A couple of minutes later Ungo returned, waddled up through the glare of the jeep's headlights.

233

"*Vamanos*," he said. "*Todos.*" He waved at some of the soldiers. They hurried over to prod at the group of peasants, poked them in the sides with rifle barrels.

The people turned and began to shamble away, out of the light, into the murk. They said nothing. R. Dale couldn't see their faces. What was going on here? Several of the children started to cry. R. Dale stepped forward, he couldn't help it. "Hey," he said. "Hey, what's going on?"

Sergeant Ungo swung around. "*¡Usted!*" he shouted. "*¡No!*" He waved his rifle at R. Dale, then at the others. "*¡Quedense aquí! ¡No se vayan!*"

R. Dale heard Mary say something. Stop it, she was saying. That's what he thought. She meant him—he knew that. Be quiet, she was saying. Please. For God's sake. Just leave it. You can't—R. Dale felt her hand clutch at his arm. He shook it off.

"No," he said. He wasn't talking to her. He was talking to Ungo. "I mean it. No." He took another step forward. He couldn't help this. He had this—this feeling, this surging in his veins, this swelling in his lungs. It was like a drug or something. It was saying, *something's happening here, something bad.* He was going to put a stop to it. He kept going. He walked right up to Sergeant Ungo, put out his hand to block the rifle barrel as it came up. "Stop it," he said. He didn't even bother trying to think of the Spanish. He just said, "Stop it." He felt Ungo step back, and he thought, okay, he could intimidate these guys. He heard someone scream, a woman—Mary?—and he didn't feel, exactly, but he was aware of the rifle stock as it rammed up into his gut, and then he was down on his knees, trying to breathe.

And there were noises all around, men's voices shouting, and the jeep's motor roaring, and screams and more screams, then gunshots that came slowly, one at a time, like the popping of firecrackers. Closer and closer. And still he couldn't breathe. He couldn't breathe. He couldn't breathe.

An Otherwise Ordinary Room

When Pablo Duarte returned to Chile in the late winter of 1983, following ten years in exile, he expected something momentous to occur. An earthquake, perhaps. Or another coup. A coup would have been ideal—General Augusto Pinochet Ugarte, wrested from power after a decade of military rule. The newspapers would be bursting with the news. Democracy Restored to Chile! Former Dictator Banished to Brazil! Millions Celebrate!

But there was no coup. There was no earthquake, either. In fact, nothing happened at all. There wasn't even a demonstration—unless you counted the presence of Aunt Sandra and Uncle Teodoro and two of their three children as constituting a sort of demonstration.

The Beltrán family stood in a group at the arrivals area of the Arturo Merino Benítez Airport. When Pablo emerged from the Customs line, carrying his very battered aluminum-frame backpack, his aunt and her daughter immediately began to wave. Pablo recognized them by the sign, hand-lettered in blue crayon, that the little girl clutched before her. It said: *Bienvenido Pablo D.*

"How did you know it was me?" Pablo asked when they'd all got into the Beltrán family car, a mid-sized Ford station wagon.

Uncle Teodoro looked both ways and pulled out onto the main highway. He had a sad, worn face with a pale complexion, and his thinning hair was mussed at the back. He sold advertising space for the main Santiago newspaper, *El Mercurio*.

"We didn't," said Aunt Sandra. She had bracelets on both her bony wrists and was smoking a cigarette. She pushed back her brown hair. "We just waved at every handsome young man we saw."

"Not every," said Clarita, the youngest, who was ten years old and now had a colouring book open on her lap. She held up a red crayon. "Only the ones with beards." She made a zigzag motion with her crayon, as though she were drawing an imaginary beard in the air.

"That's right," said Aunt Sandra. "Marta told us in her letter that you'd grown a beard." She reached over and gave her husband's head a shake. "You'll have to grow a beard, too, Teo," she said. "I think I have a weakness."

"Ugh," said Jorge. He was pressed up against the far door in the back, a thin, taciturn boy. He had both hands shoved deep between his thighs. He hunched his shoulders. "Ugh." This seemed to be about the sum of his vocabulary.

Aunt Sandra shrugged. "Thirteen," she said. She glanced back at her son, then turned to Pablo. "A difficult

237

age for boys."

Pablo nodded. He'd been just thirteen years old himself on another morning ten years earlier, when he and his mother had abandoned Chile along with dozens of others, in a specially chartered plane provided by the government of Mexico. He wondered if he'd been anything like Jorge that day—moody and grim, huddled in the airport departure lounge, responding with only a guttural "ugh" to each nervous question or tentative remark from his mother. They'd been alone that morning. Pablo's father was already dead by then. Had been for at least a week.

Pablo shifted his eyes to gaze out the window at the passing blur of broad fields and eucalyptus trees. In the distance, the faint, snowy peaks of the Andes seemed to float, like clouds, against the wan austral sky. It was still very early in the morning.

"How is Marta?" asked Aunt Sandra. She glanced at her cigarette. She and her sister had never been close. Like so many in Chile, politics had divided them. "It's amazing how we've lost touch. She still smokes?"

"No," Pablo said. "Three years ago—she quit." He shrugged. "She's all right."

"Quit cigarettes . . . ?" Aunt Sandra shook her head and took a long drag on hers. "I wish." She smiled. "You like sports?"

"Sure."

"Great. Teo can get seats for Colo-Colo games. His clients have season tickets. You follow soccer?"

"A bit."

"Then you can go."

"Great," said Pablo. "I mean. . . . " He wasn't

certain what he meant. He'd expected something else, that was all. Ten years he'd been gone—ten years, an exile. And now all anyone could talk about was soccer? Cigarettes?

They should have been talking about human rights, or political prisoners, or censorship. What about the disappearances that haunted the country still? Even now, ten years after the coup, dissidents were still disappearing. Just plucked from the street and never heard from again. Or not even dissidents. Almost anybody. Young people. Students.

Uncle Teodoro honked at a lopsided panel truck that was chugging onto the highway just ahead, spewing out black diesel fumes. He had to brake and swerve to the left, to avoid an accident.

"Oh, God, Teo, . . ." hissed Aunt Sandra.

Pablo watched his aunt—how her shoulders grew suddenly taut, how she didn't breathe, how she held her cigarette, motionless, like a statue, until her husband had eased the car back into its proper lane. Then she put her head back, released a long trail of cigarette smoke between her teeth, and closed her eyes. She moved her lips almost as though she were saying a silent prayer.

They gave him a bedroom upstairs. Irene's room. She was the eldest of the children—eighteen years old—and had started university just that year. In the car, Aunt Sandra had said her daughter was away somewhere, staying with friends. But by the time they got to the house, that story had changed. Now it seemed that Irene had taken an apartment with two or three other students, closer to downtown. That explained her absence.

Aunt Sandra guided Pablo up the stairs. "We told her it was crazy. She has this perfectly good room right here at home." Aunt Sandra stopped at the landing and placed her hands on her hips. She was breathing heavily. "But. . . . " She raised her narrow shoulders and held them there, in a show of resignation. "But. But. But." She shook her head, lowered her shoulders, and resumed her climb.

When his aunt had left him alone, gently shutting the door behind her, Pablo shoved his hands into the pockets of his jeans and closed his eyes. He was in Chile, for the first time in a decade. He saw himself in a subterranean café, huddled over a table with other dissidents, former exiles. Slow spirals of cigarette smoke melted into the darkness above terse, whispered voices. Outside—the distant wail of police sirens. He imagined riot police in a plaza somewhere, truncheons raised high.

Pablo opened his eyes again and found himself looking at a white chest of drawers, its surface cluttered with enamel boxes and small baskets stuffed with trinkets, earrings, and bracelets. In the middle of all this slouched a white teddy bear with a red bow. Pablo took a step closer. The bear seemed to be peering up at him, paws outstretched, waiting for a hug. Pablo picked the animal up, strode over to the quilt-covered bed, and plunked himself down. He held the bear loosely against his chest, idly stroked the fur on its back, and gazed about at the room.

Something was wrong. He sensed it at once. This was not the room of someone who had planned to go away for any length of time. In the first place, there didn't seem to be anything missing. He put the bear down, got up, and went over to the chest of drawers. He hesitated, then probed quickly through the drawers. They were full of clothing—underwear, socks, carefully folded blouses, corduroy slacks and denim jeans, sweaters that bore the faint scent of mothballs. Next, he looked through the closet. It was also full—skirts, dresses, and more sweaters, all arranged on a dense assembly of wooden hangers. A pair of squash rackets teetered on the floor in their presses, amid a muddle of shoes.

Pablo had a sudden intuition. He closed the closet door and went over to the bed. He got down on his knees on the rug. He hiked up the mattress and probed beneath it. There it was—a book of some sort. He eased it out. A diary. Where else but under the mattress did anyone ever hide a diary? The cover bore a pattern of flowers in red and the current year embossed in gold—1983.

He flipped quickly through the pages. They were sprinkled with entries, one every three days or so. He didn't read them. He somehow didn't want to. He simply riffled through the diary until the entries came to an end on April 14—more than four months ago. After that, there were just blank pages. He closed the book and slid it back beneath the mattress. He wondered where his cousin could have gone so suddenly that she had taken almost nothing with her. It didn't make sense. . . .

Or did it? He stood up and pushed his hands through his hair. He'd just had a bizarre thought—disappeared. What if Irene had simply disappeared? That would explain why she'd taken nothing with her.

But it was impossible. Something so terrible—surely he and his mother would have been told. He decided that his mind was playing tricks. On the plane overnight, he'd barely slept. He was just tired. He sat down and began to unlace his hiking boots. Maybe he should get some sleep.

That afternoon, Pablo went shopping for groceries with Aunt Sandra and Clarita. He was still feeling a bit dazed, a bit jet-lagged. He thought it would be good to get out.

Aunt Sandra ticked off the items on her shopping list and talked about her job. She managed a women's clothing shop at the Mall Panorámico in Providencia. She was the businesswoman in the family, unlike Marta. Marta had always been the artistic one. The radical, too.

Pablo twirled a plastic bag full of snow peas and fastened it with a wire twist. He dropped the bag into the cart. "You think my mother is a radical?"

"Well, it's all relative, I suppose." Aunt Sandra was choosing tomatoes, one by one. "I mean, she was against the coup."

"And you weren't?" Pablo already knew that his aunt and uncle had supported, not only the coup, but the years of military rule that came after. "How could you not have been against the coup?"

Aunt Sandra reached out to stop Clarita from going off on her own with the shopping cart. She pursed her lips and shook her head. "Politics," she said. "That's what I'm against. I'm against politics. That's what's done us in."

Later, at the check-out counter, Pablo tried to ask

about Irene, about when he'd get to see her. "The last time I saw her, she couldn't have been more than—"

"Eight." Aunt Sandra set a pound of butter and a jug of orange juice down on the conveyor belt. "Eight. The last time you saw Irene, she was eight." She reached for the snow peas and hesitated, holding the bag in the air. "You know what? Why don't we go out to dinner tonight? Instead of staying at home. We should celebrate. There's a wonderful place we used to go to, years ago. Do you like pasta?"

And so, that night, they all went out to dinner. The restaurant was dark, with low ceilings and candles on every table. Beside each table, a space heater squatted on the floor with orange coils glowing. There was no central heat. It was a Sunday evening, and the place was almost full—parents dining out with their children. It could have been any family restaurant in any country in the world.

Clarita became restless and was told to behave. Jorge glared at his plate. No one said anything about Irene, or the military dictatorship, or Pablo's father. Instead, Uncle Teodoro talked about cut flowers and winter vegetables. It seemed that these were two important new Chilean exports to the United States, and he was thinking of investing some money in one or the other. What did Pablo think?

Aunt Sandra smoked her cigarette, and Uncle Teodoro cupped his chin in one hand and gazed intently through the candlelight at Pablo, as though he were seeking advice from a respected colleague. And yet Pablo had almost nothing to say. Yes, cut flowers were nice. Winter vegetables seemed like a good idea, too.

Either would be fine. Both might be better.

Pablo wanted to talk about something else. He wanted to tell them what it was like to have been an exile all these years. He wanted to talk about his father. What did they remember about his father? Had they ever heard about the time in Viña del Mar when his father and mother were dancing one night at an al fresco restaurant right beside the swimming pool, and they got in an argument, and she pushed him in the water? And then remembered he couldn't swim and had to jump into the pool herself to save her husband's life? There'd been a photographer there, and he'd taken a picture later—both of them drenched and smiling, with their arms around each other.

But no one said a word about Pablo's father. They ordered coffee. No one said anything about Irene.

When they got home, Pablo went straight up to bed. Once in the bedroom, he hesitated for a few seconds, then crouched down and fumbled under the mattress again for Irene's diary. He brought it out and opened it to the month of April. He was going to read it, but then he remembered a former girlfriend of his once telling him that the only time you were allowed to read another person's diary without that person's say-so was after that person was dead.

Pablo snapped the diary shut. Immediately, he felt cold, even scared, as if it was bad luck for him to be holding the book at all. He pushed the diary back under the mattress, undressed quickly, and climbed into his cousin's bed. There was something terrible about his doing this, but he blocked it out. To make a fuss would be even worse. It would be to acknowledge that anything was wrong. He reached over to the lamp beside the bed and switched off the light.

The next morning, about an hour after they got back from church, Aunt Sandra announced that everyone was going for a drive. It was Sunday, after all, and time for an outing. They could stop for lunch along the way.

"Or maybe we could eat at one of those little seafood places along the coast, before we come back," she said. She was tying a scarf around her head. The scarf was checkered, brown and yellow, with a pattern of little riding crops and stirrups and saddles. She slipped her cigarettes into a brown leather bag. "You know, Teo. The way we used to do."

"Way back when," said Uncle Teodoro. He was wearing a turtleneck sweater and a long, dark green windbreaker. He pulled on a floppy canvas hat. "Let's go, kids," he said. "Come on, Clarita. Shoulders back. Let's go, Jorge. You too—shoulders back."

First they had to get gas. Then they had to stop at a restaurant so that Clarita could go to the bathroom, which she was supposed to have done before they'd left home.

"Sorry," she said when she climbed back into the car. "Sorry. Sorry."

She and Jorge started to fight over who was taking up more space. They traded punches, and Clarita began to cry.

"Where are we going?" Pablo asked.

"Oh . . . somewhere." His aunt lit another cigarette. She breathed out a cloud of smoke. "You'll see."

They drove out to Valparaíso on the Pacific coast. As soon as Pablo realized they were taking the Valparaíso exit, he wanted to get out of the car and start walking back the other way. He knew what was coming now.

His father's grave was in Valparaíso, along with the graves of many of the other men and women who'd been killed right after the coup in 1973, when General Pinochet came to power. A top labour organizer, Pablo Duarte senior had been an adviser to the socialist government right up until the day of the coup—September 11, 1973. He'd been taken from his bed just after dawn that morning and was never seen alive again.

Several days later, after they learned of his death, Pablo and his mother were told to leave the country. They accepted an offer of asylum in Mexico. Later, they moved to Miami, where Pablo's mother had been offered a job as a producer with a Spanish-language TV network.

Then, only a month ago, Pablo's name had suddenly been withdrawn from the military government's list of prohibited people. No explanation. That sort of thing happened sometimes—a civil servant at a computer somewhere made a decision based on who knew what. Pablo immediately gave up his apprentice-reporter's job at a Spanish daily newspaper in Miami, and came home. He hadn't hesitated for a moment.

Aunt Sandra peered back at him now through a haze of cigarette smoke. She was waiting for him to say something. But he still didn't know what to say. This was the pilgrimage he most yearned to make. But alone. He had planned to visit his father's grave alone.

"Left," said Aunt Sandra. She glanced at her

husband. "You take the next left."

Uncle Teodoro nodded and swung the car around smoothly past a small grocery store and into a narrow street lined by one-storey rowhouses with identical windowboxes, all empty. The road swooped down the edge of a long hill and then climbed back up. Near the summit, overlooking the brilliant, blue Pacific, there was a florist's shop.

Uncle Teodoro parked the car outside, and they all trooped into the store. Pablo still had no Chilean pesos and had to borrow some money from his uncle. He bought a dozen roses, red, and half a dozen Easter lilies. They got back into the car and drove to the cemetery, a little higher up the hill. They had no trouble finding the grave. Aunt Sandra seemed to know exactly where it was.

It was marked by a simple granite stone that lay flush with the ragged, yellowy grass. The inscription chiselled into the surface of the stone included only the name Pablo Duarte Suárez, the date of his birth, and the month and year of his death. The precise day of his death had never been made known. Pablo got down on one knee and placed his flowers near the middle of the grave—about where he thought his father's heart might be. He climbed to his feet and stood back.

Aunt Sandra knelt by herself at the foot of the grave. She didn't move. She remained silent, with her eyes closed and her hands clasped in prayer.

Soon, Clarita and Jorge wandered off to inspect the other graves or simply to be free of their parents. Uncle Teodoro seemed to hesitate, then ambled away behind the children, at a discreet distance. The cemetery occupied the crest of a hill, overlooking the sea. Broken clouds streamed overhead above the cypress trees, and the sunlight splattered down. Below, half a dozen merchant ships were moored in the bay, where dozens of seagulls swerved and hovered like children's kites. The ocean was a mottled blue that seemed to darken towards the horizon.

Pablo stood several metres from his aunt. He tried to conjure up a clear image of his father—a large man with longish black hair parted in the middle and swept straight back. Dark eyes with curving lashes. Bedroom eyes, his mother always said. A man shouting through a loud-hailer to the din of clapping and cheers. Pablo tried to imagine his father from different angles, but one view always prevailed—from above and behind: Pablo riding on his father's back. He heard his mother's laughter and felt the bounce of his father's stride.

A voice shrieked in delight some distance away, and Pablo started, as if awakened from sleep. It was Clarita's voice. He peered back down and watched his aunt raise her head and stare straight ahead.

"It's so important," she said.

Pablo waited for her to continue. When she didn't go on, he said, "I'm sorry . . . ?"

"This. . . . " She gestured with her hand. "A grave. To know he's there, inside."

Pablo simply nodded. He could see that it was true. All these years in exile, he'd known his father was dead. But you never quite accepted it. You needed something more. You needed to see the body or, if not the body, the grave. To say to yourself, here, now, this. This is the end. To go on from there.

248

Pablo crossed his arms, looked out at the sprawling blueness of the ocean. He realized that he would have to return to this place another time, alone, to go over this again, by himself, to put an end.

He looked back at his aunt. He said, "About Irene...."

Aunt Sandra just gazed down at her hands. She lifted them both and pressed the heels of her palms against the ridges beneath her eyes. She drew her hands down her cheeks, and Pablo realized his aunt was crying. "Yes...?" she said.

"You've had no word? You don't know where—?"

"Nothing," said Aunt Sandra. "Nothing. Not a thing. Not a word. I've tried everything. Oh, God. Sometimes I—" She shook her head. She struggled to her feet, slapped her hands together as if that was enough of that. She cleared her throat. "Well. I'm sure there's some good explanation. I'm sure it will all come right in the end. I just...." She started to fumble inside her bag, probably searching for another cigarette. She looked up. "Where have those children got to...?"

Something made her peer off to the right, and Pablo followed her gaze. Just that moment, a trio of heads emerged above the brow of the hill—Uncle Teodoro with Jorge by his side and Clarita on his back. They seemed to drift into view as one, like an ascension.

Clarita was wearing her father's floppy canvas hat. It was far too big and drooped down almost to her nose. She had her arms outstretched around her father's head, her small hands pressed against his face. She was trying to cover his eyes, to keep him from seeing the way.

249

Every few strides, Uncle Teodoro pretended to stumble, practically went right down on his knees, but he did not fall. They were all red-faced and laughing— even Jorge, who carried a stick. He was waving it in the air, like a performer in a circus act or a magician with a wand. He kept pointing it at the headstones, at every headstone he passed, as if summoning the dead to rise up and walk.

None did. Only Aunt Sandra seemed to fall beneath that spell. With her leather shoulderbag still hanging open at her side, she turned to face her husband and her two children. She began to walk towards them. Then she walked more quickly. Then she began to run.

Synonyms for War-torn

Chas Whepler got a call from a friend of his who worked at the Catholic human-rights office. The woman said about six children had gone missing that morning from a barrio over by the local cement factory. She told him how to get to the barrio. She said she thought it was six children. She wasn't exactly sure about the number.

Whepler grabbed his notebook and rode the elevator downstairs. He didn't want to be doing this, but what choice did he have? Come to that, he didn't want to be in El Salvador any more. He was thinking of getting out, thinking about it a lot. In the lobby of the hotel, he bumped into Jean-Marc Piton, who was flirting with the girls behind the reception desk. There was nobody else around.

Jean-Marc looked up, threw out his arms. "Charles!" he cried. He hurried over. He said he had a big problem. The French ambassador in Belize was coming to El Salvador on a sort of courtesy call, and he, Jean-Marc, was responsible for organizing a dinner in the man's honour. He'd just got the word in a telex from Belmopan, the capital of Belize.

Whepler shrugged. "So . . . ?" He knew that there was no French ambassador in El Salvador itself. Paris had called him home. "What's the problem?"

Jean-Marc stood back, and his eyes grew wide. "But nobody in this country will come to such a dinner. Nobody." He smacked a fleshy hand against his brow and shook his head. "It will be a *désastre,* and I will be the one to blame."

Whepler pursed his lips. Probably Jean-Marc was right. France had a socialist government, after all. Not too popular around here. "Well, do the best you can."

"You have to help me, Charles." Jean-Marc clutched at Whepler's arm. "Come. We go to the bar."

"Not right now." Whepler pulled free. "Sorry. I have to run."

"All right. Go. I will drink alone. What difference does it make? My life is over."

Whepler left the hotel and walked across the street to the Metro-Centro, the biggest shopping complex in Central America. He went up to a lone taxi parked at the stand by the curb. The driver's name was Roberto. Whepler knew him from previous trips.

"*Hola, Roberto.*" Whepler climbed in the front. "*Vamanos a la fábrica de cemento.*"

"*Muy bien.*" Roberto started the engine. He did a U-turn at the traffic lights, and off they went. His taxi still needed a new muffler.

It was one of those very quiet, very bright Sunday

252

afternoons in San Salvador when you could easily imagine what life must have been like here about a hundred years ago—goats bleating in the distance, dogs snapping at flies, everybody taking a siesta. In his mind, Whepler heard guitar music. He leaned his elbow out the window and tried to come up with some new synonyms for war-torn. He wondered what sort of adjectives you would use to describe a country where six kids went missing from the same neighbourhood on the same morning, out of the blue. War-torn didn't seem to cover it. Maybe war-crazed.

Not far from the cement factory, Whepler started to give Roberto some instructions about where to go next, but Roberto said he knew the place already. The barrio was down a wooded gully, and the only way in was along a dirt track that ran over a sort of garbage dump and then across a stream. First, though, they had to drive past a black Ford sedan that was parked in the long yellow grass at the edge of the track. Four men were hunched inside, listening to a soccer game on the radio. Someone had just scored, and the announcer cried out, "¡Gooooooool!" Probably the wrong side was ahead, because none of the four men was cheering.

They all had on aviator sunglasses and were evidently police, although they weren't wearing uniforms and they didn't show their guns. They didn't cause any fuss at all, didn't have to. They just sat there and stared at the taxi as Roberto eased by. Whepler figured they'd probably make some trouble on the way out. Maybe serious. Maybe not. He released a long breath. God, he was getting tired of this stuff.

Good for Roberto, though. He didn't blink an eye.

253

He just drove straight on. The car crept down and across the stream and came up behind a woman who was walking beneath a stand of eucalyptus trees. Whepler asked Roberto to stop just ahead of her and he got out. He didn't approach the woman—he imagined she might be a bit jumpy. He kept his distance, on the other side of the car. He said, *"Buenas tardes, señora."*

"Muy buenas tardes," she replied. She put up her hand to shield her eyes from the sun. A roly-poly woman, she had dark skin and thick black hair pulled straight back and tied behind her neck. She wore a short blue dress—the usual cheap synthetic—with a tattered yellow apron tied at her waist. She carried a white towel over her shoulder, the way they did. She looked to be in her mid-thirties.

They exchanged a few pleasantries, and Whepler said he was a reporter. He said he wanted to find out about these children who'd gone missing from the barrio that morning.

Just like that, she started to cry.

Whepler didn't make the mistake he used to, the one of thinking this was some false dramatic show. Down here, it was different. They didn't hold their emotions in. When it was time to cry, they cried. He went over to the woman and, along with Roberto, he helped her into the back seat of the taxi. She was really sobbing now. It turned out that she was the mother of one of the children who'd disappeared. Her daughter was a young girl named Alma. Just twelve years old.

They drove the woman to her matchbox adobe house, a tired affair with a smoke-charred roof. Patchy bits of croton shrub pushed through the grey earth

254

outside, and some tin cans sat on a window casement, sprouting blossomless shoots of flowers. She was trying.

The woman asked Whepler inside. She said her name was Señora Nevares. She had three other children, all younger than Alma. She said she had a husband too, but he was out in La Libertad working as a day labourer in the canefields—it was the harvest season. The children were nice-looking kids. They didn't have that withdrawn or surly look, that ground-in, smudgy quality to their faces that you sometimes saw. Whepler could tell that their mother gave them love and tried to keep them clean.

The house was rundown but tidy—a couple of dark rooms, one for cooking and one for sleeping. The chairs were homemade and creaked when you sat in them. The woman had some water in a pitcher and she got up to pour a glass. Whepler pretended to sip it, to be polite.

"It's been boiled," she said. "You can drink." She wasn't crying any more, just sniffling a bit with her towel bunched up in her hands. She watched Whepler look around at the inside of her house. She pressed her lips together. "It's very small," she said.

"Yes. But it's nice."

She shrugged.

There'd been a time when Whepler thought the consolation about poverty was that poor people didn't realize they were poor. They didn't know any better, so maybe it didn't seem so bad, the way they lived. He thought they were probably accustomed to septic water, for example, and could drink it without much effect—it didn't make them ill. But he'd changed his mind before too long. They knew they were poor. They did get sick.

Whepler pulled out his notepad, and Señora Nevares told him what had happened. Some men had come by the day before in a pair of cars, she said. They'd stopped by the garbage dump and climbed over some mounds of trash. There was a flattened section of land there where the local boys sometimes played pick-up soccer. The men started calling for Joaquín Díaz. He was a boy, a bit older, about seventeen maybe, who lived in the barrio.

As soon as the men called out his name, Joaquín started to run back towards the eucalyptus trees and up in the direction of the cement factory. Some of the men ran after him, and the others hurried to their cars, to drive up and head the boy off. The ones on foot caught him partway up the hill when he tried to double back and run down. They took Joaquín away in one of the cars. That was yesterday afternoon.

"This morning," the woman said, "they came back. The same men or maybe someone different. I don't know." She had to stop, to swallow something down. She said the men had a list of names. They went from house to house, shouting out the names—the names of children who lived in the barrio. They had rifles, and they waved them in the air. They searched the houses, door to door, banging and crashing. The commotion was terrifying—people were barely out of bed at the time. As soon as the armed men found a youngster who matched one of the names, they dragged that child out and pushed him or her into one of the cars. When it was over, they drove away.

"How many?" said Whepler. "How many did they take?"

Señora Nevares had her head lowered. She was crying into that towel of hers. But she answered his question. "Seven," she said. Her voice was muffled by the towel. "They took seven of them away."

Whepler frowned at his notepad. He was thinking about those men in that Ford up above the barrio. To get out of this place, he was still going to have to make his way past them. He grit his teeth—he'd had it with this stuff. Three years of it were enough for anybody. He'd pretty much decided it was time to get out of Central America.

After a while, he stood up and went outside with Señora Nevares to visit some more of the parents. The other people emerged from their houses to talk. They were afraid—Whepler could see it in the tautness of their jaw muscles and the way their eyes shifted to the side. But they opened right up. They were deferential and forthcoming, and he knew that here was a problem. These people thought he was going to be able to help them in some way. A gringo journalist. He was going to be able to get their kids back home, safe and sound. That was what they were thinking. They imagined he had some sort of power, some knowledge or influence, something beyond their grasp—whereas the truth was, all he had was a pretty good story for the Monday paper.

Whepler walked back with Señora Nevares to her house, where Roberto was still waiting beside the car. The woman asked him to hold on outside, along with her kids, and she bustled indoors. When she reappeared, she was carrying something—a small black and white photograph of her child. It looked like a school snapshot. The girl was a sweet-looking kid with thick, arched eyebrows, a button nose, and her hair cut short and wavy. She looked like the sort of child any parent would be happy to see their daughter bring home from school, a new friend. Whepler started to return the photograph.

"No." Señora Nevares put up her hands with the towel draped between them. "You keep it. Please. Maybe it will help you."

So there it was again.

Whepler hesitated, but then he tucked the snapshot into his money belt. It felt like some sort of IOU he'd never repay. He thought he should offer something in return and so he gave Señora Nevares his card. If she heard anything new, he said, she should try to get in touch. He said he'd do the same for her, which was true. He would. He just didn't expect the occasion to arise.

The woman peered down at the card and nodded. Then she slid it into the front of her dress. She looked up, grim-faced, as if they'd just made a secret pact. "*Gracias.*"

Whepler turned to Roberto. "Okay," he said. "*Vamanos.*" He wanted to get going. He was feeling edgy, thinking about those four men in that Ford up on the brow of the hill. He was wondering how unpleasant they were likely to be. You never knew what craziness someone might decide to pull. Whepler didn't get a thrill out of this stuff any more. He'd had enough.

When they got to the top of the hill, Roberto had to stop. The police had eased their car over into the middle of the track, to block the exit. Whepler closed his eyes, as if somehow he could imagine all of this away. But when he opened his eyes again, he was still in El Salvador.

The doors of the Ford swung wide, and the men climbed out. The gravel crunched beneath the heels of their smart black shoes. It was late afternoon now, and the sun was behind the Ford, sharp and low, casting thin, elongated shadows. The men made Whepler and Roberto get out of the taxi. A couple of them started to search it top to bottom. The other two questioned Whepler, and one kept prodding him in the chest with his hand. Every question, another shove. He got Whepler pressed with his back against the Ford, and now both these men stood close. They had shiny, bronze complexions, and their sunglasses flashed in the light. They wanted to know Whepler's name, his nationality, his occupation. They wanted to see his documents, but Whepler couldn't move to take them out. The door was open behind him, and it would not have taken much for them to push him right in.

"What were you doing down there?" Another shove.

Whepler felt the doorframe pinch into his back. "Talking to some of the people."

"What about?" The man shoved again.

"They've been having some problems."

"What business is that of yours?" Shove.

"I don't know."

"You don't know?" Shove. "What do you mean, you don't know?" Another shove. "I thought you journalists knew everything." This one grinned, and the other one sniggered.

"We only know what people tell us."

"And what did they tell you, down there?"

Whepler tried to swallow.

"Eh? What?"

"Water," Whepler said. "They—they're forming a committee. They . . . uh, want the authorities to provide clean— "

"Water? I don't believe you. You're lying to me." This time, the man didn't remove his hand. He pushed the heel of his palm into Whepler's ribs, harder and harder, worked it around and around. "Why do you lie?"

Whepler couldn't speak. The man kept his hand where it was and brought his face close, his burnished brown skin. He stared through those dark green lenses, like insect eyes. There was tobacco on his breath, stains on his teeth. His nose and cheeks were pitted, sprouting dark follicles of hair. He was the one doing the real looking. He was looking for fear, searching for it in Whepler's eyes. When he found what he wanted, which he was sure to do, there was no telling what might happen. He might go right out of control. But instead he just smiled and slowly removed the weight of his hand. All he'd intended to do was show who was the boss, and he'd done that now. No big deal.

He stood back a pace. His manner changed at once. "You must understand," he said. "We are concerned for your safety. You have to be so careful in this country. There are so many crazy people." He gestured down towards the barrio. "You shouldn't believe what crazy people tell you." He shrugged. "Now, you may go. So sorry for the inconvenience."

When they'd driven a certain distance away, Whepler turned to Roberto. He wasn't sure if he could trust his voice. He said, "Scared? Did that get you scared?"

Roberto rolled his eyes. "What do you think?" He held up his right hand. His hand was still shaking.

Whepler did the same and found his hand was shaking too. They both started to laugh, and Whepler felt a backwash of weakness sag through his chest. He thought, war-weary—a new synonym, one he hadn't thought of before. "Funny," he said. "Pretty funny country you have here." But that wasn't what he was thinking. He was thinking he'd had enough of this. He wanted out.

Back at the hotel, Whepler wrote his story and sent it off on the hotel telex machine. From his room, he phoned the paper to see if they had any questions. But Bob said nope, the story was fine. They'd even considered it for front because it was a slow day. But some oil rig had caught fire and exploded off the coast of Mexico, so that was going front instead. Couldn't have two Latin American fronters on the same day.

Whepler went down to the lobby bar, but it was empty. So he headed out to dinner alone. He walked through the darkness and a cool breeze, down the street to a place called El Rancho. A few of the other hacks were there. They all stayed on after dinner, had a couple more beers.

At breakfast the next morning, Grant Lovsted slouched into the coffee shop and flopped down at Whepler's table. "*Café*," he groaned to the waitress. "*Por favor.*" Some of the others were up at the buffet, spearing things onto their plates. It was seven o'clock. Lovsted rubbed his eyes and yawned. "Fuck," he said. "Fuck.

261

Fuck. Fuck."

"Sleep well?"

"Sleep? What's that?"

Whepler sipped his coffee. "Give me a sec. It'll come to me."

Lovsted lit a cigarette, coughed. He reached up and scratched his jaw. "That fucking Jean-Marc."

"What?"

"I had dinner with him last night. Then we went back to his place, and you know he has this collection of French brandy?"

Whepler nodded. "Yeah."

Lovsted shook his head. "Fuck." The waitress returned with a pot of coffee and filled Lovsted's mug. Lovsted stared at it, as if he had forgotten the purpose of coffee. Finally he picked it up, swallowed a mouthful, then another. He closed his eyes. "Never again. I swear to God."

"Do you want some Aspirin?"

He frowned. "I think I already OD'd on Tylenol. Don't worry. I'll survive." He had another swig of his coffee. "Hey," he said. "D'you file yesterday?"

Whepler shrugged. "Yeah."

"What was your lead?"

Whepler flapped his napkin to get rid of the crumbs. He shrugged again. "I dunno. Seven kids go missing from impoverished barrio in war-weary El Salvador."

Lovsted rubbed some sleep from his eye. "War-weary, eh . . . ?" He nodded. "Not bad. I'll have to remember that one."

It was a game they played. Editors wouldn't let

them use the word war-torn any more. It was too clichéed. So they always had to come up with something else. They weren't allowed to quote taxi drivers, either—it gave the impression they spent all their time in a car. These were the two main rules of war coverage: synonyms for war-torn, no taxi-driver quotes. They still did quote taxi drivers, though—called them small businessmen.

Whepler crossed his legs at the ankles. "Did Jean-Marc tell you about this dinner he has to organize? For the French ambassador?"

"All he talked about." Lovsted shook his head. "Poor bastard. There's no fucking way. What's the French ambassador want to come here for? They don't even have fucking diplomatic relations."

Whepler nodded, sipped his coffee. It was true. Jean-Marc was the only French guy left. He was the commercial rep, so that made sense. Couldn't stop trade.

Lovsted drained his mug. "What're you doing today?"

"I don't know. I haven't worked it out yet."

"Maybe we could take a drive. San Vicente or something. Some guys said there was fighting out there yesterday. Could still be good."

"Okay. Sounds okay." He was thinking, war-battered. War-scarred. Shell-shocked.

"Caffeine." Lovsted shoved himself to his feet and picked up his mug. "I need more caffeine." He headed for the buffet.

Whepler signed his bill and walked out into the lobby—and there was Señora Nevares with her three

263

kids. They were propped up like worn raggedy dolls on one of the big brown leather couches, beside a potted plant. In these surroundings, they looked worse than poor. They looked like refugees from another planet.

"*Buenos días.*" Whepler went over to them. "*¿Qué pasó?*"

Señora Nevares was holding his business card in her lap. She frowned down at it. "*Buenos días, Señor . . . Wayplayer.*"

Whepler pushed a chair over and sat down. Again he asked, what was up?

It turned out, not much. The four men in that car had gone away some time after dark and hadn't shown up again in the morning. That was about it. Señora Nevares wanted to know if he'd heard anything new about her daughter.

He shook his head. "No. I haven't heard anything."

"Oh." She looked down again and nodded.

Her kids were keeping perfectly quiet on the couch beside her, two girls and a boy. The elder of the girls seemed to be maintaining a watch on the other two. She reached over and started probing her brother's hair for lice.

The day was getting under way, and foreign hacks and assorted Salvadorans hurried back and forth through the lobby, calling to each other or lighting cigarettes. A lot of them glanced over at Whepler and Señora Nevares and the children. You didn't often see slum people in the hotel. Normally, they wouldn't have been allowed past the door. So there'd been a slip-up this morning.

Whepler tried to think of something to say. He

wanted to say that he had this or that enquiry out, or that he was expecting to hear a little later on from So-and-so. But the fact was, he was pretty sure that Alma and all those kids were dead already or soon would be, and he didn't want to think about it much beyond that.

He wanted to think about something else, such as how Jean-Marc was going to get anybody to attend that dinner of his for the French ambassador. Or maybe not about that. What he really wanted to think about was something else entirely—getting out of this country, calling it quits. He could call his paper today, before lunch, and announce that he'd had it. After three years down here, he wanted out. He could be gone in a week. He was war-fed-up. That was what he wanted to do. He looked at Señora Nevares. "You never know," he said. "You never know what might come up."

"*Sí.*" She nodded. "*Es la verdad.*"

It was the truth. They both just sat where they were and thought about that. Whepler heard the automatic doors gasping open and shut around the corner at the elevator well. People marched in and out of the coffee shop. A bell trilled at the reception desk. Whepler was waiting for Señora Nevares to leave. But she didn't make a move. It took him a while to realize why—she had nowhere else to go. In her search for her daughter, he was it. Who else could she get in touch with? The government? The police?

"Hey, Whepler. Fuck, man, you ready? Let's go." It was Lovsted. He had a small blue knapsack over his shoulder and was tossing his car keys with one hand.

Whepler glanced back at Señora Nevares. "Well, I'll let you know if I hear anything." He stood up. "Don't worry. I'm sure everything will be all right." He couldn't believe he was telling her this. It was stupid, cruel even. But what else was there to say?

Again, she nodded. "*Gracias,*" she said. She and her elder daughter started to get the kids up and going. "*Muchas gracias, Señor Wayplayer.*" She knotted the smaller girl onto her back with that big towel of hers, and the older girl did the same with the boy. They tottered out of the hotel on their short brown legs, in their worn rayon dresses and their flapping plastic sandals. Everyone in the lobby turned to watch them go.

"What was that about?" Lovsted said a little later.

Whepler had just come down from his room and they were heading out to the parking lot. "Don't ask. I don't want to talk about it." He double-checked to make sure he had his notebook in his hip pocket. "I'm too war-fucked-up."

"War-fucked-up . . . ?" Lovsted moved his lips around, like he was tasting a new wine. "Nah," he said. "My editors would never go for it."

It turned out the rebels had attacked a garrison town in San Vicente province. Lovsted had got the basic information from Larry Schuyler, the AP guy on the second floor at the hotel. They drove out there and soon they were crawling around in the dirt between rows of small adobe houses with bright stucco fronts, trying to get as close as they could. *Crack, crack, crack* went the gunshots. The air felt hot and raw. Lovsted yanked off his white polo shirt and tied it to the end of a stick he'd found, to use as a white flag. Each time they got to another corner of the narrow cobbled streets, Lovsted and Whepler waited until they saw some soldiers or

266

rebels on the other side. When the way was clear, the fighters would sometimes wave them across.

They crept around like that, with the white flag suspended in front. They were trying to get a fix on things, figure out what was going on. For a time, they got pinned down at a gas station. They'd been scurrying across the street when shooting broke out—and there'd been nowhere else to hide. They had to lie down right behind the pumps, a stupid place to take shelter, but there was no choice. The bullets hurtled and smashed against the low tin roofs of some shacks right behind them. There must have been rebels back there, but they weren't returning fire, or not yet.

Whepler had his head pressed down flat on the sticky, tar-covered earth. The ground burned into his chest. Lovsted's shirt was crumpled a few inches away, streaked now with grease and dirt—so much for their white flag. Whepler closed his eyes. The bullets hissed overhead and crashed into the wood and tin behind. He couldn't believe he was out here, doing this. This was the last time. It was. It was. If he got out of here alive, he'd never come back. He'd leave this country as soon as he possibly could.

The gunshots tore into the tin-sheet awnings behind the gas pumps, wrenched away bits of wood so that the nails shrieked. The sun burned down, and now Whepler could feel the pressure of the gasoline storage tank swelling up underneath him. It was probably right below him. It felt as if it was bloated or something, straining up against his chest. All they needed was a little spark around here—a direct bullet hit—and the obituary writers would have their hands full.

Whepler opened his eyes. He could see the top of Lovsted's head, little flakes of dried tar mixed in with the dense brown hair. "Now what?" he hissed. "Now what do we do?"

"Stay down," Lovsted shouted. More bullets slammed into the shacks behind them. "And don't fucking smoke, either."

Whepler wanted to do something, anything, to get them out of here. He couldn't stand this being so helpless, but it was no use. There was nothing to do but wait until the shooting finally moved off somewhere else, and he followed Lovsted, scrambling away from those pumps over towards some shabby market stalls and an adobe wall. They both slumped down there. Rifle shots snapped like whipcracks, a block or so away, maybe two blocks. Now and then, the boom of an exploding mortar rumbled through the earth, and Whepler felt it in his groin like a contracting fist. He started talking about deadlines. He was worried about his paper's deadline.

Lovsted slapped some of the muck from his shirt so that it would look halfway like a white flag again. He glanced up. "Deadline? What are you talking about? We've got loads of time. Come on. We need to find an officer. We don't have any officer quotes."

They did keep going. They did find an officer, too—a cocky young lieutenant jabbering into a radio behind a sandbag barricade. The barricade was set up against the wall of a building—a bodega or something—and overlooked a small square planted with cypress trees and some scraggly lemons. The rebels and the army were shooting across the square.

Lovsted and Whepler waited until they caught the

lieutenant's eye. Then they skittered along an alley and ducked down behind that barricade, right beside him. When the officer got off the radio, Lovsted asked what was going on.

"*Combate*," the lieutenant shouted. "*Mucho combate.*"

Lovsted shook his head. "Ask a stupid question..."

The rebels didn't appear to have an angle on this barricade, so it was possible to peer over the top and see what was happening in the square. Not much, it seemed, apart from flying bullets. Then Whepler saw something. At first he thought it was a soldier, a dead soldier, lying on his chest on the cobbles. No—not lying. He was moving. He looked like he was trying to crawl out of the square. And he wasn't a soldier, either. He was far too small, and he wasn't wearing a uniform. He was barefoot, and he had on brown pants and what looked like a blue T-shirt. He was a boy, just a kid.

Christ. What was a boy doing out there? He looked about ten, maybe twelve years old, and he was on his stomach. Whepler saw now that he had a large, dark stain on the back of his shirt—blood. He'd been shot. If you looked carefully, you could see a long, broken streak of blood from the point where he'd evidently been hit, over by a little fountain in the middle of the square. A lumpy brown parcel lay over there, and it oozed something, some brownish liquid. Medicine? It looked like it might be medicine or something, leaking from a broken bottle.

Whepler wanted to cry out. But what would be the point? That boy wouldn't hear him anyway. So he hunched his shoulders and just watched. The boy was trying to get out of the square, but it was slow going. He dragged himself forward a foot or so with his hands and forearms, before slacking off to rest. Then he pulled himself forward a little more. He was trying to get to some kind of cover.

"Can't you do something?" Whepler shouted at the lieutenant. "Can't you get in there and bring him out? He's just a kid."

"You crazy?" the lieutenant roared back. "He's dead. He'll be dead soon, anyway." The officer dropped down onto his knees and started barking again into the radio. It turned out he was calling in mortar rounds against the rebels.

"Better get down," Lovsted shouted.

But Whepler couldn't. He couldn't take his eyes off this one young boy, who'd somehow got himself caught all alone in this square at just the wrong moment. Probably he'd been running across it, thinking the way was clear. Maybe the boy had been sent to get medicine for his little sister. She was ill, maybe dying. Something like that. He'd had to go straight to wherever the local doctor lived, get some medicine from him. Then he turned and started to run back, took the shortest route home. Stupid little idiot, to get caught out in the open like that.

The child was close enough now that Whepler could just about make out the features on his face when he raised himself up a bit, to heave forward. He looked even younger than Whepler had thought, maybe not even ten. Once or twice, Whepler thought he almost caught the boy's eye, but probably not. The child probably wasn't thinking of anything or anyone but himself just now. There he was, out on the sagging cobbles of that square, with the war busting a gut just above his head, and he was all alone. There was no one to help him. Nobody else was even looking his way.

Whepler had the idea that if he just kept watching, just kept his eyes peeled, then maybe that kid would be okay. He'd crawl out of there alive. Maybe there was some kind of karma, some kind of good-luck force, in having somebody keep their eyes on you. At least you wouldn't be alone. Whepler grit his teeth and clenched his fists and tried to will that boy across the square to safety. It was just a matter of a few yards, a question of two minutes, maybe three. Whepler kept watching until the first of the mortars exploded, too short, and dust and bits of wood and brick clattered down. After that, Lovsted grabbed him and hauled him to his knees. He tried to get up but Lovsted wouldn't have it, climbed right on top of him.

"You crazy?" Lovsted shouted. Another mortar exploded, and more debris rained down. "You fucking crazy?"

Whepler flailed out with his arms, but it was no use. There was nothing he could do. Lovsted was too damn big.

Before long, the lieutenant was back shouting into the radio, and three or four more mortar rounds crashed and shuddered somewhere ahead, at the side of the square. Whepler's teeth shook like they'd broken loose from his gums. He was thinking about that young boy. He kept hoping someone would go out there and rescue that kid, some brave soul. Finally the shooting seemed to quiet down, either because that group of rebels had

271

been hit or, more likely, because they'd moved away. Lovsted got off him, and Whepler struggled onto his feet. He peered out over the barricade, wondering where that boy had got to.

There he was. He hadn't got far, hadn't really moved at all, and he wasn't moving now. He sprawled on the cobbles with his arms pinned underneath him and with a pale grey dusting on his backside. His trousers were torn at the side. His mouth hung open. He lay still. Then some soldiers darted out from the edge of the square to drag him to shelter, but Whepler was pretty sure from the look of the boy that he was dead.

Right away, the shooting started up again a few blocks farther along. The lieutenant took Lovsted and Whepler back a short distance, into a dark one-room building that seemed to be some sort of secretarial school. It had old typewriters set up on all the desks. The officer rattled off some numbers about the dead and wounded—lots of rebel casualties, of course, and very few on the army side. Probably he made the numbers up on the spot. He also provided some passable quotes about the grimness of war. Whepler asked him to check on the radio about whether that boy was still alive. The answer crackled back a few minutes later. No. Dead.

After a while, the fighting seemed to calm down for a bit—the lieutenant said he thought the rebels were starting to withdraw, which sounded unlikely—but the lull meant Lovsted and Whepler could work their way back to the car. At first, Whepler didn't want to leave. He wanted to find that young boy, look at his body, make sure the soldiers did what was right by that body. Or he thought maybe he should try to pay a visit to that boy's family, tell his mother what had happened to her son. But it was impossible. He didn't even know the kid's name. So he just kept low and darted through the streets and lanes behind Lovsted. They finally got to the car and climbed in.

Lovsted started the engine and pulled out, headed straight back to the capital. "Whoo!" he shouted.

Once they were on the Pan-American Highway, Lovsted's foot hit the floor, and he kept it there. He still didn't have his shirt on, and he was covered all over in grease and dirt. Whepler looked down and saw that he was just as bad.

"Whoo!" Lovsted shouted again. The windows were open, and the wind blurred his hair. He was having some kind of adrenalin fit. "Whoo! Whoo!" He kept punching the wheel, shaking his head, and laughing. "Whoo!"

"Yeah, yeah," Whepler muttered. He popped open the glove compartment and started rooting around in there for a pack of cigarettes. He really needed a cigarette. He was thinking, war-wired. The guy was war-wired. Whepler got out a cigarette, but the car lighter didn't work. He had to poke around in his money belt for a book of matches. Instead, he came up with that picture, the one of that little girl—Alma.

"What's that?" Lovsted reached over and took the snap from Whepler, glanced at it, and handed it back. "Cute kid. Yours?"

"Yeah," said Whepler. "Sure thing. My illegitimate daughter."

"Take good care of her, pal." Lovsted hit the brakes, and the car shook through a patch of dirt and washboard. He wailed out an old Bobby Vee refrain about taking good ca-are of someone's ba-aby! He punched the wheel again. "Whoo!"

"Yeah." Whepler slid the photo back into the pouch and got out some matches, lit his cigarette. He had to be careful, because of the way his hands were shaking. "Yeah, yeah, yeah."

The paper loved the story, though.

"Fantastic!" said Bob on the phone. "Great stuff! Great colour!" He said he especially liked the bits Whepler had woven into the story about that poor kid dragging himself across the square. He said it was really moving, like a symbol for the futility of all war. The story was going front for sure. "Keep your head down," he said. "It sounds pretty hairy down there."

"Yeah," Whepler said. "Yeah, thanks." He had to admit, though, that the praise didn't hurt too much. It wasn't too unpleasant to hear.

Whepler went downstairs and met Lovsted in the lobby bar. Lovsted said he'd got the same reaction from his paper. His story was going front, too. Whepler said it was ridiculous. It was stupid.

"What is? What are you talking about?"

"This." Whepler dug a cigarette out of Lovsted's pack and lit up. "This whole thing. What did we do today? We went out and got shot at, saw some other people getting shot at. Big deal. It doesn't mean anything. We write about it, and nothing happens. It's just description. What's the point? The people still die. The war just keeps on going."

"Damn right." Lovsted drained his beer and slammed down the mug. He asked Pedro for another.

Whepler shook his head. It was ridiculous. He sipped his beer and tried to think of some more synonyms for war-torn, but it was no use. He'd run out.

"*Ah! Mes amis!*" It was Jean-Marc. He waddled into the bar from the lobby, climbed onto a stool beside Lovsted, ordered a cognac. He shook his head. "It's terrible," he said. "Terrible."

"What?" said Lovsted. "Don't tell me. Still no takers for the Ambassador's Ball?"

"You laugh," said Jean-Marc. He was quiet for a time, waiting for his drink. When it came, he warmed the glass in the palm of one hand. "But it isn't funny. It is terrible."

Apparently, he'd been on the phone all day, coaxing and pleading with local businessmen and bigwigs to show up at the dinner he was organizing. No one was willing to come. He gulped his cognac, swallowed, and clucked his tongue. "I am finished," he moaned. "Destroyed."

"Looks like it," said Lovsted. "Too bad."

"No one understands me." Jean-Marc swallowed the rest of his cognac and called for another. He was already pretty lit. "No one has ever understood me."

There was nothing anyone could do to help, so Lovsted and Whepler left him there and headed out to dinner across town at El Bodegón.

That night, in bed, Whepler thought about the young boy he'd seen in the plaza, the one who'd got himself killed. He kept thinking, if only he hadn't taken his eyes off that kid, then maybe something would have been different. Maybe that boy might somehow have survived, got that little bit of strength he needed to pull himself out of there alive. It was just seeing that kid out there all alone. It was that dying all alone.

Next morning, Whepler wasn't out of bed yet when he got a call from Manuel, the concierge in the lobby. Manuel said there was a woman at the hotel entrance who needed to talk to him.

"*Bien, está bien.*" Whepler hung up the phone and peered at his watch. It was just a few minutes past six.

When he got downstairs, Señora Nevares was out in front, with her three kids. She was perched on a low stone wall just across from the hotel entrance, under the flame trees. She was surrounded by several grimy, barefoot boys, the ones who came by each morning to sell newspapers to the hotel guests. They rough-housed and squabbled around her. Whepler walked over. He had to squint in the sun. Señora Nevares was full of apologies for bothering him. Whepler said it was all right, no problem. What was up? Any news?

"Nothing," she said and shrugged.

It was an exact repeat of their conversation the previous morning. She wanted to know if Whepler had heard anything. Whepler said no, not a word. He said he was sorry about it.

She nodded. She said she was sorry too.

They stayed like that for a minute or more, both of them staring off into space. It was another beautiful morning, and the traffic lurched and growled past along the Boulevard los Héroes. Señora Nevares reached over and straightened her elder daughter's dress. Whepler was trying to think of something he could say, but he wasn't coming up with much. What was he supposed to do? It was awful—but no one was going to find her

276

daughter again. She was gone. That was it. There was nothing anyone could do.

Maybe that was what he should have said, but somehow he couldn't say it. He was thinking, what the hell. Maybe he could go around to some government offices, ask some questions, get a lot of blank stares and curt denials, even a threat or two. But at least he'd have done something. He'd have something to tell this woman, some activity to report. Señora Nevares would have the feeling that something was being done about her girl. Whepler figured he could at least do that. Besides—you never knew. He might just find her. There was always that chance.

"Look," he said. "Why don't you come back tomorrow morning? I'll see what I can do. Maybe I'll have some information for you by then."

She didn't say anything. She just closed her eyes and fumbled with her towel. Whepler thought she was going to start to cry. But she didn't. Maybe it wasn't time yet. Instead, she just looked up at him. She said, "Gracias. Gracias, Señor . . . "

"Wayplayer," he said.

"Sí. Perdóname. Muchas gracias, Señor Wayplayer."

And off she went, with the kids in tow. Whepler stood there and watched them—Señora Nevares with one daughter clinging to her back, the other daughter carrying the boy. They looked like little elves, hobbling away along the street in front of the Metro-Centro.

Whepler did what he said he would do. He made some enquiries. He poked around. Once a week or so, he even went down to the Catholic human-rights office where his friend worked, to leaf through the black and white photographs they kept there—pictures of the dead bodies that turned up around town each morning, victims of the death squads. But he didn't find any trace of that little girl. Her mother came around each morning for the rest of that week, and then twice a week for a time, then once a week, then every month or so.

One day, probably a year later, Whepler took a taxi up to the barrio where Señora Nevares lived. She was still there. She seemed to be doing okay. He tried to give her back the photo, the one of her daughter, but she wouldn't have it. She started to cry. She probably thought it would be bad luck, an admission that there really was no hope. So Whepler put it in his wallet and he has kept it there.

Poor old Jean-Marc. He never did find any Salvadorans to attend that dinner of his for the French ambassador. What he did instead was, with about an hour left to go before the dinner itself, he came barging into the lobby of the Camino Real, high as a kite, and he invited the entire foreign press corps to come on over to the room he'd rented at the Sheraton Hotel, just in order to fill the seats. And they all did.

Decked out in their jeans and hiking boots and polo shirts, they slogged over there aboard a fleet of taxis and rented cars. They filled the seats and wolfed down the free paella they were served, and the wine. Then they took turns climbing to their feet and proposing long toasts in Spanish. *¡Viva Mitterrand! ¡Viva D'Aubuisson!* Long live French-Salvadoran solidarity! One toast after another, each more ridiculous and pompous than the one before.

But maybe the ambassador didn't suspect. He was

a bilious old guy with a bald head and possibly not a lot of brains. Besides, he didn't speak a word of Spanish. He just sat there in his baggy brown tweed suit and nodded and stroked his moustache and tipped back his glass at the end of each toast, as though everything was going just the way he'd anticipated. El Salvador—a strange and inscrutable land. At the end, he even got up and made a speech himself, in French, which Jean-Marc translated. Then he sat down, and the hacks all started banging their glasses on the table and clamouring for beer. Not wine. Beer. By the time he left, the French ambassador must have had a pretty interesting impression of Salvadoran high society.

Grant Lovsted went back to the States not long after that. He got married to some woman up there, and they have a couple of kids now, both girls. He was on the education beat at his paper, last Whepler heard. Most of the other hacks have moved on, too, replaced by newer faces, younger scribes. Whepler has stayed down here, though—he doesn't know why. Just war-torn, maybe.

He used to get into a taxi sometimes, usually in the afternoon when it was sunny out and there was nothing else to do, when the city was glazed in that Salvadoran light, that polished, waxy glow. He'd go for a tour around town, tell the driver to slow down each time they came upon a group of children. He was looking for some echo, some semblance, of that girl. Maybe the police had let her go and she was being raised by strangers. Maybe she'd lost her memory—you never knew.

Then he realized she wouldn't be a child any more. She'd be a young woman, hard to recognize now. But still he finds himself scanning the faces in a crowd, wondering if he might see someone who looks like her, a girl miraculously returned to life. He never has seen her, never has caught a glimpse of her that he knows of. Yet he keeps his eyes peeled for that moment. And sometimes he still drops by different government offices, maybe once a month, asks questions about this girl named Alma Nevares. He doesn't expect any answers, just wants them to remember that someone wants to know.

He still thinks about heading home, or even putting in for a new assignment someplace else—possibly Delhi, maybe Cairo—but somehow he never manages to make up his mind. Something always gets in his way. There's seventy thousand dead civilians in this war so far, and the number just keeps on growing. The war never quits. They say it's going to end someday, but they don't say when.

Acknowledgments

Many of these stories have appeared, in the same or slightly different form, in other publications: 'Bang-bang' in *The New Quarterly*, later reprinted in *The Journey Prize Anthology 5* (Toronto, McClelland & Stewart); 'So Far, She's Fine' in *Story* (U.S.A.), later reprinted in the British anthology *Best Short Stories '94* (London, Heinemann); 'Guerrilla Beach' in *Descant*; 'Dangerland' in *The New Quarterly*; 'The Disappearance of Pepe Vásquez' in *Quarry*; 'Welcome to the War' (under the title 'War Stories' in *Grain*; and 'Synonyms for War-torn' in *Saturday Night*.

Many people helped with their advice, criticism, or encouragement while I wrote these stories. I want to thank Lawrence Hill, Cynthia Holz, Janice Kulyk Keefer, Paul McLaughlin, Kim Moritsugu, Gregor Robinson, Leon Rooke, Ron Ruskin, Mark Sabourin, Bert Simpson, and Christine Slater. I'd like to thank my agent Jan Whitford. I also want to thank Jan Geddes at Cormorant Books and the editors of the various publications where many of these stories first appeared—with special thanks to Lois Rosenthal at *Story* and to John Fraser at *Saturday Night*, and with extra special thanks to Mary Merikle and Kim Jernigan at *The New Quarterly*. Finally, my gratitude to the Ontario Arts Council for a work-in-progress grant that made a big difference.